Praise for

T.M. Logan

'A tense and gripping thriller'
B A PARIS

'Assured, compelling, and hypnotically readable – with a twist at
the end I guarantee you won't see coming'
LEE CHILD

'A compelling, twisty page-turner, and that's the truth'
JAMES SWALLOW

'Outstanding and very well-written debut psychological thriller.
This book was so gripping I genuinely found it hard to put down'
K. L. SLATER

'A terrific page-turner, didn't see that twist!
A thoroughly enjoyable thriller'
MEL SHERRATT

'I can do no better than recommend *Lies*, a brilliantly plotted
psychological thriller by TM Logan, whom I have no doubt is
going to be a major exponent of this genre . . . Exceptional
and highly recommended'
ALISON WEIR

'Even the cleverest second-guesser is unlikely to arrive at
the truth until it's much, much too late'
THE TIMES

'Fraught with tension, with a compelling lead character who
becomes more and more unsure about who he can trust'
COSMOPOLITAN

'Creepy, creepy, creepy . . . a winner if you like thrillers'
WOMAN'S WAY

TM Logan is a former science reporter for the *Daily Mail* and subsequently worked in higher education communications. He was born in Berkshire to an English father and German mother. His debut novel *Lies* was a number one bestseller and has sold over 300,000 copies. He now lives in Nottinghamshire with his wife and two children.

Also by TM Logan

Lies

29
SECONDS

T.M. Logan

ZAFFRE

First published in Great Britain in 2018 by
ZAFFRE PUBLISHING
80-81 Wimpole St, London W1G 9RE
www.zaffrebooks.co.uk

A CIP catalogue record for this book is available from the British Library.

ISBN: 978-1-78577-080-7

also available as an ebook

1 3 5 7 9 10 8 6 4 2

Typeset by IDSUK (Data Connection) Ltd
Printed and bound by Clays Ltd, St Ives Plc

Zaffre Publishing is an imprint of Bonnier Zaffre,
a Bonnier Publishing company
www.bonnierzaffre.co.uk
www.bonnierpublishing.co.uk

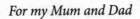

For my Mum and Dad

If we say that we have no sin, we deceive ourselves . . .
Christopher Marlowe, *Doctor Faustus*

There were three conditions.

She had 72 hours to provide a name.

If she said no, the offer disappeared. Forever.

And if she said yes, there was no going back. No changing her mind.

She stared at this stranger, this man she had never met before and never would again after tonight. A powerful, dangerous man who found himself in her debt.

It was strictly a one-time deal, a once-in-a-lifetime offer. A deal that might change her life. A deal that would almost certainly change someone else's.

It was a deal with the Devil.

PART I

TWO WEEKS EARLIER

1

The Rules were simple enough. Don't be alone with him if you could possibly avoid it. Don't do or say anything which he might take as encouragement. Don't get in a taxi or a lift with him. Be extra careful with him when you were away from the office, particularly at hotels and conferences. And most of all, the number one rule that must never, *ever*, be broken: don't do any of the above when he had been drinking. He was bad when he was sober, but he was worse – much worse – when he was drunk.

Tonight, he was drunk.

And Sarah realised, too late, that she was about to break all of the Rules at once.

One minute they were standing on the pavement outside the restaurant, the six of them, breath steaming in the cold night air, hands thrust deep in pockets against the November chill, contemplating their journey back to the hotel after an evening of good food and lively conversation. Just colleagues relaxing at the end of a long day away from home. The next minute he was striding out into the road to flag down a taxi, taking her firmly by the arm, guiding her into the back seat and following her in, his breath a hot fug of red wine and brandy and peppered steak.

It happened so fast, Sarah didn't even have time to react – she just assumed the others were following right behind them. It was only as the car door slammed shut that she realised he had separated her from the rest as deliberately and efficiently as a jungle predator.

'Regal Hotel, please,' he said to the driver in his deep baritone.

The taxi pulled away from the kerb and for a moment Sarah sat frozen in the seat, still in shock at this sudden turn of events. She twisted to stare out of the taxi's rear window at the rest of their little group stranded on the pavement and receding as the taxi picked up speed. Her friend and colleague Marie's mouth was open slightly as if she was speaking, a look of surprise on her face.

Always stick together. That was another one of the Rules. But now it was just the two of them.

The interior of the taxi was dark and smelt of old leather and cigarettes. She turned back and hurriedly put her seat belt on, edging as far over to the right side of the taxi as she could. The pleasant warm buzz from a couple of glasses of wine had fled, and she suddenly felt stone-cold sober.

If I play this right, I'll be OK. Just don't make eye contact. Don't smile. Don't encourage him.

He didn't put his seat belt on, but instead lounged, open-legged, across his side of the back seat, facing towards her. His right arm stretched along the shelf behind the passenger seats, right hand draped casually behind her head. His left hand rested on his thigh, inches from his crotch.

'Sarah, Sarah,' he said, his voice slow and deep with alcohol. 'My clever girl. I thought your presentation this afternoon was fantastic. You should be very pleased. Are you pleased?'

'Yes.' She clutched her handbag in her lap, staring straight ahead. 'Thanks.'

'You're very talented. I've always seen it, always known you had the right stuff.'

The taxi took a sharp left turn and he slid another inch nearer to her along the back seat, his knee touching hers. Sarah had to stop herself from flinching. He didn't move his knee away, but let it rest there.

'Thanks,' she said again, thinking of the moment – *please let it be only minutes away* – when she would be able to put a locked door between them.

'I'm not sure I mentioned it, but did you know BBC2 have commissioned another series of *Undiscovered History*? And the production company have talked about me having a co-presenter on the next series.'

'That's a good idea.'

'A *female* co-presenter,' he emphasised. 'And you know, seeing you present up there today, I really thought you might have the potential for television. What do you think?'

'Me? No. I'm not keen on having cameras pointing at me, to be honest.'

'I think you've got the talent for it.' He moved his right hand nearer to the back of her head. She could feel him touching her hair. 'And the looks.'

He had been OK-looking once upon a time, she supposed. Maybe even moderately handsome as a young man. But forty years of alcohol and fine food and debauchery had taken their toll, and now he resembled nothing so much as an ageing Lothario gone to seed. He was carrying too much weight on his tall frame, a pot belly hanging over the waistband of his jeans, his jowls fleshy and his nose and cheeks dappled red with booze. His grey ponytail was thinning, strands of hair gathered over his increasingly bald pate. The bags under his eyes were heavy and dark.

And yet, Sarah thought with a trace of amazement, *he still walks around acting like he's bloody George Clooney.*

She tried to edge further away, but she was already hard up against the door, the door handle digging into her thigh. The inside of the taxi was intensely claustrophobic, a temporary prison she couldn't escape.

She felt a pulse of relief when her mobile rang in her handbag.

'Sarah? You OK?' It was Marie, her best friend at work – and another woman with direct, first-hand experience of Lovelock's behaviour. It was Marie who had first proposed the Rules for dealing with him the previous year.

'Fine.' Sarah spoke quietly, turned towards the window.

'Sorry,' Marie said, 'I didn't see him flagging the taxi down. I just turned around to get a light from Helen and when I looked back he was virtually pushing you into the back of that cab.'

'It's fine. Really.' She could see him staring at her, his image reflected in the dark glass of the window. 'Did you find a taxi yet?'

'No, we're still waiting.'

Shit, she thought. *I really am on my own.*

'OK, no problem.'

'Text me when you get back to your room, all right?'

'Will do.'

In a quieter voice, Marie said: 'And don't put up with any of his crap.'

'Yup. See you in a bit.' Sarah ended the call and tucked the phone back in her handbag.

He shifted a little closer on the seat.

'Checking up on you?' he said. 'Thick as thieves, you and young Marie.'

'They're on their way. In a taxi just behind us.'

'But we shall be there first – just the two of us. And I've got a surprise for you.' He tapped her leg just above the knee, letting his hand rest there. His fingers felt heavy on her thigh. 'I *do* like these stockings. You should wear skirts more often. Your legs are *fab*ulous.'

'Please don't do that,' she said in a small voice, twisting her wedding ring around her finger.

'Do what?'

'Touch my leg.'

'Oh? I thought you liked it.'

'No. I'd prefer it if you didn't.'

'I *love* you playing hard to get. You're such a tease, Sarah.'

He pressed himself closer again. She could smell his sweat, acrid and sharp, and the post-dessert brandy he'd swirled in his glass as he stared at her across the restaurant table. He moved his fingers a few inches higher, stroking her thigh.

Carefully and deliberately she lifted his hand up with hers and moved it away, aware of her heart thudding painfully in her chest.

Then he was stroking the back of her head, caressing her long dark hair. She flinched away, sitting forward against the seat belt and shooting him a look. He ignored her, cupping his right hand around his nose, eyelids fluttering closed for a second.

'I love your smell, Sarah. You're intoxicating. Do you wear that perfume just for me?'

Her skin crawling, she tried desperately to think of a way to stop this happening again.

Option one: she could just get out of the taxi right now. Rap on the glass divide and tell the driver to stop, then find another taxi back to the hotel, or walk the rest of the way. Perhaps not a great idea alone in a strange city – and besides, he'd probably follow her. Option two: she could politely ask him – again – to respect her personal space and respect her as a colleague. As likely to be effective as every other time a woman had said that to him. Option three: do nothing, stay quiet, make a note of what he said afterwards and report him to HR as soon as she was back in the office on Monday. About as likely to be effective as . . . well, see option two.

Then of course there was option four. The option her seventeen-year-old self would have taken: she could tell him to *get his damn hands off her and just piss off, and then keep on pissing off until he couldn't piss off any further*. She could feel the shape of the words on her tongue, picture the look on his face. But of course she wasn't going to blow everything by actually saying them out loud. She wasn't seventeen anymore and there was too much at stake now, too many people depending on her. Fifteen years on, she'd learned that just wasn't the way things worked. It wasn't the way to get on in life.

And the worst thing was, he knew it too.

2

Sarah took a deep breath. She had to be better than that. She just had to take a minute, stay calm, walk the line between anger and acquiescence.

Which meant it would have to be option five: try to get him thinking about something else.

'You know, Alan, I've been following up on that research grant we won from the Bennett Trust recently,' she said, a steadiness in her voice that she did not feel. 'I've been looking into other sources of funding and I think I've had some luck – there's something called the Atholl Sanders Foundation who've match-funded Bennett awards in the past and I think they might do it again with ours.'

'The what foundation? I've never heard of it.'

'Atholl Sanders. Based in Boston, in the US. Quite secretive, made a fortune in property, pharmaceuticals, that kind of thing. Normally they keep a low profile but I think they'd be interested in funding some of our studies. The chairman has a personal interest in Marlowe.'

He clasped his hands together in his lap.

'That's good work,' he smiled. 'Go on.'

Despite herself, she smiled back. With a glance over his shoulder, she scanned her surroundings. There was the train station, and the bridge, and the court building she recognised from earlier – they were close to the conference hotel now. All she had to do was keep him talking.

'I've been in touch with the chairman of trustees,' she said, 'and they're keen to find out more about what we can do.'

'*That's* why you're our clever girl, Sarah. I think you should present your idea at the departmental meeting on Tuesday. The dean will be there – lots of brownie points on offer.'

'Sure. Sounds good.'

'Aren't I nice to you?'

She said nothing.

'Which reminds me,' he continued, producing an envelope from his jacket pocket. 'I've been meaning to give you this. I do so hope you can make it.'

He handed her the envelope, his hand brushing her leg again. It was heavy, expensive cream-coloured paper, her name on the front in swirling handwritten ink.

'Thanks,' she said, tucking it into her handbag.

'Aren't you going to open it?'

'I will do. When we're back at the hotel.'

'I am nice to you, aren't I?' he said again. 'You can be nice to me, too, you know. Once in a while, at least. Why don't you try it?'

'I just want to do my job, Alan.'

The taxi finally pulled to a wheezing halt outside the white stone façade of the Regal Hotel.

'Here we are. Now, I'm going to treat you to a very special nightcap. Don't you dare go anywhere.'

He leaned forward with a twenty pound note in his hand as the driver's light came on.

'Sorry, I'm exhausted,' Sarah said hurriedly. 'Going to call it a night.'

As fast as she could, she undid her seat belt, pulled the door handle and got out, walking quickly around the front of the cab, through the revolving door – *come on, come on, hurry up* – and into reception, her heels clicking on the shiny tiled floor.

Please let there be a lift. Please. Just let me get to my room, with a door I can lock behind me.

There were four lifts. As she speed-walked past the concierge, the one on the far right opened and a lone woman stepped in. The doors began to close.

'Wait!' Sarah half-shouted, breaking into a run.

The woman saw her and hit a button. The doors slid back open again.

'Thank you,' Sarah said as she entered the lift, flattening herself against the wall.

The woman was an American whom Sarah recognised from one of the seminar sessions earlier in the day. A name badge on her lapel said *Dr Christine Chen, Princeton University*. She had straight dark hair and kind eyes.

'Which floor?' she asked Sarah.

'Five, please.'

Dr Chen pressed the *Door Close* button just as Lovelock strode through the revolving doors at the far end of the lobby.

'There you are,' he boomed, starting to walk briskly towards them.

Pretending not to hear, Sarah hit the door's close button again. Nothing happened.

'Sarah!' he shouted again. 'Wait!'

With agonising slowness, the lift doors began to close.

'Sarah! Hold the –'

His barking command was lost as the doors slid shut.

3

'Why do you put up with that creepy bastard?' Laura said, slicing peppers at her kitchen worktop.

'You know why,' Sarah replied.

'Doesn't give him the right to grope you and harass you. If he was my boss I'd report him to HR so fast he wouldn't know what fucking day it was.'

'I know. But it doesn't always work like that at the uni.'

Laura turned away from her chopping for a moment and gestured with the knife, a long black-handled blade that tapered to a wicked point.

'It bloody *should* work like that,' Laura said. 'It's like you're working in the 1950s.'

Sarah smiled. Her friend swore and drank more than anyone she knew, and had an ingrained Yorkshire habit of speaking her mind without any thought of the consequences. Sarah loved her for it. Laura took absolutely no shit from anyone.

They had met at antenatal classes when Sarah was pregnant with Grace and Laura with her twins, Jack and Holly. At first Sarah had been a bit taken aback by Laura's directness – and her assertion that she wanted all of the drugs available for childbirth, preferably from a week before labour started – but it turned out they had a lot in common. They'd both studied English at Durham, they lived in the same north London neighbourhood and were both keen to get on at work. Laura was head of digital content for a large high street retailer.

Friday night sleepovers had become a monthly feature in their diaries. The four kids all got along well and played endless dressing-up games, even if Harry, as the youngest and smallest, usually seemed to be cast in supporting roles, as a servant, baddie or farmyard animal. He didn't seem to mind too much, as long as he was included.

They were tucked up in bed now. Laura's husband Chris was at the pub with mates from his five-a-side football team. Sarah sat at the large kitchen table while her friend busied herself preparing a stir-fry for the two of them. The air was rich with the smell of beansprouts, cashews and chicken already sizzling in the wok.

'I know it should work like that, Loz, but it doesn't. It just depends who's getting accused. In any case, it's been tried before.'

'And?' Laura took a swig of red wine from her glass.

'And nothing. He's still there. That's why they call him the bulletproof prof. And why I have to play the long game, until I get a permanent contract.'

'Bulletproof prof,' Laura repeated. 'What genius came up with that one? Makes him sound like some kind of fucking superhero.'

'It's been his nickname for years, long before I got there. Unofficial, of course.'

'Someone has shopped him before, though?'

'It's all whispers in corridors. No one talks about what's happened openly, it's all very hush-hush.'

'Have you talked to any of them? To whoever reported him to HR before?'

Sarah shook her head and took a sip of wine.

'God no, they're gone. Long gone.'

'Shit, really? Gone as in fired, asked to leave? Or gone voluntarily?

Sarah shrugged.

'It was before my time, but I don't think most of them are even in academia anymore. There have been a variety of students as well, over the years.'

'People know, then?'

'The thing is, Loz, there are two sides to Alan Lovelock. There is the famous Cambridge-educated TV academic, charming and charismatic and incredibly clever, next in line for a knighthood. That's the public side, the one on display to people most of the time. It's only when you're unlucky enough to be a woman on her own with him that you see the other side.'

'So how many notches on his bedpost have been students and members of staff?'

'I'm hoping I'm never in a position to see his bedpost.'

Laura snorted and refilled her glass from the nearly empty bottle of red. She was already a glass ahead of Sarah.

'I don't get it, though. Why don't HR just come down on him like a ton of shite? Surely he's in their sights?'

'Hmm. I'll try to explain: imagine the crappest thing you can think of.'

Laura leaned on the countertop, facing her friend.

'OK. I'm thinking . . . Southern Rail?'

'Now multiply its crapness by a factor of ten: that's how effective our HR department is. At best, they'll give him a slap on the wrist and "Guidance training on appropriate behaviour". At worst, they'll say it's his word against mine and nothing will happen except I'll find that the next time my contract could be made permanent – in three days' time – instead it will be *Oh sorry, I'm afraid we're going to have to let you go.* Bye-bye contract. Bye-bye job. And either way my career, in my field of expertise, will basically be buggered.'

'I can't believe the university still lets him work there. Should have been sacked years ago.'

'He's smart. Double first from Cambridge. Never does it where there are witnesses, so it's always your word against his. There's never any hard evidence, so the university hierarchy end up giving him the benefit of the doubt.'

'Someone should record him. Catch him in the act.'

'Except if he catches you doing it you can kiss goodbye to a permanent contract.'

'Getting him on record would at least give you a fighting chance.'

Sarah indicated the wall-mounted TV, a muted news bulletin showing Donald Trump holding court on the White House lawn.

'Right – because being caught on tape boasting about harassing women really scuppered his ambitions, didn't it?'

Laura pulled a face.

'Ugh. Don't even get me started on that one.'

She grabbed the remote and flicked to BBC2. Professor Alan Lovelock filled the screen, standing amid medieval ruins and gesticulating at the camera.

'Jesus,' she muttered, switching to a film channel, 'can't get away from the lanky bastard.'

Sarah sighed and took a sip of her wine.

'Anyway, the university has a lot of reasons to want to keep him. Nine point six million reasons, to be precise.'

'So he can do what he likes?' Laura said. 'Because of the money?'

There was no question that Professor Alan Lovelock was an outstanding scholar and a gifted researcher – he was one of the best in the world, in his specialist area. That was what had drawn Sarah to his department at Queen Anne University in the first place. But what made him untouchable was that he had landed one of the biggest grants given out to an English department ever: a seven-year grant from an Australian philanthropist worth £9.6m.

'It's a massive grant – more than the whole faculty got for the last five years put together. Queen Anne's top brass are petrified that if life gets uncomfortable here, he'll just take his grant, and set up somewhere else. And that will blow a massive hole in our research profile, we'll drop in the league tables, they won't be able to go on every five minutes about having this famous professor who has his own BBC2 series. Every so often he'll drop a hint to the dean that Edinburgh and Belfast universities have been sniffing around, just to make it clear that he might walk if he feels like it.'

'It's a shame he doesn't walk off a cliff,' Laura said and Sarah smiled, but it faded quickly.

'You know what really gets to me?'

'Apart from the groping and harassment and discrimination and all the rest of the crap?'

'What really gets me is that I've got an MA and a PhD, a full-time job and a mortgage; I'm married, I've got two children, and yet he still calls me "the clever girl" in meetings like I'm the fourteen-year-old work experience kid. I don't know why I let it wind me up but it's just maddening. I'm thirty-two years old, for Christ's sake. He wouldn't dream of calling any of his young male colleagues something like that.'

'You won't change your mind about going elsewhere?'

'Where would I go? There are only three universities in the UK that have specialist centres on Christopher Marlowe: Belfast, Edinburgh, and us. And Lovelock's not just *one* of them, he's the best, with the biggest grant, the biggest team, the biggest reputation. Switching disciplines now would be like going back to zero and starting again.'

'I don't see why you *should* bloody move, anyway,' Laura said. 'You've worked hard for this, you love what you do and you haven't done anything wrong. It would be taking your kids out of good schools to move hundreds of miles away; away from your dad, too. Bugger that.'

'Quite. Anyway, while we're on the subject, I'm hoping that there might finally be some good news around the corner.'

Laura raised a quizzical eyebrow.

'How so?'

Sarah reached for her handbag and found the expensive cream envelope that Lovelock had given her in the taxi two nights previously. She handed it to her friend.

'Bet you can't guess what that is.'

'No idea, love,' Laura said, turning the envelope over in her hands. 'You're going to have to give me a few clues.'

'Open it.'

Laura reached into the envelope and took out the thick embossed card, giving a low whistle.

'You've got to be kidding me.' She looked up, the smile fading from her face. 'But you're not seriously thinking about going to this, are you?'

Sarah nodded.

'Yes. I think I am.'

4

Laura was incredulous.

'You are *kidding* me. Have you gone mad?'

'I have to show my face. He holds this party every year, on his birthday, but it's the first time I've been invited in two years of working at the university.'

Laura held up the creamy white card and read from the text inside in her best *Downton Abbey* voice.

'*You are cordially invited to Professor and Mrs Alan Lovelock's annual charity gala on Saturday 11th November.*'

'His parties are legendary in the faculty. He uses them to raise money for his foundation.'

'His what?'

'He has this charitable trust called the Lovelock Foundation. Does lots of fundraising for disadvantaged kids, scholarships, bursaries, all that kind of stuff. And this year he's also celebrating the publishing deal for his new book. There's a tie-in with his BBC show so it's bound to be massive.'

Laura frowned, tossing the invitation onto the kitchen table.

'But after everything we just talked about, you're still going to go?'

'Yes.'

'You *have* gone mad. A few days ago he was putting his hands on you in a taxi and chasing you into your hotel. From what you've told me, he's acted like a massive lecherous pervert for as long as you've worked there. And now you're going to accept an invitation to his party, at his house, like that's all OK?'

Sarah shifted uneasily in her chair. She desperately wanted her friend to understand why she was doing this. To see the thread of cold, clear logic that ran through everything. If she couldn't convince her best friend, she couldn't convince anyone.

'It's not OK. That's not what I'm saying.'

'So what *are* you saying?'

'It's like . . . like a test, Loz. A rite of passage. You get senior professors who basically do their utmost to make you feel like shit as you're coming through the ranks, especially if you're a woman. It's like they're flexing their muscles, showing you your place for a while so you can learn the hierarchy. They want you to be blooded. But now it feels like I'm finally coming out the other side.'

'You're justifying it.'

'I'm not saying it's right, it's just how it is. He holds all the cards. But this party is normally only for other professors and associate professors, all the senior staff – never the temporary contract people like me. It's normally off-limits to us little people.'

'Thank Christ for small mercies, I would have thought. That's a blessing, isn't it?'

'Not if you want to move your career forward. Play along to get along, as they say.'

'Even when the person in question is a complete and utter shitweasel with absolutely no redeeming features?'

'Especially then. This invitation – I think it's a sign.'

'A sign that he still wants to get into your knickers?' She held her hands up. 'I'm sorry, I didn't mean that. Actually, I did. Because he clearly does.'

'A *good* sign.'

'You sure you're not reading too much into this?'

'He's never invited me before! The promotions committee is due to meet on Monday, three days from now. And I've just had my first invitation to his big, swish, annual fundraising party. Think about it. It can't be a coincidence – it's like he's welcoming me into the inner circle, or something.'

'Well, it's about bloody time. But you deserve it, lady.'

'Thanks, Loz, it feels like it might finally be happening.'

'Just don't get carried away before you've got the contract, signed, sealed and delivered. OK? We've been here before, haven't we? Last year.'

'I know. But last year was different. I've got a really good feeling about this. This party invitation is basically him telling me that I've got the permanent contract.'

'Tell me you're not going to go on your own, though? I don't like the idea of you flying solo when he's anywhere nearby.'

'It's a plus-one invite, but obviously I can't go with Nick, so . . .'

She tailed off, raising the wine glass to her lips. She still found it hard to talk about her husband without emotion getting the better of her. Anger and love and despair and hope, all mixed up in a toxic cocktail that tasted as bitter now as when he'd first left.

Laura gave her a sympathetic smile.

'Has he been in touch this week?'

'Not since last weekend. That text.'

'How long is it now?'

'Four weeks on Monday. Almost a month already. And the kids still ask about him every day.' She swallowed hard. 'Every sodding day.'

'Come here.' Laura held out her arms and enfolded her friend in a hug. 'You poor thing. He'll be back, you'll see.'

Sarah nodded into her friend's shoulder but said nothing, tears welling up.

She'd fallen in love with Nick when she was twenty, fallen for the handsome, charming dreamer who did everything so well, so effortlessly, that it was impossible not to be swept along by his enthusiasm. It was impossible not to believe in his dreams of acting on stage and screen – not when he always had the audience eating out of the palm of his hand. But the breakthrough had never quite happened for him. He had had roles here and there, touring productions and stage plays, even the odd bit of TV, but his acting career had never really taken off. And after a dozen years of trying, one day he had just upped and left – gone to 'find himself', he said. What a cliché. It was the second time he'd left in eighteen months.

She had no idea when he was going to be back this time. *If* he was going to be back.

'He's still in Bristol?' Laura asked gently. 'With what's-her-name?'

'Arabella. Yes, I think so.'

'He always was a daft sod.'

Sarah nodded. It was true enough.

'Hey,' Laura said finally, disengaging from the embrace, 'I could go with you to the party, if you want? Although I'd probably throw a drink in Lovelock's face in the first five minutes.'

'You think you'd last five minutes, do you?'

She shrugged and smiled.

'Maybe five would be pushing it a bit.'

Sarah sniffed and wiped her eyes on a tissue.

'I appreciate the offer, Loz. But I've asked Marie to be my wingman. She's seen first-hand how he operates. We'll stick to The Rules, stay together, make sure neither of us are caught alone with him.'

'And you're absolutely sure about this?'

Sarah took a breath then looked her in the eyes.

'It's something I have to do.'

5

Professor Alan Lovelock lived in Cropwell Bassett, a neat little south Hertfordshire village forty minutes from the Queen Anne University campus, in a sprawling, late Victorian six-bedroom pile tucked away at the end of a tree-lined gravel drive. Two saloon cars – a large black Mercedes and a white BMW convertible – were parked in front of a triple garage away from the main house.

'I had another Midnight Mail last night,' Marie said as they crunched up the gravel driveway. 'My third this week.'

Midnight Mail was a trademark of Lovelock's management style. So-called because it usually arrived in the recipient's inbox between midnight and 1 a.m. Almost always critical – if in a slightly oblique way – frequently impenetrable, and usually copying in three or four colleagues to increase the embarrassment factor for the recipient. Everyone in the department dreaded waking up to them: a lurking Midnight Mail had the potential to ruin your entire day.

'What was this one about?' Sarah said.

'The research council visit. He slated me publicly a few days ago for not having the arrangements in place, told me to use my initiative and just get on with organising it. Then last night he picked apart what I'd done in forensic detail, explaining how I'd got it wrong and asking if I'd like Webber-Smythe to take over.'

'Webber-Smythe couldn't organise a piss-up in a brewery. Just tell Lovelock you're sorry and you're happy to carry on with it.'

Marie snorted.

'Should I curtsy and call him sir, as well?'

'You know what I mean. Just play the game, like we all do. He's half-drunk when he sends them, apparently – not that it's any consolation.'

'He'll be drunk tonight.' She gestured to the grand house looming in front of them. 'Anyway, how does he afford this? Surely it's too posh for a prof's salary?'

'Family money. His dad was an earl, or a baronet or something.'

'He's kept that pretty quiet, hasn't he?'

'And he's made a squillion pounds from his TV series and books and everything else.'

'Smile,' Marie said, gesturing to a small CCTV lens mounted discreetly above the front door.

A delivery van was idling by the porch, the driver on the doorstep handing over a package to a slim, middle-aged woman in a spotless white apron.

'Domestic staff?' Marie said out of the corner of her mouth.

'Well, it's not Mrs Lovelock, that's for sure.'

The driver went back to his van and pulled away in a crunch of gravel. The woman in the apron held the door open, smiling and gesturing to Sarah and Marie to come in.

Sarah had to stop herself from staring when she walked into the kitchen they'd been taken to. It was the size of the whole downstairs of her little semi-detached put together. Broad oak beams in the ceiling, black granite worktops, creamy-white marble floor. She felt a pang of jealousy.

There was a low murmur of chat over soft jazz music, small groups of people standing in threes and fours, holding drinks and canapés. It seemed to Sarah that everyone looked around when she and Marie walked in, then they all returned to what they were doing a half-second later. Sarah moved over to a long table where a white-jacketed caterer was pouring glasses of champagne. She picked up two glasses and handed one to her friend.

Lovelock was holding court. He stood with his back to the Aga, a large glass of red wine in hand, talking and gesturing expansively to a rapt audience of colleagues from the faculty. Despite the chatter in the room, Lovelock's booming baritone was clearly audible above the hubbub. *Talking about his book, as usual.*

'And so I just said to the BBC chaps, well, it's entirely your choice.' He shrugged and raised an eyebrow at his audience, their faces turned towards him like flowers towards the sun. 'Either the BBC shifts its transmission dates to tie in with the publication of my book, or I shift the whole show to Channel 4. Simple as that.'

There was a polite ripple of laughter from his audience.

Sarah recognised the dean of the faculty, Jonathan Clifton, standing in another corner of the kitchen talking to Lovelock's wife, Caroline. A slim woman in her late forties, she had sculpted cheekbones and thin lips, perfect blonde hair falling to her shoulders. She was a good ten years younger than Lovelock.

Sarah had heard mention of Caroline Lovelock but had never spoken to her before. She was his second wife, she knew that much, and had worked with Lovelock as departmental secretary in his last job at Edinburgh University. The departmental gossip was that she spent her days overseeing a cohort of domestic staff – cleaner, cook, gardener, handyman – to keep everything in perfect order for the master of the house.

Sarah wondered idly whether he'd behaved with her the same way he behaved with most of his female colleagues. And she had ended up marrying him. *Jesus*. To Sarah they looked like an odd match: she was an attractive woman and he was clearly punching way above his weight to have landed her. Either way, she had left her husband when they first got together, and Lovelock had left his wife and young daughter. But that was years ago.

Caroline's eyes roved over the room, stopping momentarily as she looked at her husband addressing his crowd in the corner, then moving on. Sarah smiled and gave her a little wave, but got a blank stare in return. She wondered if Mrs Lovelock had any inkling of what her husband was like now. Did she realise? Perhaps she knew better than any of them.

Sarah checked her watch. It was only just gone eight o'clock.

'Two hours,' she whispered. 'Then we're out of here.'

'Stick to the Rules,' Marie whispered back.

'You too,' Sarah replied.

6

Sarah stood in a corner of the sitting room, at the edge of two or three conversations, watching groups of people as they made polite conversation and picked at buffet food from fine china plates. Swooping, incomprehensible jazz music played on the stereo. Colourful tropical fish swam in a long tank set against one wall. With Marie gone to join the queue for the bathroom, it suddenly felt to Sarah that none of this was real, that she had stumbled through the looking glass into an alternative reality – a place where she didn't belong and didn't know the rules.

But all of these people were like her once, she reasoned to herself. All of them had been on the outside looking in, waiting for the tap on the shoulder that meant someone thought they were good enough, smart enough, tough enough to move onwards and upwards. Once it had been their time. Soon it would be *her* time. She just had to be patient, that was all. She had to play the game. She sipped her drink, smiling politely at anyone who caught her eye.

Her mobile vibrated in her pocket. The display showed *Home*. She hit the green icon and put the phone to her ear.

'Hello?'

The sound at the other end was muffled, indistinct against the buzz of conversation and music in the room. She put her drink down and pushed a finger into her other ear, catching the eye of a man across the room as she did so. His expression seemed to say *How dare you be so vulgar as to take a phone call at the great Professor Lovelock's party, the social event of the season?* She ignored him, but still could barely hear over the noise of conversation. She headed for the wide patio doors.

Out on the patio, the night air was cool and sharp against her cheeks after the heat of the room. The lawn was long and wide and strung with Chinese lanterns down both sides, illuminating it with a soft glow. She moved away from the house and strained to hear the voice of the caller.

'Hello?' she said again.

'Mummy?' Grace's voice.

'Yes. Are you OK, Gracie?'

'We're having popcorn.'

Sarah moved across the patio to be nearer one of the tall outdoor gas heaters, feeling it warm her face. She seemed to have the space to herself.

'That's nice,' she said. 'What flavour popcorn are you having?'

The line went muffled again and she heard raised voices. Harry and Grace, both shouting. After a moment, her dad came on.

'Sorry about that, Sarah, Harry wanted to say goodnight. Hang on a second.'

More shouting and then her son's tiny, high voice came on the line.

'Hello?'

'Hello, Harry. What are you up to?'

'Mummy?'

'Yes, darling?'

A pause, more muffled noise in the background, and then: 'Grace pinched me.'

'Oh dear, well I'm sure she didn't mean it, darling. Are you going to have a story with –'

'Night!' he said.

'Night, Harry. Love you.' But he was already gone – he had never been one for long phone conversations. Her dad's voice came back on the line.

'How's it going, love? Everything OK? Are you still with Marie?'

She had never told her dad about the trouble she'd had at work with Lovelock. He knew about Nick, about their marriage problems, but she had compartmentalised the work part of her life. Partly because she wanted him to still be proud of her, proud of his clever daughter, and she was worried that Lovelock's behaviour would somehow besmirch that. Partly because she didn't want to bother him with it. Since Sarah's mother had died nine years previously, she didn't want him to worry. He did that enough already.

'It's fine, Dad. It's . . . nice. Marie's just nipped to the loo but we're going to grab a taxi back together later.'

'As long as you're all right.'

'Listen, Dad, I should probably go and do a bit more mingling, show my face. Kiss the kids goodnight for me.'

They said their goodbyes and she hung up. She put the phone in her pocket and was about to go back inside when she heard a familiar voice behind her, loud and deep and already blurring at the edges with alcohol.

'Hello, Sarah. I'm *so* glad you could come.'

7

It was him. Standing between her and the house, blocking her path.

She looked past him, praying Marie had reappeared. But her colleague was nowhere to be seen.

'Oh, hello, Alan.'

'You seem to be without a drink, Sarah. This cannot be allowed at my party under *any* circumstances.' He held out a large crystal tumbler, ice clinking against the glass. 'Gin and tonic, isn't it?'

'I probably shouldn't, I've already had a couple and I had a –'

'Nonsense,' he said, proffering the glass again and giving her a wolfish grin. He was slurring his words slightly. 'It's my party, and I insist. Anyway, I made it specially for you.'

'OK. Thanks.'

'Cheers,' he said, taking a step towards her, raising his own crystal tumbler of whisky and touching it to hers, before swallowing half of it in one gulp.

'Cheers,' Sarah said.

'Aren't you going to drink? You can't toast without drinking.' His lips curled upwards again. 'Not in my house, anyway.'

Sarah raised the glass to her lips and took a sip. It seemed OK. Maybe the strongest G & T she'd ever tasted – probably half gin and half tonic – but otherwise OK.

Lovelock leaned closer.

'Sarah, it's so lovely that you could make it. Glad I caught you, actually. I'd like to talk to you about Monday.'

Monday. Promotions committee.

'Sure,' she said, trying to stay calm as her stomach did somersaults. *This is it*, she thought. *This is where he gives me the good news.* 'Here? Now?'

He looked around.

'There's no time like the present.'

'OK,' she said, taking another small sip of her drink. *Damn*, but there was a lot of gin in there.

'Why don't we have a seat?' He indicated an ornate stone bench at the edge of the patio, flanked by two winter shrubs in upturned chimney pots. He sat down on the bench and patted the spot next to him. Sarah hesitated and then sat at the other end, perching on the edge of the weathered stone seat.

'Is Marie not here?'

Sarah felt the cold of the stone bench through her trousers and shivered involuntarily.

'She just went to the ladies. Should be back down in a minute.'

'So: are you looking forward to Monday?'

Sarah looked at him, searching his face for clues as to how she should react to this. On Monday, he and four of the other senior professors from the department would sit down and make final decisions on who would be put forward to the dean for promotion this year. The five professors – all of whom were here at the party tonight – would shut the door and work through a lavish lunch, into the early afternoon, discussing and voting on each application. Then they would call in all the candidates one by one to give them the news. This year six staff were up for promotion to the next rung of the academic ladder. One to full professor, another to assistant professor, two to senior lecturer and two more – Sarah included – looking to move up to a permanent lecturer's position from their current temporary contracts.

Folklore in the department was that they gave out the bad news first – mid-afternoon – and saved the good news for the end of the day. Lovelock's secretary would fire off the six emails inviting each hopeful member of staff to a fifteen-minute 'outcome meeting', one after the other.

Sarah forced a smile, and shrugged.

'I suppose I'd really just like it to be over with, if I'm honest.'

'Promotion is a momentous step. You know that, don't you?'

'Yes, I know.'

'It means one putting one's faith in a colleague – and trusting that faith won't be misplaced. What I mean is, you've really got to want it.'

'I do want it. More than anything. I know I have lots to offer the department and the students.'

'You need to be able to make sacrifices.'

'I understand that. Completely.'

'Marvellous.' He smiled, leaning closer. 'That's what I wanted to hear.'

She wondered, for the thousandth time, how the voting might go at the promotions committee. Five middle-aged men deciding each application according to a majority decision. Giles Parkin was one of Lovelock's close friends and would vote with him, whatever happened, Roger Halliwell was super ambitious and so wrapped up in himself he barely even registered junior members of staff. He would do whatever he perceived might yield him some small advantage, either now or in the future. The fourth member was Quentin Overton-Gifford, one of the cleverest people Sarah had ever met but also one of the most arrogant. His obnoxiousness was legendary and he was particularly fond of telling administrative staff how they were merely low-level functionaries feeding off the university's scholarly body. He was also of the firm opinion that women were not – and never could be – the intellectual equals of men. Lastly there was Henry Devereux, a decent guy who Sarah knew to be fair and reasonable – and happy to disagree with Lovelock. But even if he did, there was no hope of Devereux getting a majority.

Departmental folklore said that no one had ever carried a majority against Lovelock's wishes. If she had his backing, she was home and dry. But he wasn't about to give her anymore clues now, it seemed: the work conversation appeared to be over. Abruptly, Sarah realised that he was staring at her chest.

'You have a very nice house,' she said, just to be saying something.

'Let me give you a guided tour. We've had the upstairs completely remodelled, the master bedroom is really quite –'

He stopped in mid-flow, distracted by a noise. Footsteps clicking on the stone patio.

Someone was behind them.

Sarah turned and saw a woman in a black jacket and jeans, her blazing eyes fixed on Lovelock.

'There you are,' the woman said. 'Finally I fucking found you.'

'Hello, Gillian,' he replied coolly. 'What a surprise.'

8

She was a little younger than Sarah, maybe thirty, with dark bags under her eyes and her brown hair scraped back in a ponytail. Her face was twisted with anger. Ignoring Lovelock, the woman turned and walked towards the house. She opened the patio doors, swinging them wide open so the hubbub of conversation and music spilled out onto the patio. Some of the conversation died as the guests saw her.

She beckoned them closer.

'Come on, I want you to hear this.' She pushed a hand into her handbag. For a moment, Sarah thought she was going to pull out a weapon of some kind and she shrank back into the stone bench. But instead she produced a folded sheet of paper. She held it out and addressed the group of partygoers.

'Your wonderful colleague here, Alan Lovelock, had the university get rid of me when I complained about him. After he spent a year harassing me, stalking me and finally sexually assaulting me on five separate occasions. He refused to promote me unless I slept with him. And now,' she opened up the folded paper and flourished it, 'having tried and failed to fuck me, he's fucked my career instead.'

A murmur went through the crowd. Sarah felt like she wanted to be somewhere, anywhere, else. Lovelock said nothing.

'I couldn't work out why I couldn't get another post,' the woman continued. 'Most places I didn't even get an interview, even though I was qualified. It didn't make sense. But then I managed to get hold of a copy of the reference you gave me, Alan,' she turned toward him, 'and it all started to fit together.'

Lovelock shook his head, slowly.

'You're embarrassing yourself, Gillian.'

'You warned everyone off, didn't you, you bastard? Everywhere I've tried to get a job – at Edinburgh, Belfast, even bloody Harvard. All run by your little cosy club of bloody crusty old men who've known each other for decades. You've given the same shit reference to all of them.' She unfolded the paper. 'But guess what? The last place, their fucking useless HR department accidentally copied me into an email with your reference attached. It really is quite a read, isn't it?'

'I have an obligation to the truth. Anything less would be to do a disservice to colleagues at other universities.'

'The truth, is it?' She dropped her eyes to the paper and began to read. '*Unreliable, unstable, prone to outbursts of anger and highly critical of colleagues. Abrasive, not a team player. Corrosive effect on team dynamics within the department. Tendency to make wild and unsubstantiated allegations about colleagues.*'

'I'm really sorry that things haven't worked out career-wise, for you, Gilly,' Lovelock said. 'Really, I am.'

'It's all bullshit though, isn't it? Complete and utter bullshit, from the first word to the last. You warned them all off.'

Sarah stared at the woman, wondering if she was looking at her own future, her own destiny, brought to life. There was even a physical similarity, she realised: the new arrival was about the same height as Sarah, same long dark hair, slim figure, similar age.

I suppose Lovelock has a type. A particular look that he goes for. But this is not me. It is a warning, but it is not me.

Lovelock gave the woman a calm, sympathetic smile.

'You're drunk, Gilly.'

'Of course I'm fucking drunk,' she spat back at him. 'It's the only way I can get through the days.'

She seemed to notice Sarah for the first time.

'Are you his latest?' The woman gestured towards Sarah, turning to face her. 'Has he tried to get you into bed yet? Because if he hasn't yet, he will. Believe me.'

Party guests who had spilled out onto the patio watched in silence, their eyes moving from Lovelock to the woman, like rubberneckers hoping to see blood at a road accident. Marie appeared, squeezing her way through the crowd.

Sarah hesitated, feeling the eyes of the department on her. The eyes of the man who was going to promote her on Monday. It didn't seem like the right time for the truth.

'No,' she said. 'No, he hasn't. Nothing like that.'

'He hasn't tried to shag you yet?' She looked Sarah up and down. 'You're just his type.'

Sarah shook her head quickly, feeling herself blush.

'No.'

The woman stared at her for a moment, her eyes narrowing.

'If he hasn't yet, he will do soon. In case you didn't know, he's a repeat offender.'

Sarah felt like saying *Yes, I do know.* But instead she stayed silent and hated herself for it. Her cheeks felt hot.

'You heard her,' Lovelock said. 'She doesn't know what you're talking about.'

'You're a liar and a predator and a serial abuser!' she spat back at him. 'I know it, most of the people at this party know it. Even the dean of the faculty has known it for years.'

'That's simply not true, Gilly.'

'Of *course* it is.'

'Well, why don't you just ask him, if you're so convinced?'

'Ask who?'

'The dean.' Lovelock gestured towards the house. 'He's here. In the kitchen. I don't think he'd have come to my annual party for the last ten years if he thought I was some sort of bad egg. Ask him what he thinks of you coming here and throwing wild slanders and accusations at a member of his senior team.'

Charlie Webber-Smythe, one of Lovelock's young acolytes from the department, emerged from the crowd of party guests.

'Alan, you should probably know that some woman tried to talk her way in at the front door just now –'

'Yes. I know.' He gestured to the woman. 'She came through the side gate instead. Caroline must have left it unlocked again. But she was just about to leave, weren't you, Gilly?'

'Screw you! You can't tell me what to do anymore. I'm not finished yet.'

'I think you are.'

She made a lunge for him but Webber-Smythe grabbed one of her arms, holding her away from Lovelock.

'Get off me!'

Webber-Smythe was much bigger and stronger than her, but she had fury on her side. She wriggled free and made another lunge for Lovelock, swatting for his face. Lovelock merely sat back on the stone bench and watched, a look of mild amusement on his face. Webber-Smythe tried to grab the woman's other arm but caught her handbag instead, the strap breaking away and the bag tumbling to the floor. The zip was open and some of its contents fell onto the patio – purse, lipstick, mobile, pens, papers, diary and everything else tumbling out and scattering across the stone tiles. Marie crouched down and began gathering it all up.

Webber-Smythe got a firm grip on the woman's arm, and with another party guest on her other side, they marched her off towards the side gate.

Her shouts of anger receded as she was led away.

9

'These are yours,' Marie said, holding out the woman's things.

She looked up, tears streaking her face.

'Thank you.'

'You're Gillian Arnold, aren't you? I know you from LinkedIn.'

The woman nodded, tucking her belongings back into her handbag.

'Hey,' Sarah said, catching up to them. 'What you did back there . . . it was really brave.'

Gillian sat on a low stone wall at the end of the drive, swaying slightly. She spoke without looking at Sarah.

'For all the good it will do me.' She zipped her handbag and clutched it in her lap. 'Anyway, what do you know about being brave? You knew exactly what I was talking about back there. I saw it in your eyes.'

Sarah looked at the ground.

'I'm sorry. I just . . . just couldn't say it in front of all those people.'

'Good luck with that.'

'With what?'

'Staying quiet. I tried it too, until I couldn't look at myself in the mirror anymore.'

A tear rolled down Gillian's cheek and she brushed it away, angrily. She looked defeated. Broken.

'I'm sorry, I don't mean to have a go at you. It's just that I'm so angry all the time now; I have so much anger I don't know what to do with it. Every day I think about what he did to me, *every single day*. The nights are the worst: he's always there, in my head.' She paused, staring straight ahead. 'For a long time I thought about killing him.'

Sarah hesitated, not sure how to ask the next question.

'How long did he do it for?' she said quietly.

'Does it make any difference? A day, a month, a year, does it matter? It's what he does, it's who he is. He'll never change. Neither will the university – not until they have to.'

'He's been targeting me since soon after I joined, about two years ago.'

'Well, you've lasted longer than me. I only made nineteen months.'

'What happened?' Marie said.

Gillian shrugged.

'What happened is that it's a business and they've got too much invested in their prime asset to let him go. People like us are just the collateral damage.'

Sarah sat down next to her on the low stone wall and passed her a tissue from her handbag. She saw now that, beneath the anger, Gillian had a kind, open face. Beyond the lines of worry and stress there was a genuine warmth and intelligence.

'People like us?'

'Anyone who threatens to expose him for what he really is. I thought I'd get a fair hearing – I didn't realise until it was too late that the university's number one interest was to protect itself. It's one hundred per cent about their brand. Colleagues told me in private that if I spoke up, the attack dogs would come after me. But I didn't listen.' She laughed bitterly. 'I thought I knew better.'

'Did you have evidence that you could give them?'

'I used to write transcripts, from memory. Details of the things he said and did – or *tried* to do – during our one-to-one sessions, at conferences away from the university, at social events when he cornered me. After six months, when I thought I had enough evidence, I went to the dean.'

'So you had him bang to rights.'

Gillian shook her head, slowly.

'No. What you have to realise is that when the dean does an investigation like this, he's not on your side. You *think* he is, but he's not. His role is to neutralise the threat. He told me to think of the consequences for my career, suggested I was partly to blame anyway, but that he'd talk to Lovelock and get him to back off.'

'He persuaded you not to take it further.'

'For a few months.' Her voice caught with the anger. 'But it was such *bullshit*. Lovelock just carried on exactly as before, until finally I'd had enough and went ahead with a formal complaint to HR.'

'What happened?'

Gillian snorted.

'What do you think happened? Absolutely fuck all. The university went into cover-up mode, there were lots of highly confidential meetings and letters and forms to fill in, policies to follow, arbitration meetings. Lots of arse-covering by every manager involved. Then Lovelock made a counterclaim and it all went completely to shit. He basically accused me of all the things I was accusing him of, to muddy the waters, and privately made it clear that my career in the field was over unless I took the voluntary severance package on offer and signed an NDA.'

'NDA?'

'Non-disclosure agreement. A couple of months' extra salary in exchange for keeping my mouth shut. By that time I was a wreck. I wasn't sleeping, I wasn't eating, it had been going on for months and I didn't know what the hell I was supposed to do. I was even getting abusive texts and emails from Caroline, his wife. Can you believe that? Like it was all my fault for trying to steal her husband away. I was massively behind with my work by this point and I was barely functioning. So in the end I signed the agreement.'

'I'm so sorry, Gillian.'

The woman focused on Sarah, her eyes bloodshot.

'You should get out while you can. Before it's too late.'

'I can't, not yet.'

'Whatever you do, it doesn't matter. It won't change him or the university: he's too valuable. He's untouchable.' She blew out a breath and stood up. 'I should go. I've said far too much already.'

'We'll wait with you,' Marie said. 'Until you can call a taxi.'

Gillian indicated the end of the lane, where a saloon car was parked on the grass verge.

'I asked him to wait for ten minutes. Didn't think it would be long before I got thrown out.'

*   *   *

They watched the tail lights of the taxi receding into the distance then walked back down the drive to the house, back towards the party. Sarah looked up to take in the grandeur of the house again as they approached the front door. There was a face at one of the bedroom windows. A face dark with such fierce anger that Sarah had to look away.

Caroline Lovelock glared down at them, arms crossed, eyes filled with fury.

10

The end of Monday couldn't come soon enough. Yet Sarah didn't want it to arrive. As a young girl, she'd been the same at Christmas. She loved everything about Christmas Day – the presents, the food, the games, having her nana and grandad there from Southend – but she also loved the anticipation beforehand almost as much. Of knowing that it was all still to come.

Her email from Lovelock's PA – summoning her to a so-called 'outcome meeting' – had duly arrived just after two o'clock. She had stared at it in her inbox for a full minute, knowing that six other emails would be dropping into colleagues' inboxes at virtually the same moment. Jocelyn Steer prepared all the drafts at the same time and then sent them in a quick sequence, *bang bang bang*, so everyone received them within the space of a minute.

Sarah clicked on the email. Her meeting with Lovelock was booked in for five o'clock.

She'd been holding her breath without realising it. She exhaled heavily and allowed herself a little smile: the timing was good. A five o'clock meeting time meant she was one of the last, if not *the* last to be booked in. She read the email twice to make sure she hadn't misunderstood, clicked *Accept invitation* to add the meeting to her Outlook diary.

The meeting time was pretty much as late as she could push it to still get to after-school club in time to get the kids, without getting fined for being late. Again. Ordinarily she'd ask her dad to pick them up but Monday was his walking day, when he and his friend Pete would head off into the countryside for an eight or ninemile walk, stopping at a country pub on the way. They were both widowers and their Monday walks had become an established habit over the last few years. He'd have skipped it without a second thought if she'd asked him, but she didn't want him to miss out.

Her phone buzzed. A text from Marie.

How are you doing? Am in the most boring Senate meeting in history. x

Sarah knew what her friend was really asking. She typed a reply: *Good. Got promotions outcome meeting booked for 5. x*

The reply was emojis rather than text: ☺☺☺

A moment later another message followed it: *Nice and late! Good luck – rooting for you! Let me know how you get on. x*

Sarah smiled. She hoped that next year, when promotions came around again, it would be her turn to give Marie encouragement as she made a move up the ladder.

Will do. Thanks. x

She was aware that she was about to break one of the Rules: don't be alone with him. But there was nothing she could do about that – all the meetings were held in Lovelock's office because there had to be privacy for those receiving the news.

Knowing the meeting was coming, she'd worn trousers and a blouse buttoned up to the neck, with a jacket. Lovelock always kept his office unseasonably warm but she had no intention of taking her jacket off, even if it was thirty degrees in there.

She sat at her desk for a moment longer, trying to concentrate on her breathing. *Relax. It's a formality, it's going to be fine. This is what you've been waiting for, what you've worked for.*

She stood up and headed for his office.

* * *

Lovelock beamed at her when she came in, gesturing to the empty seat in front of his desk.

'Ah, Sarah, lovely to see you. Sorry for keeping you hanging on until the end of the day.'

She sat, straight-backed, in the empty chair.

'It's no problem.'

'How are you feeling today?'

'Good.' She felt herself starting to sweat in the warmth of his office. 'I think.'

'How's the teaching going? Not taking on too much, are you? With all that admin as well?'

'No, it's fine, it's a bit of a juggling act sometimes, but, you know . . . The students are lovely. I'm enjoying it.'

'Excellent.' He dragged the word out, rolling it around his mouth. 'Glad to hear it. And that latest journal publication?'

She shifted uncomfortably in her chair, wondering how long he would string out the small talk.

'Should be published any day now.'

'Great. Would you like a cup of tea, by the way? I can get Jocelyn to make us one.'

'I'm fine, really.'

It was always weird when he was like this – normal, reasonable, professional – because she knew what he was capable of, the depths his behaviour had plumbed in the past. She had never been able to understand how these two different characters seemed to coexist quite comfortably inside his head. Or how fast he could switch between the two.

Lovelock reached for a folder on the desk in front of him, flipping to a page marked with a green Post-it note.

'So: we held the promotions committee meeting earlier today, as I'm sure you know.'

'Yes, I was aware.' *Here we go,* she thought. She wanted to remember the details of what he said because she knew Marie would ask her later. Her dad would ask her too. This was the day, the hour, the minute, that her life was going to change for the better, and she wanted to remember everything.

'There have been some big decisions this year,' Lovelock said. 'We're lucky to have so much stellar talent in this department.'

He let the silence ring out for five seconds. Then ten. Sarah thought about jumping in, but didn't want to talk over him. So she held her tongue.

He smiled again, his lips stretching back to show small, yellowed teeth.

'In fact,' he continued, 'I'm struggling to remember when we had so many committed, talented colleagues around the table. It's a wonderful team we have, it really is.'

Another pause. This time Sarah couldn't stand to let it go on.

'Yes, it is lovely to be part of such a great team.'

'I'm so glad you agree, Sarah.'

It occurred to her that he was enjoying this. Immensely. Drawing it out, savouring the moment, holding her future in the palm of his hand. It was a power thing, she supposed. She made a mental note to never, ever, drag it out like this when she was delivering good news to junior colleagues in the future.

She couldn't bear the silence any longer.

'So were you able to – to reach a decision on all of the candidates today?'

'Yes. We were.' He paused again, nodding, his unblinking eyes on hers. 'It's bad news, I'm afraid.'

11

Sarah was sure she hadn't heard him correctly. She blinked quickly and swallowed hard, feeling the ground shift beneath her feet. This wasn't happening. It was a joke, surely? A bad joke, but a joke nonetheless. In a moment he would crack a smile and say *Only joshing, my girl, of course you've got it, do you think I'm mad? Oh, my dear, the look on your face is absolutely priceless!*

But he didn't smile. He didn't move. His eyes never left hers.

'Bad news?' she repeated, her voice cracking.

Lovelock nodded slowly, lips pursed together, like he was a doctor giving a terminal diagnosis.

She felt the emotion bubbling up in her chest, long-suppressed.

'You're not putting me forward? For a permanent contract?'

'I'm afraid not.'

'Are you . . . are you sure?' she said. It had to be a joke.

Lovelock leaned forward on his big oak desk, crossing his arms.

'It's just not your time, Sarah: you're not quite ready yet. Almost, but not quite.'

'I *am* ready.' The words felt inadequate. 'More than ready.'

'Believe me when I say this is not easy for me either, but it wouldn't be in your best interests to put you up for a permanent post at this stage. I know it's tough to hear now, but in the long run, you'll thank me.'

The anger started to burn hot in her cheeks.

'*Thank* you? For what? Once again denying me the promotion that I should have had last year? Denying me progression in my career? Denying me recognition for what I've done?'

'I know you really want this. But you need to demonstrate your commitment to the discipline. You've already got two little children; how do I know you're not going to be disappearing off to pop out more babies as soon as you get that permanent contract? Leaving your colleagues in the lurch while you go for a nice maternity leave holiday and we don't see you for another year.' He gave her a lascivious smile. 'More to the point, *I* don't see you for a year.'

Sarah sat up straighter. The prospect of her *popping out more babies* was distant indeed considering Nick was off with his girlfriend in Bristol. But she was staggered that Lovelock had dropped it into the conversation so casually.

'Hang on, you can't use that as a –'

'In a year's time, in the next promotions round, I think you'll have a solid chance. In the meantime you need to keep building, keep moving forward. Embrace all the opportunities that come your way – grab them with both hands.' He leaned forward. '*All* of them.'

Sarah felt her anger flare, and fought hard to keep her voice level.

'I set up the new masters programme this year, basically ran the whole thing. We've had a good first year. *Really* good. All the signs are positive.'

He sat back in his big chair, the leather creaking under his weight.

'I do love to see you angry, Sarah.'

'What?'

'You're so sexy when you're angry.'

'Why do you think you can say that? Why do you think it's OK?'

He shrugged.

'It's true. You are.'

'Why did you tell me at your party on Saturday that I'd got the position? Why did you say that if you were never going to put me forward?'

'I didn't say you'd *got* it, I asked if you *wanted* it. How badly you wanted it. Your behaviour over the last few months illustrates perfectly that you don't want it badly enough.'

'That's not fair! I want this more than anything and I deserve it, you know I do.'

'Let's not be bitter about this, Sarah. You're better than that.'

She felt tears threaten and bit her tongue, the sharp pain distracting her. *Don't cry. Don't you dare. Not in front of him. Don't let him see that.*

'This is not fair,' she repeated, her voice rising.

'I'll tolerate all kinds of behaviour in my office,' he smiled again. 'But I won't tolerate hormonal junior members of staff shouting at me. So why don't you come back a bit later when you've calmed down and you're a bit less . . . hysterical, and we can discuss this like adults?'

I should have recorded this on my phone, she thought. *Could I get it out now and set the recording app going? No chance. Not without him noticing. Shit.*

With a huge effort, she managed to get her voice back under control.

'Who have you put forward for a permanent post? Who have you picked?'

'You know very well that I can't tell you that, it's confidential. In any case, I have to wait until my recommendation goes to the dean, and then it has to be ratified in the usual way.'

'Just tell me.'

'I can't. It's confidential.'

'You've picked Webber-Smythe, haven't you? Picked him over me for promotion, even though he's five years younger than me and I've been bloody mentoring him for the last year. *I* have been mentoring *him*.'

Lovelock gave her a small smile.

'You've done a very good job with him. You're a good mentor.'

'So it is him?'

'You know I can't comment.'

'This is bullshit,' Sarah said, her voice choked. 'And you know it.'

'I'd be the first to admit that it's a cruel process. We just can't please everybody, every year, I'm afraid. That's not the way the world works.'

'What's my right of appeal?'

He smiled.

'Appeal? It's not a court case, Sarah.'

'I'll speak to the dean, then.'

'By all means, take it up with Jonathan.' He stood, his angular frame unfolding from the leather swivel chair. He came around the desk. 'But he doesn't tend to make policy on the basis of hysterical girls stamping their little feet until they get what they want.'

'This is wrong. It's not the way it's supposed to work.'

She stood up and turned to leave, wanting to get out of his office before she said something even worse than she had already. But he was blocking her way, leaning back against the door with his arms crossed. At six feet four he was almost a foot taller than her.

'Let me out.'

'It doesn't have to be this way, Sarah. You can still make the promotions list. You just have to show me your commitment to this department.'

'I *am* committed.'

'So show me.' His eyes flickered. 'Show me how committed you are.'

12

'No,' Sarah said quietly.

He moved towards her, dropping his hands to his sides.

'Show me.'

She took her phone out of her bag, not taking her eyes off him the whole time.

'I'm calling security, and then I'm going to scream until you let me out.'

She found the number for Campus Security stored in her favourites, dialled and put the phone to her ear. It started to ring.

Lovelock smiled and moved away from the door. He spread his hands.

'When you change your mind, I'll be here.'

Sarah ended the call and tore open the door. Lovelock's secretary, Jocelyn, was standing right outside, a shocked look on her face. Sarah had never seen her frosty demeanour disturbed for anything before – and it threw her for a moment. Jocelyn seemed to be about to speak, but with one look at Sarah's thunderous expression she backed away to her desk instead.

Sarah hurried back to her own office, praying she didn't see anyone on the way. But the corridors were empty this late in the day. Once inside she slammed the door behind her and began ramming folders of papers and her laptop into her bag. She hated him. She hated everything about him. And she hated herself for believing – against all the evidence – that when it finally came down to it he would do the right thing.

Her phone beeped. A text from Marie. No words, just a single emoji of a champagne bottle, cork popping, and three question marks.

This time Sarah couldn't stop the tears. She stood with both hands on the back of her chair, head down, shaking with emotion as great racking sobs tore through her. *This wasn't happening.* But crying was a luxury she couldn't afford: she didn't have the time. She found a tissue and wrenched her office door open, stumbling down the stairs, wiping at her eyes as she went. She ignored the concerned looks of two students in the front lobby, pushed through the double doors into the car park and almost bowled over Marie coming the other way.

'Sarah,' Marie said, taking a step back. 'You OK? What happened?'

Sarah shook her head but kept on walking.

'Fine. I have to go.'

'You don't look fine.'

'I have to get the kids.'

'What did he say? Are you OK? I texted you.'

Sarah stopped and turned, still shaking with anger.

'I think I've finally had enough. God, I *hate* him.'

Marie handed her a tissue.

'You didn't get the contract?'

'No, I didn't bloody get it!' Her voice cracked as she tried to get the words out.

'I'm sorry, Sarah.'

'Sorry.' She swiped angrily at fresh tears. 'I'm not having a go at you.'

Marie placed a comforting hand on her shoulder.

'I know. I can't believe it, though. What are you going to do?'

'No idea. I have literally no idea.'

'D'you think he gave the contract to Webber-Smythe?'

'I don't know. I think so. Look, I have to pick up the kids from school.'

'I'll text you.'

Sarah nodded and turned away. She got straight into the driver's seat of the car, shoved the phone into its cradle on the dashboard, and turned the key in the ignition. She reversed out and gunned the engine, weaving through groups of students as she headed down the hill.

There was a painful tightness in her throat and a pounding in her head, and she knew she should slow down, pull over and take a minute just to calm herself, get her emotions in check. She should do what she'd always done – stop, count to ten, take deep breaths and wait until it passed. Sarah was an expert at that. She'd been doing it for years. It was her coping mechanism, her safety valve when life was getting on top of her.

Not today.

Today she carried on driving, revving the engine, flashing past the security booth on the edge of campus, across the junction as amber turned to red and out towards the main road. She slammed the car into fourth gear and stepped down hard on the accelerator.

Then she turned the car stereo up as loud as it would go, gripped the wheel tightly, and screamed. She screamed with frustration and humiliation. She screamed at the injustice of it all. She screamed with bitterness, with helplessness, and with anger.

But it was more than mere anger. Much more.

It was rage.

13

A few minutes of speeding south on the A10 came to a halt as the dual carriageway slowed to a crawl. Traffic was solid: too many cars and not enough road, as usual.

'Come *on!*' Sarah shouted, slamming her palms on the steering wheel.

She sat for a few minutes, her anger simmering, before gunning the engine once more and forcing her way through a gap between two cars, pulling off down a slip road in search of another route. She was trying to concentrate on the road and the traffic but it was difficult with all the thoughts whirling around in her head. *Should I report him for what just happened? Why did he invite me to his party? Why go to the trouble if he was just going to slap me down again when it came to promotion?*

But deep down she knew the answer: power. It was part of his power trip. And another way to humiliate her. Another chance to get her alone. For him to show who was in control.

Her phone beeped with a text. It was from Marie.

Are you OK? I want to help. Call me xxx

She came off the slip road, through a junction, and found herself on an industrial estate, parallel to the ring road, taking a left and another right before she saw the signs up ahead. It was a no through road. A dead end.

It's not the only thing that's at a dead end, she thought bitterly.

She did a hasty U-turn, retraced her route and found herself back at the junction, ready to rejoin the mass of crawling traffic. The light was red.

The dashboard clock said it was 17.16. Only fourteen minutes before she got another twenty-five pound fine from the after-school club. *Shit*. She reached towards her phone in the dashboard cradle, to ring Nick's number, but her hand stopped halfway as she remembered he was not around to help out anymore. She thought about calling her dad.

No. He had done enough these last few weeks.

She called up Google Maps on her phone and typed in the school's Wood Green postcode. It gave her three routes, two of which would take her further into the traffic and the third which went around the houses but gave her at least an outside chance of reaching the school by five thirty. It was longer in distance, but should be quicker overall if it meant avoiding the logjam of rush-hour traffic.

She turned left as soon as the light turned green, pure frustration making her push down hard on the accelerator. Merging with another main road, she took another left and then a right as the satnav directed her diagonally away from the ring road. She drove faster, through amber lights and narrow gaps, following the blue line of the Google route. Turning the wheel as she thought again of her ill-fated meeting.

What do I do now? Who do I tell?

She scanned the street as she drove. She didn't know this part of Muswell Hill. Wide, tree-lined streets, handsome three-storey properties, at least a million pounds more than she could ever afford. So far out of her reach, she thought, they might as well be on the moon.

Is that it for another year? Or should I make a complaint?

A car pulled out sharply in front of her. A big black Mercedes saloon, wide and long with windows tinted dark. She braked hard and slammed the horn with the heel of her hand, twice, shouting her frustration at the driver. The Mercedes showed no sign of having heard her – neither did it speed up as it finished its turn in front of her. Sarah changed down into third gear, then into second. Still the Mercedes didn't speed up, crawling along in front of her at barely twenty miles per hour.

'Come on!' Sarah shouted. 'Let's go!'

She thought perhaps the Mercedes was picking someone up, looking for a place to pull over. Her eye was caught by two people on the pavement, a man and a girl, both with their backs to her. These two?

The girl was young, primary school age, with a blue blazer, dark pigtails, a pink backpack with little fairy wings on each side. Grace had the same backpack for school. The man was in a dark suit and walked alongside her, on the street side like every responsible adult would do. *Not holding her hand, though*, Sarah thought. That was a bit odd.

For a moment, she caught herself thinking that this was Nick; he had come back to them and finally he was going to face up to his responsibilities. He would come home, and ask for forgiveness, and they would go back to how they'd been before. But it wasn't her daughter. And it wasn't her husband, either. Wrong girl, wrong man, wrong place, wrong time. Wrong bloody everything, today. This man was taller than her husband, broader, more powerfully built. He was walking slowly, keeping pace with the child, arms by his sides.

Not Nick. Not Grace.

Two things happened in the next few seconds. First, the little girl on the pavement turned her head to the right and Sarah knew for sure that it was not her daughter. Then the black Mercedes jerked forward, mounted the pavement, and ran down the man in the dark suit.

14

The man went down hard as the big black saloon car mounted the kerb and knocked him to the ground. His foot seemed to get caught and he fell beneath the wheels, the Mercedes bumping on its suspension as it drove over him. The little girl jumped back in alarm, her scream of fear drowned beneath the revving of the engine.

Sarah cried out too, an involuntary shout of alarm at the collision of flesh and metal.

'Oh God!'

Everything snapped into vivid, slow-motion detail: a little girl who'd escaped injury by a matter of inches, her mouth open in a scream; the man flat on the pavement, moving slowly; the Mercedes reversing back over him, bumping viciously on its suspension again as it drew back onto the road; a smear of dark blood on the grey pavement. The passenger side door of the Mercedes swinging open, a bald man in a black leather jacket jumping out and moving quickly towards the girl. The little girl shaking her head quickly, her back to the high iron railings at the side of the pavement. Tears starting from her eyes, the tips of the pink fairy wings from her backpack visible over her shoulders.

Sarah gripped the steering wheel, helplessness rising up as she watched the scene unfold. Questions colliding in her head. *Does he know her? Is he her father? Who is the man in the dark suit? Is he OK? Should she call an ambulance?*

Dark Suit pushed himself up into a sitting position, his face a mask of blood, and tried to stand up. The bald man shifted his attention away from the girl and grabbed the lapel of the other man's suit, raining punches on his unprotected face. Sarah looked around frantically for a policeman, hoping there would be a patrol car coming down the road that she could flag down. *Police. Of course.* She fumbled in her purse for her mobile, her shaking fingers bringing the screen to life and stabbing in 999. It rang three times as she checked both ways up and down the street, desperately craning her neck to look for someone, *anyone*, in uniform to step in and put this right. The call connected and she asked for police and ambulance to attend a traffic accident immediately, scanning for the nearest street sign to give to the operator. Wellington Avenue.

There. A man was coming towards them, walking towards the little scene playing out on the pavement. A younger man in a tracksuit, mid-twenties, looking like he was fresh from the gym. Tall and fit-looking. Hair still wet from the shower, rucksack over one shoulder, earphones in.

Thank you, God, Sarah thought silently. *Thank you. Now help them. Intervene.*

The young man seemed to register what was happening in front of him for the first time. He slowed his pace slightly as he took in the bald man standing over his bloodstained victim.

Help him, Sarah thought again.

Then the young man was checking over his shoulder and crossing the busy street away from them, keeping his eyes fixed on the pavement. Studiously ignoring the fight, the injured man being beaten to a pulp.

'Hey!' Sarah shouted to him through the closed window of her car. He made no indication that he'd heard her.

'Hey! You!' she shouted again, her voice higher and louder, slapping her palm so hard on the car window that the sting of it travelled up her arm.

The young man kept on walking, not looking back, increasing the distance between him and the girl.

Sarah slapped the window again, in mute desperation. *Coward. Bloody coward.* She turned her attention back to the two men, one on his feet and one on his back. As she watched, the bald man let his bloodied opponent flop to the pavement. Satisfied that he was no longer a threat, he turned his attention back to the little girl.

She was trying to hide, crouching down between two parked cars a few yards away, a look of such pure terror on her face that Sarah felt something stir deep within her.

Come here, she thought, *come to me. I will protect you.*

The bald man moved towards her but the little girl darted away from him at the last moment – Sarah's heart in her mouth as she thought for a second she was going to run straight out into the traffic. Instead the girl turned, coming up alongside the big Mercedes, then turned again and ran in front of Sarah's car, pigtails flying behind her, backpack bouncing up and down as she ran. She stopped when she reached the pavement, holding her hands up as if that might keep him at bay. Her face was streaked with tears.

The bald man continued stalking her. In a couple of seconds he would be through the gap between the two cars and then he would take her. An innocent child at the mercy of a man of violence. At the mercy of a man who believed he had the right to impose his strength on those weaker than himself. He was going to take her, do God knows what to her, for the same reason that men like him had always done such things: because there was no one who could stop them. No one who could stand up to them.

He was about to come through the gap between the front of her car and the back of the Mercedes.

Time seemed to stall.

And suddenly all the emotion of the last week, all the anger and frustration and helplessness, was bubbling up inside her.

All the rage surging from her brain down into her hands and feet.

Fuck that.

There was no real thought, no decision. Just emotion.

She took her foot off the brake and stamped on the accelerator pedal.

Her Fiesta jerked forward and caught him sideways on, smashing his knees into the back of the Mercedes. There was a sickening *crunch* of metal colliding with bone and flesh and cartilage and the bald man was hurled backwards, his legs crushed between the two cars. The impact flung Sarah forward against her seat belt. She watched in horror as the bald man crumpled to the ground, his face twisted in pain, hands grasping his shattered knees. She was momentarily stunned by what she had done, a flash of guilty horror at the damage she had inflicted on this stranger.

But at least the girl was safe. Sarah caught a glimpse of her running away down the pavement and saw, in amazement, that Dark Suit had got up and was now limping slowly and painfully after her, his right arm hanging uselessly by his side.

The driver's side door of the Mercedes opened. A second man got out, his shirt stretched taut across a large belly.

Shit.

She turned the key in the ignition. The Fiesta coughed and refused to start.

Oh no.

A flutter of panic.

She turned the ignition once more. The Fiesta's engine coughed again.

He was almost at her door, his hands bunching into fists.

At the last moment, just as Sarah thought he was going to tear open her door and attack her, he turned and bent down to his injured friend. Lifting him up by his armpits, he dragged the moaning man around to the rear door of the Mercedes, opened it awkwardly, and bundled him in.

Slamming the passenger door, the driver pulled something from his pocket – for a moment Sarah thought it was a gun – and held it up towards her. A mobile phone. He took a picture at a low angle to her car.

As soon as he'd done it, Sarah knew why.

Not a picture of me. A picture of my number plate.

The driver got back behind the wheel and the car pulled away in a squeal of tyres.

15

The young detective constable handed Sarah a cup of tea in a white styrofoam cup. He sat down opposite her at the interview room table, retrieving a pen from his jacket pocket and flipping back a page in his pad. He could only have been in his late twenties but had a pale complexion and flecks of grey at his temples that made him look older.

'No sugar, right?'

'Yes. Thanks.'

It was the first time Sarah had ever seen the inside of a police station. She had attended voluntarily after the incident on Wellington Avenue, and felt the weight of guilt pressing down on her now the surge of anger and emotion had passed. Guilt for deliberately driving her car into the bald-headed man.

She had sorted the kids' pickup with a shaky phone call to her dad, asking him to help out. Roger had duly obliged and taken Harry and Grace back to her house for their tea, Sarah promising to be back as soon as she could get out of the police station.

The tea was strong and dark and scalding hot. She took a small sip and set it down carefully on the table in front of her.

'This is all just totally surreal,' she said. 'This whole thing. A couple of hours ago I was sitting in my office, and now – this. Did you find the little girl yet?'

'Not yet.' The detective, whose name was DC Hansworth, clicked his ballpoint pen as he studied her. 'Still working on that.'

'She can't have been more than eight or nine years old.'

'Yup. So you said. Let's get back to the incident itself, shall we? You said your vehicle collided with a pedestrian as he walked in front of your car. A white male.'

'Yes. Have you found him?'

'Let's just concentrate on your statement first, shall we?'

'Right. Of course.'

'You were concerned that the man was going to take this child. Abduct her.'

'Yes. That's what it looked like to me.'

'And did he?'

'No. After my car went into him, he collapsed. She ran off.'

'And then what?'

'His friend picked him up and put him in the back of the Mercedes. Then they drove away. I got out and tried to find the girl but there was no sign of her.'

'What about the other man, the one the girl was with when you first saw her?'

'He looked to be in a really bad way but he still went after the girl. There was a big 4 x 4 there very quickly – I think perhaps they were both picked up further down the street. Did you find him?'

The detective put down his pen and clasped his fingers in front of him.

'Here's the problem, Dr Haywood: there was no sign of this bodyguard, or whatever he was. No sign of the little girl. No sign of the two men from the Mercedes, either.'

Sarah felt a stab of concern.

'No sign of the girl? You don't know where she is? Hasn't anyone reported her missing?'

DC Hansworth shook his head.

'No child of that description reported missing. No adult reporting an attempted abduction. No middle-aged white male turning up at any of the two nearby hospitals suffering leg injuries consistent with a traffic accident. All we have is a dent on the bumper of your car.'

'I don't understand,' Sarah said.

'We can't find any of them. Basically, all I've got is your statement.'

'What about eyewitnesses? There was that young guy walking along who passed right by us? And the van behind me when it happened. Have you spoken to the driver?'

The detective shook his head again.

'No pedestrians have come forward. We've got a couple of car drivers who were behind you, but they didn't see much because the van was in the way. One of them thinks he saw a black Mercedes when it went up onto the pavement, but then his view was blocked by a parked car. The other one thought he heard shouting or screaming at one point, but he had his radio on and his windows up, so he can't be sure. None of them saw a little girl.'

'I didn't make the whole thing up, if that's what you think. I'm not some sort of mad attention-seeker.'

'Of course not.' His voice took on a world-weary tone. 'The problem with incidents like this, Dr Haywood, is people often assume that someone else will come forward. Someone else will take the time. They might be happy to film it on their phone and put it on YouTube, but when it comes to helping the police – *sorry officer, too busy.*'

'What about CCTV?'

'We've pulled the local footage and have a late-plate Mercedes a bit further down the street, at a time that corresponds with what you describe. But the plates are bogus – they're from an Audi stolen a couple of days before.'

'Surely there must be *something.*'

He shrugged.

'If it was what you say it was – a kidnap attempt – then it would seem likely the plates were changed for that reason.'

'Someone needs to find that little girl – that's my biggest worry. I just want to know that she got home OK.'

'If she's not reported missing, and she doesn't turn up anywhere, then we have no name and no picture to go on. We have nothing to progress an enquiry.'

'You have my statement.'

'I know – and you did the right thing to report it. But if I'm honest, in the absence of a complainant or any other witnesses, I'm going to struggle to progress any of this very far.'

Her mobile phone vibrated on the table between them. Her dad.

'I need to take this,' Sarah said.

'Of course.'

Her father's voice came on the line, tight with tension.

'Sarah, are you on your way home? Where are you?'

'I'm all right, Dad. Are the kids OK?'

'They're both absolutely fine. I've given them tea and Grace is about to have her bath.' There was a measure of relief in his voice now. 'Are you all right?'

'I'm fine. I'll fill you in when I get back.'

'How did everything go at work? Did you find out about your job today?'

Sarah took a deep breath and closed her eyes. He had always wanted the best for her, always encouraged her without ever pushing. It was her father who'd calmly told her at the age of sixteen – when she'd been suspended from school for the second time in a month – that she had reached a crossroads in her life. Her mum had ranted and raved and talked about grounding Sarah for a month, stopping her pocket money for a year, banning her friends and taking her bedroom door off. But her father had just taken Sarah aside and said quietly, gently: '*You are at a fork in the road, and you have to choose which way you're going to go. You can carry on kicking against anything and everything, getting in trouble, doing everything on your terms. Or you can make the most of your ability, play by the rules for a while and see how far you can go. You could be the first in our family to get to university. I know you have the ability to go as high as you want. But you need to decide – right now – which way you're going to go.*'

She had turned it around, got the grades she needed for Durham University, and had been playing by the rules ever since.

Fifteen years on, she had arrived at another crossroads – except all the roads seemed to lead nowhere.

More than anything, more than ever, she wanted to speak to Nick about what was going on in her life. Share a bottle of wine with him, feel him close to her, be held by him and feel she wasn't facing this alone.

But she couldn't do any of that. Because he was gone.

Her father's voice interrupted her thoughts.

'Sarah? Are you still there?'

'I'm here.'

'Did you get any news today? Did you have your meeting?'

She couldn't bear to hear the hope and expectation in his voice.

'I'll tell you later, Dad. Give the kids a kiss for me.'

She hung up and turned back to the detective.

'Sorry about that. Are there some more questions you wanted to ask?'

'I think we're done for now.'

'There was one other thing,' she said, trying to think how best to phrase it. 'The driver of the Mercedes took a picture of my car while I was in it. And my number plate.'

'OK.' The detective reopened his notepad. 'You're sure?'

'Yes. I was thinking, well, what if they try to find me after what I did to that man?'

'How do you mean?'

'They've got my car registration – maybe they can use it to find me.'

He shook his head, giving her a little smile.

'They wouldn't be able to do that. All that kind of information is on secure DVLA servers, very carefully protected.'

'But what if they somehow get my home address?'

'I don't think you have anything to worry about.' He slid a business card to her across the desk. 'But give me a ring if you see anything that concerns you. Anything at all.'

16

It was two days later when she saw him for the first time.

She'd just given a seminar to her favourite group of final-year students and – as usual – it had overrun by half an hour as they discussed the finer points of Christopher Marlowe's most famous play, *Doctor Faustus*, in which the eponymous doctor sells his soul to the Devil for twenty-four years of charmed life. The students who made up the group, just out of their teens, could not comprehend a situation in which they would be willing to hand over their immortal soul. His willingness to do so seemed to register with them only in the most abstract way, so she had guided the discussion towards reasons why he would have chosen that path. And so the seminar had overrun and now she found herself hurrying back up the hill, laptop bag in one hand, handbag over her shoulder, checking her watch and doing a mental calculation as to whether she could fit in a quick sandwich from the library café before her next lecture. She didn't mind being busy: it meant she had less time to think about Alan Lovelock and whether she should put in a formal complaint about him.

That was when she saw the scarred man. Just an outline at first, a shape, a deviation from the outline of the wall he stood beside.

Standing at the corner of the main library building, he was half in the shadows thrown by the building's concrete façade. He stood out among the undergraduates milling about, who were talking, smoking, laughing, checking their phones and either drifting off down the hill towards the halls of residence or up to the students' union bar.

In the midst of this throng of students, the man was motionless, and silent, and alone.

He was staring straight at her.

She slowed her pace and kept her eyes on him, expecting him to move, to turn away, to break contact somehow. But he remained where he was, absolutely still, eyes on her, looking for all the world like a statue cast in stone. He was powerfully built, thick through the shoulders and chest, with arms that stretched the sleeves of his jacket. Dark clothes, dark hair. Arms loose by his sides. Even from fifty feet away she could make out a strange white line reaching from his hairline down through his dark stubble to his jaw. It looked like a scar.

She looked right as she crossed the road, pausing as one of the campus hopper buses lumbered past in a huff of diesel fumes, windows steamed up against the cold autumn afternoon. Maybe the man was waiting for someone, looking for someone, there were all kinds of reasons why . . .

When the bus had passed by and she looked towards the library again, he was gone. She scanned the surrounding groups of students for any sign of him, but he was nowhere to be seen. Vanished. Had he even been there at all, or had she imagined him?

Whatever. He was gone now. She dismissed it as the product of an overactive imagination and hurried on to the café.

You don't need another thing to worry about, Sarah Haywood, she told herself. *So don't make him into one.*

Marie caught up with her later that afternoon as they both waited to use the departmental photocopier. They'd still not had a chance to have a proper chat about any of Monday's events.

'How are you doing?' Marie said, putting a hand on Sarah's arm. 'Are you OK?'

Sarah nodded slowly.

'I'm all right. You know, plodding along as usual.'

'You still haven't told me how it all went down on Monday, after the promotions committee.'

She would tell Marie soon, but not yet. That was for another day. She still couldn't talk about it without feeling like crying.

'It was the usual Alan Lovelock bullshit.' In a low voice, she added: 'Listen, have you noticed anyone weird on campus in the last few days?'

Marie raised an eyebrow.

'Weird?'

'Anyone hanging around who looks out of place? A man too old to be an undergraduate, slightly weird-looking?'

'Sounds like most of the male staff in the faculty.'

'I mean, weird as in . . . potentially dangerous.'

Marie frowned. Shook her head.

'Don't think so.'

'You haven't seen a man with short black hair, stocky build, a white scar down the side of his face?'

'Nope. Who is he?'

'Not sure. Just some guy I saw hanging around earlier.'

'You think you've got a stalker?'

'No. I mean, I don't know. Maybe.'

'You're worrying me now, Sarah. What's going on? Have you told security?'

She shook her head.

'I just . . . want to keep it low-key if I can.'

'Do you know him?'

'Never seen him before.'

'Well, if you see him again I think you should call the police.'

'It's probably nothing, I don't want to overreact. But will you let me know if you see him?'

'Of course. I still think you should call someone.'

Sarah nodded, thinking of the young policeman's card in her handbag.

'I will.'

17

Sarah felt herself sagging with relief when Saturday came. Away from work, away from Alan Lovelock, she busied herself with the children and their activities, chores and shopping and play-dates and meals. She was busy all day and glad of the distraction. She would spend two or three hours marking papers tonight when Grace and Harry were in bed. For now, she was grateful to be away from the university, away from the daily reminders of how little control she had over her own destiny.

Away from the stranger who had been watching her by the library.

Two days had passed since she'd seen him. She'd not spotted him again, and in that time she'd convinced herself that he was probably just a visitor, maybe a scout for the rugby team, or someone spending a few days with a younger sibling on campus and drunk or stoned or otherwise messed up in a way that explained his odd behaviour. And was it really odd behaviour, on a university campus? Where the rowing club had been repeatedly warned over initiation ceremonies that involved drinking a pint of spirits or running naked from one side of the campus to the other? Where the campus security team had recently had to deal with twenty-five rugby players dressed as chickens who had manhandled a pool table onto the roof of the union building?

No. It was one man. Probably nothing.

Standing on the touchline of a football pitch at Lordship Rec, she shook off thoughts from the week and tried to pick Harry out among the gaggle of small boys chasing a football across the muddy pitch. Harry's seven-a-side team, the Cavaliers, were playing their local rivals the Typhoons. Saturday afternoon football was another one of the things that Nick had started off doing, but then lost interest. Instead he would invent some DIY task that he *had* to crack on with, but which would remain mysteriously uncompleted when Sarah and Harry returned home from the game.

At school, Sarah had played hockey, netball and rounders, none with any particular distinction, but she knew the rules and how they should be played. She'd never played football – apart from kickabouts with Harry in their small back garden – but she was fairly sure this was not quite how it was supposed to be played. Apart from the goalkeepers and one other boy who was standing to one side picking his nose, every other player on the pitch was following the ball like a swarm of lively bees pursuing an intruder in the hive. Defenders, attackers, the ones in the middle – whatever they were called – all of them were trailing the ball in an enthusiastic scrum, despite the shouts of both coaches from the touchline. The relatives belonging to each team stood on opposite sides of the pitch, a couple of dozen parents, grandparents, brothers and sisters, all hunched in overcoats, parkas, hats and gloves.

She shifted her umbrella from one hand to the other. It was drizzling with slow, steady monotony and her jeans and shoes were already soaked through. She had reluctantly allowed Grace to go back to the car park and sit in the car rather than stand in the rain, with strict instructions to keep the doors locked and not to turn the radio on in case she ran the battery down.

One of the boys managed to kick the ball clear of the pack and the mass of mud-spattered five-year-olds surged towards the other team's goal. The goalmouth, for some reason, was empty. Sarah quickly saw why – the other team's green-shirted goalkeeper had wandered off the pitch and was heading towards the catering table laid out with chocolate bars and drinks at the edge of the pitch.

The coach of the Typhoons, a blond, bearded man in a track-suit, threw his hands in the air.

'Will! Will! What the bloody hell are you doing?' He pointed desperately at the vacant goalmouth. 'Get back in goal!'

The absent keeper turned and looked blankly at him, his mouth open. The biggest boy in the gaggle of charging players, bearing down on the empty net, miskicked the ball and fell over into the mud, another boy falling on top of him. The ball trickled wide of the empty goal and out of play.

The other coach covered his face with his hands. There was a smattering of applause and more shouts of encouragement for both teams.

'Hard luck,' shouted one of the dads next to Sarah.

'What's the score?' Sarah asked him.

'Not sure. 12–8? 12–7? Actually, it could be 11–8. I've lost count.'

'When they get an even dozen goals each can we call it a day?'

He grinned, shaking his head. He wasn't wearing a hood and his greying hair was plastered to his head with rain.

'No such luck, Sarah. It's not even half-time yet.'

She indicated the Typhoons' wandering goalkeeper, who was now standing on the touchline with tears pouring down his face.

'I think their coach has his work cut out for the half-time team talk. Looks like the goalie's dad is not very pleased either.'

The boy's father, hands on his hips, was speaking to the coach. Sarah was too far away to hear what was being said but could tell from their body language that it was not a polite conversation. The boy was left on his own, still crying, as the two red-faced men argued and jabbed their fingers at each other. Their voices got louder.

Sarah felt sorry for the boy, willing his father to comfort him, to at least –

There was a gap in the crowd. She felt her whole body tense.

He was there. The man with the scar.

Standing behind the mums and dads of the opposition team, wearing a black puffa jacket and dark blue jeans. His black hair was cropped close to his head and was short enough to show off the deep white scar that ran all the way from his crown, above his ear and down to his jaw.

It was him. She was sure of it.

18

As she watched him, the scarred man turned his head slightly to look in the direction of the car park next to the clubhouse, where Sarah's Fiesta was parked. He nodded, once, then turned back to look at Sarah again. A very slight movement, but the meaning was clear.

The breath caught in Sarah's throat.

Grace was in the car. Alone.

She turned towards her car, forty or fifty yards away, the fear surging so hard that her legs almost buckled. The little blue Fiesta was still there. *But was Grace still inside?*

She began to hurry to the car park, dropping her umbrella and digging in her coat pocket for her phone. Then stopped dead.

Harry. She ran back to the pitch. Harry was still there, trotting gamely after the ball with his teammates.

The man was still there too, his square-jawed face impassive. He had his hands in his pockets, his black jacket glistening with rain.

Sarah was torn with indecision. Stay or go? Was Grace still there? Would he take Harry if she turned her back? Surely not in front of all these people?

She grabbed the arm of the touchline dad she'd just spoken to.

'I have to check on my daughter,' she said, her voice rising. 'Can you watch Harry? Keep an eye on him?'

The grey-haired man gave her a concerned look.

'No problem. You OK?'

'I don't know,' Sarah said, hurrying off across an empty pitch towards the car park. She broke into an unsteady run, her shoes slipping on the muddy grass, groping in her pocket for her mobile. She knew she had to be ready to ring the police if Grace was gone from the car. No delays. No wasted time.

Please be there. Please don't say they've taken her.

'Grace!' she shouted, panic rising. 'Grace!'

She hit the tarmac of the car park, sprinting strides taking her straight into the path of a car pulling out. The driver honked angrily and braked hard, stopping just short of her. Sarah waved an apology at him and kept on running, desperately trying to see into her car, to see the back of Grace's head in the front passenger seat.

The windows of her car were steamed up.

She slid to a stop by the passenger side door of the Fiesta and pulled hard on the handle of the driver's side door. Locked. Of course. She had given Grace the keys.

'Grace!' she shouted, the flat of her hand slapping on the opaque window. She hit it a second time, putting her eyes right up to the glass in a vain attempt to see in. Was her daughter inside? It looked like there was something there, a shape, or maybe a –

The passenger side door opened with a metallic click and Grace leaned her head out.

'Is the game finished?' she said.

Sarah almost laughed with relief, but it caught in her throat. *She's OK. It's OK.*

'Not yet, Grace. Are you all right?'

'I finished my book. Where's Harry?'

Another thought, like a punch in the stomach: *This might just be a distraction to take him.*

'He's still there. You need to come with me now.'

'Why?'

'You just need to come. Quickly, now.'

Grace began to climb out of the car.

'S'boring, though.'

Sarah craned her neck to look back at the pitch and, as she watched, there was a whistle and all the players slowed to a stop. She slammed the door and hit the remote to lock the car.

'There's not long left of this half – come on.' She took her daughter's hand. 'I'll race you.'

She started running back towards her son, back towards the game, knowing nothing except that she had to get back to him. Had to be there to protect him. The heavy mud sucked at her shoes, threatening to tear them off. Grace ran alongside her, telling her to slow down until they both reached the edge of the pitch, breathless and mud-spattered. The grey-haired dad was nowhere to be seen and the players were in a huddle surrounding the coach for the half-time team talk.

Sarah strained to see Harry, moving towards the group, looking for his blond hair in among the scrum of small, blue-shirted boys.

Felt the raw fear filling her head, pushing rational thought away.

He's gone he's gone he's gone –

She looked around wildly, searching the park, the trees, the road, for any sign of the scarred man.

Harry appeared in front of her, looking pleased with himself.

'I nearly scored a goal, Mummy. Did you see?'

She knelt down and hugged him tight, holding him close, not caring that he was drenched with rain and splashed with mud. Breathing in his smell, feeling his little arms around her neck, his hot breath in her ear as he described the goal he had almost scored.

She brushed the hair off his forehead.

'Well done, Harry!'

Her children were safe: that was all that mattered. She scanned the far side of the pitch again.

The man was gone.

She dug into her handbag for the detective's card and dialled his number, not sure whether he'd pick up after working hours. But the call was answered after two rings, and Sarah launched into a hurried explanation of the man she feared was following her.

'He looks . . . dangerous,' she said.

'Do you know this man – do you recognise him from the traffic incident you reported?'

'No, but as I told you: one of the men took a picture of me and my car that day, including my number plate.'

'Has this man approached you, spoken to you?'

'He's never there for long enough.'

'Have you received any unusual or threatening mail, email or phone calls recently?'

'None.'

'Any males at work, or in other areas of your life, who might have taken a particular interest in you?'

None that I can tell you about, she thought.

'No, but I've seen this man twice in three days now: once on campus and just now while my son was playing football, he was there on the other side of the pitch.'

The detective sounded unconvinced.

'And you're sure it's the same man?'

'Pretty sure. He's quite distinctive, he has a long white scar down the side of his head. Isn't there anything you can do?'

'The problem, Dr Haywood, is that he's not committed an offence at this stage. It still seems to be possible that it could be a coincidence, and –'

'It's not a coincidence! He turned up at my five-year-old's football match, for God's sake!' She turned away from the rest of the parents and lowered her voice, aware of the curious stares she was attracting. 'What am I supposed to do? I'm a woman on my own and, frankly, I'm scared of what might happen next.'

The young detective ran through some basic measures: Sarah should always carry a mobile phone and an attack alarm, alter her daily routine if possible, avoid being alone, start making a record of incidents, avoid engaging or talking to the man. He gave Sarah the name and number of a colleague, a Detective Sergeant Jane Irons, who had many years of experience of stalking cases. Sarah made a mental note to give her a call.

It was only when she was back at her car, clipping on Harry's seat belt across his booster seat, that she turned the question over in her mind: this man had tracked her down, he had found her at work and at home – and he'd done nothing. *Yet*.

But who was he?

19

It was exactly a week since Lovelock had told her she would not be getting a permanent contract. Sarah felt like she'd entered a parallel reality, where everything had been turned on its head and nothing made sense anymore. For months she had been waiting for good news about her job, struggling towards it like a drowning sailor flailing towards the last life raft, the one thing that was keeping her going. Ignoring any fears that the life raft would drift away and leave her behind. Leave her to drown.

But the life raft had turned out to be a mirage. It had never been there in the first place.

She had upped her dose of sleeping tablets since the bombshell about her job, to try and get more than three or four hours of sleep a night, but it was no good. She just lay there in the small hours, alone in the big double bed, listening to the tiny tick of her watch on the bedside cabinet, the sheets pulled tight to her chin. In idle moments she increasingly found herself thinking *Could I do it? Could I sleep with him to save my job? For my kids? To keep up the mortgage payments?* She would dismiss it, discard the idea, but then it would come creeping back again when she was least expecting it. Sitting at her desk with a stack of essays. Waiting in traffic at a red light. Pushing a meal around her plate as she wondered where her appetite had gone.

The question came creeping back now as she flipped off the lights of the arts faculty lecture theatre, plunging the auditorium into darkness, the last of her students sloping off down the corridor towards the union building. As an undergraduate and then a postgraduate, she had slept with a grand total of six people before meeting Nick and had been faithful to him since then, despite his betrayals. But were there any among those six that she actually didn't like? Any of them that she didn't enjoy sleeping with?

Of course there were. Probably two or three. She had done it for the wrong reasons – for stupid reasons – and regretted it afterwards. With Marco, she'd allowed herself to be convinced by his colossal self-belief in his abilities between the sheets (which turned out to be sadly inaccurate). Adam because she was worried he would split up with her (which he then did anyway). A guy in her final year – she couldn't remember his name – because she was pissed off with Adam and thought in some abstract way that sleeping with someone else would ease the hurt and betrayal he'd left her with.

Is that so different to what Lovelock wants? You slept with them and didn't enjoy it, so why would this be different? And more to the point, could you do it? If it was sink or swim?

No. Just no. This was not how the world was, not anymore. Or at least not how it was supposed to be. There was a world of difference between a few bad decisions and the degrading, hor-rifying prospect of sleeping with Professor Alan Lovelock, CBE.

She rebuked herself, again, for even thinking it. She would never sink that low.

No. Not that. Not ever.

She dug in her bag for her car keys. Trying to locate them in among the lucky dip of biros, mobile, tissues, chewing gum, lipsticks, purse, keys, half-finished packets of Polos, and a palm-sized aerosol that her cousin had brought back from America. Her fingers located the keys and she looked up, trying to remember which end of the row she'd parked. It was dark. Sometimes the days just blended into each other, she forgot from one day to the next where she'd found a space – and as usual, she had been late onto campus after dropping the kids at school, all the spaces near her office having been taken. She'd had to circle back, further away, to a little row tucked away at the back of the engi-neering building. It was her fallback option when the main car park was full because not many people even knew it was –

She stopped walking.

The scarred man was waiting for her.

But this time he wasn't skulking at the back of the lecture theatre, or watching her from a distance. This time he was lean-ing back onto the bonnet of her Fiesta, arms crossed. And he'd brought another man, younger, dark hair pulled back in a pony-tail, but with the same blank-eyed stare. Both men regarded her with expressionless faces.

She stared back, an icy sensation at the back of her neck. *Think. Stay calm.*

The engineering building in front of her was in darkness. It formed a natural cul-de-sac against the long boundary fence – the only way out was back the way she'd come. She checked over her shoulder, back towards the main road through campus. A couple of students, heading the other way perhaps thirty or forty yards distant. No one approaching. Could she shout to them for help, attract their attention? No. Stay calm. No shouting. Not yet. *Don't let yourself be intimidated by these thugs.*

Her hand was still in her bag, holding her keys. She released them and reached for her phone instead. *Campus security or the police?* The campus security team knew every inch of the university and would be here faster. And she needed someone, anyone, to intervene. *Fast.* Their office was a three minute walk back down the hill and she had the twenty-four hour control room number stored in her phone. She would just head in that direction, call them, and get them to meet her. Then call the police for good measure.

She put the phone to her ear and turned to walk quickly away.

Straight into another man. Barrel-chested and heavily built, he had come up behind her silently and now placed a big hand on her shoulder, freezing her in place. His after-shave was sharp and pungent. With his other hand he prised her phone roughly away and terminated the call, shaking his head. Sarah reached back into her handbag, fear and anger flowing through her in equal measure, and her fingers closed around the little aerosol can. She brought her hand back out of the bag, the little canister in her palm, and fired red dye spray straight into his face.

He recoiled instantly and took a step back, swearing in a language she didn't understand, but his other hand still gripped her. She sprayed him in the face again and this time he staggered back. She turned to run.

But it was too late. There were already footsteps behind her.

The man with the scar grabbed her arm and pulled her back, roughly. He took the little can of self-defence spray from her and put it in his pocket.

None of them had said a word to her yet and somehow this made the situation even more terrifying. But now he spoke, in heavily accented English.

'Don't do this again.'

She opened her mouth to scream but the ponytailed man clasped his hand over her mouth before she could get the noise out. A ripple of pure panic went through her, like an electric shock.

The scarred man shook his head.

'And no screaming.' He opened his jacket to reveal a black pistol in his belt. 'Understand?'

She nodded quickly, eyes wide. Her mind was racing.

A gun. He has a gun. What the hell is going on?

But deep down she already knew the answer: the man she had driven her car into a week ago. His friends had found her. Her legs felt weak, as if they might buckle at any moment.

The ponytailed man propelled her towards a black BMW 4 x 4 with heavily tinted windows. He opened the passenger door and she struggled against his grip. She wouldn't let them put her in the car. Some primal instinct told her that it was better to stay out here in the open for as long as possible. But it was an uneven struggle that was over before it had even begun, and in seconds she was manhandled into the BMW as the door slammed behind her. Ponytail climbed into the driver's seat and started the engine.

'Please!' Sarah gasped. 'Please, I have to get my children. I have to pick them up. They'll be expecting me to be there. Please, they're waiting for me.'

She was on the back seat, the scarred man beside her. Calmly, he took her phone from her bag and held it out with a single word.

'Unlock.'

She reached out a shaking hand and unlocked the phone with her thumbprint. The scarred man navigated quickly to text messages, selected 'Dad Mob' and scrolled down before selecting one from a previous week. *He knows what he's looking for*, Sarah thought. He copied the text and pasted it into a new message.

Running late, can you pick kids up from after-school club and take back to mine? See you in a bit. Thanks. S x

'Now they are not expecting you,' he said, and pressed *send*.

A moment later the reply dropped in.

No problem, see you later. Dad x

The scarred man switched the phone off and opened its case, took the battery out, and slipped the three parts into the pocket of his coat. He then produced a black silk hood from his other pocket and in one quick movement he hooded her.

Sarah's world went black. The inside of the bag smelt musty and sour, like someone else's sweat. She went to take a deep breath but there wasn't enough air. Not enough to fill her lungs. She suddenly felt light-headed and for one horrible moment she thought she was going to faint or suffocate. She lurched backwards as the car began to move.

Close by her ear, close enough to be a lover's whisper, a voice said: 'Lie down on your side.'

She did as she was told, the man's hand heavy on her shoulder, trying to calm her breathing. *Slowly. Calmly.* In through the nose, out through the mouth. She wondered what had happened to the last person who had been forced to wear this hood.

The BMW swung through a series of turns and she knew they were leaving the campus. She imagined the possibilities, her breath hot inside the bag. There still wasn't enough air, but in this lying position she was able to shift her head on the seat, creating a tiny gap at her neck to allow more air through. She shivered involuntarily, a violent spasm that went through her whole body. The hand pushed down a little heavier on the top of her arm, pinning her in place on the BMW's back seat.

Think. If this was about the man she'd hit with her car, what would they do to her in return? What about her dad? How long would it be before he raised the alarm when she didn't come home later? Another thought pierced her like a blade: what if these men were going to take Grace and Harry, too? In her head, she said a silent prayer: *Please let this be about me, not about my children. Please let them be safe with my dad.* The thought of Grace and Harry and her dad sitting around the kitchen table made her eyes fill with tears. She swallowed hard and fought them back.

This is no time for crying. Not now. You don't have that luxury. Think.

She tried to count in her head, and guess how quickly the car was travelling. Were they on a fast road, a dual carriageway? No. Lots of traffic. Lots of stops. Traffic lights and twists and turns which suggested they were heading further into the city, rather than away. But the journey seemed to be taking forever. She began counting as best she could, one to sixty, then starting again. Not too fast. Count the minutes. The act of counting kept her mind off other possibilities, helped her stay calm. One to sixty, then start again.

She reached what she thought was fourteen minutes, near enough.

The car stopped.

Then the hand was on her arm again and she was pulled sideways, edging along the car seat and stepping carefully down onto hard ground. The sounds of the road fainter now. For a second she just stood there, smelling diesel and rain and cold night air. Men talking in low voices, muffled through the hood. Car doors slamming. The grip on her upper arm loosened slightly. She was still hooded, but her hands were free and she had a sudden urge to rip the hood off and just make a run for it, look for a gap between these men and sprint through it, as fast as she could. She thanked the instinct that had made her wear flat shoes this morning. She could run in these shoes. She used to run for her school, and she had been good, too. 100 metres,

200 metres, 4 x 400 metres relay. She could do this. It might be her last chance – her only chance. Instinctively, she knew that if it came it would only be a second or two and she would have to be ready to react without hesitation.

More voices, but she couldn't make out what they were saying. The smell of cigarette smoke. The metallic *chuck* of the BMW's doors being central-locked.

The hand came away from her arm.

Now.

She ran.

20

She pulled the hood from her head and threw it down, leaning away from a man who lunged for her as she ran past. His fingertips brushed her jacket but she was past him, sprinting now, eyes squinting in the brightness of two tall floodlights at each side of a courtyard, chain-link fence in front, open concrete, warehouses, more dark buildings behind them. Startled shouts behind her. Footsteps. *There.* A gap between two buildings. She veered towards it, sprinting, pumping her arms and drawing great breaths of cold night air deep into her lungs.

'Help!' she shouted. 'Help me!'

She ran into the corridor of darkness between two warehouses, headlong, trying to make out what was at the far end, more buildings and a hint of street light. Her lungs were already starting to burn. She would run to the street and flag down a car, find a café or a pub, get someone to call the police, just get around this corner and –

A strong hand shot out and grabbed her, grasping her arm in a steel-hard grip. Another man, one she didn't recognise. Panic pulsed through her. She swung a slap at his face with her free hand, feeling it connect with an impact that stung her palm. She kicked him in the shin and then pistoned her knee up into his crotch with as much force as she could muster. She heard a grunt of pain, there was a momentary loosening of the grip, then the man flipped her around, put an arm around her waist from behind and lifted her off her feet. He began carrying her back to the BMW.

'Help me!' Sarah screamed again.

The man put his other hand over her mouth.

He carried her all the way back to the car like that. The scarred man and his two colleagues were there. The one with the pony-tail looked shaken, and he stepped forward as if to strike her. She flinched back as his hand came up, but it was just the black hood again. He pulled it down over her head and her world went black once more. The cotton was wet where it had landed on the ground and the musty damp smell filled her nose.

She heard an exchange of what she recognised as Russian between two of the men and then they laughed. More Russian. The sound of a heavy punch landing on muscle, breath escaping and a body falling to the wet concrete. Groaning and coughing, a scraping noise as the struck man got back to his feet. A loud spit and a string of fast, angry Russian.

Then more laughter, the sound cruel to Sarah's ears. She was suddenly terrified of what was going to happen next.

'What?' she said, trying to keep the panic out of her voice. 'What's happening?'

The answer, when it came, was right next to her ear and she jerked away from the sound, a heavily accented Russian voice, deep and slow. The scarred man, the one who had spoken to her on campus.

'I said: "Mikhail needs more time in gym and less at keyboard".'

More laughter. More fast Russian from Ponytail, the one who had been punched – whose name seemed to be Mikhail – talking and trying to catch his breath at the same time.

Then the hand grasping her arm tightly was half-guiding, half-pulling her along. She stumbled on a step up, tripping and almost falling forward, her hands going out instinctively to break her fall but the grip on her arm keeping her upright. The slam of a door. Echoes of their walking feet. They were inside. Through a gap at the bottom of the hood she could see a rough concrete floor, a pair of feet either side of hers. Another doorway – the heavy metallic slam of a large metal bolt being shot home into its lock – then thick carpet beneath their feet.

She was being pushed down into a straight-backed wooden chair.

Oh God. This is it.

The hood was snatched off her head and she sat, blinking, not wanting to move or turn around in case it provoked them further.

There was a soft click as the door shut behind her.

Her eyes slowly adjusted to her new surroundings and she saw that she was in a large windowless office, a huge desk in front of her with an empty leather chair. The far side of the room was dark, deep in shadow but there were spotlights angled towards her, one in each corner, that made her feel like she was about to be interrogated. A large closed door behind the desk.

Sarah took deep breaths, glad to be free of the hood. The room smelled of cigar smoke and aftershave and old leather. She waited. A minute. There was sweat on the palms of her hands but she willed herself to stay calm. *Please let my children be safe.* Two minutes. *If they were going to hurt you, they would have done it by now. Wouldn't they?* As she was considering rising to find the man who had brought her here, the door opened in front of her.

A tall man came through the doorway, dressed in a dark suit and white open-necked shirt. Squinting into the light, Sarah struggled to make out his features. He looked to be in his mid-fifties, with short black hair and a black beard, neatly trimmed. He sat down behind the desk, settling back into the leather chair, hands laced together in his lap. He stared for a moment, dark eyes seeming to consider her.

Sarah stared back, blinking fast, heart thundering in her chest. Praying that whatever was about to happen wouldn't hurt too much.

Let's just get it over with.

Finally, the man spoke.

'Do you know who I am, Sarah?' His voice was deep and soft, the trace of an accent.

She shook her head quickly.

'No.'

'You can call me Volkov. It is a name that some people use for me. Do you know why you are here?'

'No.'

'Let me show you.'

He stood up and returned to the door he had come in from a few moments before. He opened it, beckoned to someone, and said something in Russian. He beckoned again and a girl appeared, hesitant at first, peering around the door frame with wide eyes. She was small, about Grace's age, her dark hair in pigtails.

Sarah recognised her instantly. The girl from Wellington Avenue.

21

Volkov beckoned to the girl again, said something to her in rapid Russian. He turned back to Sarah, his face softer.

'Do you recognise this girl?'

Sarah nodded and leaned towards her.

'Hello there. Are you all right?'

The girl gave her a shy smile and a little nod in return, but said nothing.

Sarah said: 'Thank God she's safe, I was so worried about her.'

'You've seen her before, yes?'

'I saw her, last week. Some men were . . .' She trailed off, looking from man to girl, and back again. 'This is your daughter?'

'Very good.' He put his big hand on her shoulder. 'Aleksandra, you have something to say to Dr Haywood?'

'Thank you,' the girl said in halting English, her eyes fixed on the desk between them. 'For stopping the bad man.'

'You are very welcome, Aleksandra. I'm just glad you're OK.'

Volkov spoke to the girl in Russian again and she disappeared back into the side room. The door shut and Sarah was alone with him once more. The rush of relief she felt was almost overwhelming, as she realised for the first time since being taken from the campus that these men might not want to hurt her.

He gestured towards her and Sarah noticed the watch on his wrist, heavy and wide-faced, inlaid jewels glinting in the spotlights.

'I'm sorry for this unpleasantness.'

'It's all right.'

'Soon we will take you back to your university. But first let me tell you why I've brought you here. Will you indulge me?'

Sarah nodded.

'Good.' He took a bottle and two small glasses from a desk drawer, filled each glass and set one on the desk in front of Sarah.

'Drink,' he said.

She took a small sip, the vodka burning the back of her throat.

He raised a toast to her, drank half of his, and settled back into his chair.

'So, I had a son, once. Aleksandra's brother.' His face darkened. 'He was taken four years ago, in Moscow. Kidnapped. This is one of the reasons why I am here now, in UK.'

Sarah waited for him to continue, noting his use of the past tense. But he stayed silent until she couldn't bear it any longer.

'I'm sorry,' she said. 'What happened to your son?'

'There were men who thought they could change my mind by threatening me, who thought they could bend me to their will by threatening my son, my oldest child. I looked for him, day and night. Bled my enemies white searching half the city. But I was too proud to negotiate. Too proud to make a deal for his life.' He was silent for a moment. 'So one day they sent a finger. I continued searching. The next day another finger. Still I would not bow down to these men. The day after that, they sent his hand. That was all we had for the casket when we buried him. I never saw him again.'

'I'm so sorry, so very sorry . . . '

He touched a picture on his desk.

'My wife Katerina died very soon after. She couldn't . . . she was not able to deal with losing our boy. She stepped in front of an express train at Kazansky Station.' He gestured towards Sarah. 'You remind me of her. Very much.'

Sarah didn't know how to respond to such personal revelations from a stranger, so she said nothing.

'But their blood is on my hands,' Volkov continued. 'And it always will be, until the day I die.'

'What was your son's name?'

'Konstantin. He was eight years old.'

Sarah tried to imagine the trauma of losing her child in such horrific circumstances. The black cloud on every parent's horizon.

'My little girl will be eight next month,' she said softly.

'So, what you must understand, Sarah, is that by saving my daughter you have saved my future. You have saved the last piece of my family.'

'I just saw red, that was all.'

'They could have taken your life . . . ' He clicked his fingers. 'Like *that*. You have no idea how close you came to it. You acted with courage, when others chose cowardice. And in doing this, you gave me a gift without price.' He flipped the lid of a box on the desk, withdrawing a long cigar. 'Sarah, I have been blessed with remarkable success in my working life. I have much property, private jets; I have more money than I can spend in a hundred lifetimes. But all of it is pointless, worthless, unless there is someone to pass it on to when I am gone.'

'Your child.'

He used a cigar cutter to snip the end off the cigar with a sharp *snap*.

'Exactly. And so a man who wants to take her away from me threatens everything. He threatens my whole world.' He lit the cigar and drew on it heavily, clouds of smoke rising to the ceiling. 'When you saved Aleksandra you gave me a gift that is so . . . so immense, that it is impossible to measure. And I have never been in debt, not one day in my life. Never owed anything to anyone. Until now. In Russia we say that debt is beautiful – but only after it has been repaid.'

'You don't owe me anything,' she protested.

He considered the tip of the cigar, glowing cherry red.

'Do you know what a truly good deed is, Sarah?'

'When you do a good turn.' She shrugged. 'When you help someone. You know.'

He shook his head emphatically.

'No. A *truly* good deed is one that is totally unselfish, without any hope or expectation of a reward. By its nature, a truly good deed *cannot be repaid*.' He rolled the cigar between thumb and forefinger, before pointing it at her. 'But I am going to try. Because in my life I have learned that to be a great man, to be a leader, we cannot simply strike back against the evil done to us. We must also reward loyalty, bravery, brains, to truly elevate ourselves above the masses. My colleague Mikhail, for example: you met him already this evening, I think. At the age of fifteen Mikhail hacked my company's computer network, planted viruses, made a mess. Not to steal, just to have fun. We caught him, of course, and he was punished. But I recognised his genius with the computer and asked him if he wanted to come work for me, to stop such attacks happening again. And he has provided loyal service ever since.'

'I don't want anything from you. I'm just glad your daughter is safe.'

'You don't seem to understand, Sarah. Listen to me: *I am in your debt*. Every good deed must be rewarded. And the reward should match the deed, so I'm going to give you something very special – a gift like no other.' He took a deep drag on the cigar, smoke coiling from his nostrils. 'Back home in Russia one of my other nicknames was *volshebnik*. Do you know what this means?'

'My Russian is about as basic as it gets, I'm afraid.'

'It means "The magician". Because I could make things disappear – money, evidence, problems.' He paused for a moment, his dark eyes boring into her. 'Sometimes people, too.'

'O-OK,' Sarah said, hesitantly.

'The men who took my son in Moscow – I made *them* disappear. All of them. The men who tried to take Aleksandra last week, they were members of an Albanian gang who want to carve a niche for themselves. They too will disappear soon. So here is my offer.' He put the cigar in an ashtray and leaned forward, hands clasped together on the desk. 'You give me one name. One person. And I will make them disappear. For you.'

22

Sarah stared at him. Was this a trick? A joke?

She swallowed. 'Disappear?'

'Yes. No comebacks for you, no connections. No one would ever know.' He made a chopping motion with his hand. 'It happens. And then that is it.'

'Disappear as in, well . . . ?'

His unblinking eyes stared back.

'Gone, vanished. They vanish off the face of the earth as if they never existed. Then you and I will be even. Your deed will be repaid and my debt will be settled.'

There were three conditions, he told her. She had seventy-two hours to provide a name. If she said no, the offer disappeared forever. And if she said yes, there was no going back. No changing her mind.

Sarah sat for a moment, trying to make sense of his words.

'You're talking about . . . well, that would be . . . it would be illegal.'

'Legal, illegal? Who decides this? Who makes it so? I am not talking about the law, I am talking about *justice*. Justice for you, justice for your family, for anyone you love. I intend to repay my debt – if a man does not have honour, he has nothing.'

'But you can't just arbitrarily make someone disappear. That's not . . . it's not . . . you just can't . . .'

'Perhaps not in your world. But in my world?' He shrugged. 'People vanish all the time. Most of them don't even merit more than a few paragraphs. Not unless they are a pretty young woman or a child or a celebrity. Are you telling me there is no one in your life who doesn't deserve it? No one who has wronged you? Your faithless husband, for example?'

'No! Of course not.'

'Or perhaps his little girlfriend in Bristol?'

Sarah hesitated. Volkov grinned.

'Aha! You see? You are thinking about it, this is good. So: your husband's girlfriend?'

'No. Not her.'

'But you hesitated.'

'How do you even know about that?'

'We know all about you. I wanted to find out all I could about the brave woman who saved my family.'

'I just can't believe what you're saying. I can't get my head around it.'

The man's smile vanished. He leaned forward.

'Give me a name. And I will make you believe.'

A memory rose to the surface of her mind.

'The men who came for your daughter – one of them took my picture, my car registration number. I'm worried they might find me, come after me or my family.'

He waved his hand dismissively, smoke billowing from his cigar.

'Don't worry about them. Amateurs. They are already being taken care of. I'm asking for a name from *you*, from *your* life.'

She fought against her instincts. *It wasn't right. It couldn't be right.*

But why not? Why not let the hammer fall on this most deserving victim?

She lifted her gaze to look at Volkov again.

'I don't . . . I don't have a name to give you. There isn't anyone.'

'Nonsense. Everyone has someone they would like to punish. To have just a little bit more justice in this world.'

'Maybe I'm the exception.'

He considered her for a long moment.

'Are you sure?'

She felt like a traveller who had been on the same straight road for a thousand miles, expecting it to be straight for a thousand more, and then suddenly arriving at a fork in the road. A choice she had never anticipated. And was he even serious?

'Yes. I'm sure.'

'Everyone has a name to give. Everyone. Whether they admit it to themselves or not.'

'There's no one.'

'I advise you to think very carefully about this.' He pressed a button under his desk and a moment later the scarred man came in. He handed Sarah two mobile phones – one of which was hers, the other an unfamiliar Alcatel handset with a clamshell design that she hadn't seen for years.

Volkov indicated the Alcatel phone.

'This is a single-use phone. A throwaway. There's one number in the memory, you can reach my staff on it. If you change your mind, you have seventy-two hours to give me a name.'

She pocketed both phones.

'Thank you.'

'I ask only one thing of you.' He leaned forward until his face was inches from Sarah's, his breath sulphurous with old cigar smoke. 'Show me the respect of keeping my confidence. Don't tell anyone that we've met, or this offer I make you. Do you understand?'

'Of course,' Sarah said.

'Can I trust you?'

'Yes.'

'Good. Let me just be clear how serious I am.'

The man with the scar placed four glossy 8 x 10 photographs on the table in front of her.

One of her house. One of her dad's house. Two that were street views of school playgrounds filled with primary-age pupils. Small children in red jumpers, running, playing, talking. Harry's school. Another image of a school playground, with bigger children, Grace there, in the centre of the shot.

Sarah felt her stomach contract as she studied the pictures.

'How did you –'

'Research.'

'You've been spying on me?'

'I told you: I wanted to know the woman who saved my child.'

The knot of fear in her stomach tightened.

'You could have just asked me.'

'And you would tell me?'

'I'll tell you now, if you like. There's not much to tell.' She paused, swallowed. 'But then you must give me these pictures back.'

He smiled. Shook his head.

'I don't think so. I need to be sure that our conversation stays private. If you tell the police or anyone else we have met, you will force my hand, and then who knows who will be next to disappear. Do not tell Nick, your friends Laura Billingsley, or Marie Redfern, your father, Roger. No one.'

He knows all their names, Sarah thought.

As if reading her mind, Volkov continued: 'Yes, I know who they are and where they live. I know where you live and where your beautiful children go to school. But please be sure that this is just for insurance. A man like me has to be careful; he has to have options. Nothing will make me happier than to burn all these pictures, forget all these names. And I will do this, after I have repaid what I owe you. But not yet. For now, I keep them in my safe. Insurance. Do you understand?'

Sarah thought for a long moment, contemplating the danger of lying to this man.

'Yes. I understand.'

'Good. And now we will take you back to your car, and then you will drive home, kiss your children and put them to bed. You and I will not see each other again, and we will not speak again.'

He stood up and held out his hand.

'Goodbye, Dr Haywood.'

She stood and shook hands with him, his grip strong and dry against her palm.

PART II

23

Sarah sat in her car in front of the house, the events of the past hour turning over and over in her mind. The words bouncing around inside her head until they drowned out everything else.

Give me one name. One person. And I will make them disappear.

She felt exhausted, as if she'd just returned from a long journey to a foreign country. As if she could sleep for a month. Finally, she got out of the car, locked it, and walked wearily into the house.

Her dad leaned on a mop in the corner of the kitchen. Tall and straight-backed with a full head of curly white hair, he was a regular visitor since becoming a widower some eight years previously. Still fit and trim in his mid-sixties, his face crinkled into a smile at the sight of his daughter. Sarah kissed him on the cheek, gave Grace a hug and admired the story she'd written at school, then sat Harry on her lap so she could give him a proper cuddle, her son chattering on about the football cards that Grandad had bought him at the sweet shop, showing her each of them in turn.

Home. Familiarity. Safety.

It was the same as it had always been. But also subtly different, shifted on an angle, as if she was looking at her life through a pane of frosted glass. She had glimpsed the people in the shadows, and now she knew they were there.

They took the children upstairs at seven o'clock for teeth cleaning, pyjamas and stories. Harry was always finished with stories first – was first to fall asleep and first to wake in the morning – so Sarah soon found herself back at the table in the little kitchen. She dug in her purse for DC Hansworth's card, stared at it for a long moment. Two numbers, mobile and landline. She should call him. Report what had happened. She took the landline out of its cradle and held it in her other hand.

Tell no one.

The instruction had been clear. But she felt like she was stepping over some line by not telling anyone about what had happened to her this evening. It already felt like a heavy weight that she wanted to put down, but she couldn't. Not yet, anyway. Perhaps not ever.

Footsteps on the stairs. She put the policeman's card back in her handbag.

Her dad appeared in the kitchen doorway, leaning against the frame, hands in his pockets.

'Princess Grace is officially asleep.'

'Does she want a mummy kiss?'

'Dropped off before she could think to ask.'

'Harry only managed a few minutes before he zonked out. What were you mopping the floor for earlier? That's definitely above and beyond.'

'Jonesy brought a squirrel in.'

'Alive or dead?'

'Alive to begin with, I think, then he made a bit of a mess of the poor little chap all over the kitchen floor.'

'Ugh. Did the kids see it?'

He nodded, gritting his teeth.

'Grace was a bit upset. She wanted to give it a proper funeral, with flowers and a headstone.'

She smiled. 'Thanks for sorting it out.' She looked over at her ginger cat, who was sitting on a box next to the radiator. 'Bad boy, Jonesy. Poor squirrel.'

Jonesy blinked slowly at her and began to purr.

Her dad pulled out a chair and sat down next to her at the table.

'Are you going to tell me what's going on, Sarah?'

'What do you mean?'

'What happened today? You look like you've been to hell and back.'

She thought quickly.

'I got stuck in a horrific traffic jam and my phone was about to die, so I thought I'd just text you before my battery went totally flat. Thanks so much for helping out.'

He raised an eyebrow and for a second Sarah thought he was going to call her out on the lie, but he seemed to think better of it.

'You look as if you're carrying the world on your shoulders.'

'Busy at work, that's all. Lots to keep up with.'

He studied her for a moment longer, then went to the kettle on the kitchen side.

'Cup of tea?'

'I'll be up all night if I have tea now.'

'How about a snifter instead, before I head off? I bought you a new bottle of single malt, your stocks were getting low.' He opened the cupboard and took out the bottle of Glenmorangie from the back, with two glasses.

Sarah was about to say no – ordinarily she would never drink whisky on a school night – but this had been no ordinary day.

'Go on then.'

He poured a generous measure, then the same amount again of water, and set the glasses down on the kitchen table.

'So, are you going to let me in on it?'

'On what?'

'Just want to know what's up with my youngest girl, that's all.'

Proper chats with her dad were still a relatively new phenomenon. When she and her sisters had been growing up, most of the real heart-to-hearts had been with her mum. The long discussions about friends and fall-outs, school, boyfriends, breakups, anxiety and exams had always been her domain. Handing out tissues and hugs along with calm advice – not always what they had wanted to hear, but what needed to be said. Her dad had been there, but usually in the next room, one step removed from the emotional whirlpool that was living in a house with three teenaged girls, hearing about it afterwards from his wife and getting involved only when he deemed the situation required his intervention, as with Sarah's year of teenage rebellion at sixteen. Her dad had spent the eight years since his wife's death trying to bridge that gap, to fill the void left by her passing. And as it turned out, he was a good listener.

Sarah picked up her tumbler and took a sip, trying to get the thoughts straight in her head, trying to disentangle the things she could tell him from the things that were forbidden.

'Things have been tough at work, Dad. They aren't really going the way I expected them to.'

'I wish there was some way I could help, Sarah.' He rested his chin in the palm of his hand. 'Has Nick called you? Has he . . . said something to you?'

'No. He still hasn't called.'

'Is there something else bothering you?'

Tell no one.

'No.'

'You're sure?'

'I'm sure.'

* * *

Tidying the kitchen alone later, Sarah realised she didn't even know Volkov's real name. Or his daughter's full name. Or the surnames of any of his men. Or where they had taken her. What exactly *could* she tell her dad, or the police? The implied threat to her family was real enough – the pictures of the children's schools, her house and her dad's house. But what meaningful information could she give the police? What could she tell them that would make her family safer, rather than putting them at even greater risk? The man said he was rich, and was some kind of businessman; he had a daughter who was maybe eight or nine years old. But that was it.

That night, she lay in bed alone, listening to the tick of her watch on the bedside table, turning the situation over and over in her mind. Sleep wouldn't come.

She wished so hard that Nick was here to talk to. Someone she could share the burden with, so she didn't feel so utterly alone with this secret. Would she have told him everything? Probably. But could he be trusted to stay silent? She wasn't sure. He certainly couldn't be trusted to keep his marriage vows.

Tears sprang to her eyes and she blotted them on the duvet cover.

The smart thing to do would be to just pretend it had never happened. Put it behind her and never mention it to anyone. The risk to her family – to her children – was too great. She didn't know much about Volkov, but it seemed clear enough that he was highly dangerous. The best thing to do would be to move on with her life.

Forget the offer he had made to her.

Give me one name.

But she couldn't forget. She couldn't.

Because as soon as he'd made his offer, the very instant the words had left his lips, she'd had only one thought. One overpowering thought, drowning out everything else. It had not taken minutes, or even seconds for it to come to her. First name, last name. Two words, four syllables.

Of course she had a name to give him.

Everyone had a name to give, didn't they?

24

Harry had dressed himself – or tried to – but had only got as far as pants, odd socks and his red school jumper, back to front. No shirt or trousers. He lay on his bedroom floor, surrounded by Lego and *Star Wars* toys, oblivious to the rapid approach of the school day.

Sarah leaned against his bedroom door, a fierce bloom of love in her chest.

'Time to get you ready for school, young man.'

'I've done school already,' he said to his toys.

He had been at infant school for all of two months.

'Not for a while yet, Harry boy.'

'I want to do playing now.' He parked the Millennium Falcon in its Lego garage, carefully pushing the doors closed behind it. 'A playing day.'

Don't we all, she thought.

'You can have playing days on Saturday and Sunday.' She realised as she said it how lame and inadequate this must sound to a five-year-old.

'Is today Saturday, Mummy?'

'No, darling, it's Tuesday. Come on, let's finish getting you dressed, shall we?'

In films and on TV, she thought as she poured out bowls of cereal, people's rosy-cheeked children trotted out of the house and got in the car holding hands, smiling at their mother and sitting quietly on the way to school. Maybe the big one would help the little one put his seat belt on. And the little one would give the big one a hug, then they'd sit quiet and smile angelically whenever mummy turned to check on them.

Her children had never done that.

She finished getting them both ready, checked Harry's book bag and made sure – in between quick bites of toast – that they'd both cleaned their teeth and had everything they needed. She knelt down to do up the Velcro on Harry's little black shoes for him, used her thumb to wipe away a trace of toothpaste from Grace's top lip as she flinched away in protest. They stood side by side in front of her for a moment, dark-haired daughter and blond-haired son, junior school and infant school, and she felt a burst of pride. *These two.* They were everything, *they* were what mattered. Whatever happened with her and Nick, whatever happened at work. Whatever she had to do, she would do it – for them. They were the rock her life was built upon. *I must remember what this is like*, she thought to herself. *What they're like when they're little. Before I know it they will be grown and gone, and I will miss them being like this.*

'Right,' she said. 'Are we ready to go?'

Harry shot off out of the kitchen and down the hallway, getting a head start on his sister, his unzipped coat billowing out at the sides. Grace caught up with him in five quick strides and grabbed his hood, hauling him back. It threw him off balance and he collapsed backwards as if poleaxed. Lying full-length on the hall floor he began to cry, a loud and piercing air-raid siren wail that cut through her like broken glass.

'First to the door!' Grace said triumphantly, putting her hand on the front door handle.

'Grace!' Sarah said, catching up to them. 'Stop that! Say sorry to your brother.'

'He was in the way.'

Sarah picked Harry up and stood him back on his feet, before his crying could reach full volume. Experience as a mother told her that crying was not always a cause for alarm. It was when they were hurt but quiet that you really needed to be worried.

'There's enough room for all of us. Say sorry.'

Grace stared at her brother, eyes blazing.

'Cry baby,' she said.

'Say sorry,' Sarah repeated.

'He is, though.'

'Grace!'

'Sorry,' her daughter mumbled to no one in particular.

Sarah straightened her son's coat and brushed his hair off his forehead. She checked her watch: 8.46. They were still OK for time – just.

'Let's try again, shall we?'

Harry put his little hand in hers and they walked to the front door. As they passed Grace, he swung his book bag in an exaggerated arc so it slapped against his sister's back, then clung tighter to Sarah's hand as Grace tried to swing her bag to retaliate.

Sarah hit her car remote to unlock the doors and turned to secure the front door behind them.

Harry released his grip on her hand and hared off across their short drive, grabbing open the rear passenger side door and clambering up on to his booster seat.

'First in the car!' he said, beaming.

Following him, Sarah strapped her son into his booster seat and glanced quickly at her reflection in the rear-view mirror. She'd had all of sixty seconds to put a bit of make-up on, in between sorting the children out, and it wasn't enough to hide the tiredness she felt.

Grace went around the other side and climbed into her seat, glowering at him.

'First in the car,' Harry said again, bouncing in his seat. 'I was first.'

Grace leaned over and pinched him, hard, on his forearm.

'Ahhhhhhh! Mummy, Gracie pinched me!'

Sarah shot her daughter a look. She loved her children more than anything else in the world. But she also longed for harmony, for something to be easy, once in a while, for a time when she didn't feel like she was continuously policing a fragile truce between the Crips and the Bloods.

'Didn't,' Grace said, with a look of angelic sweetness.

'It hurts!' Harry cried.

'Stop it, both of you,' Sarah said.

The children got their competitive streak from her, she supposed. Nick wasn't the competitive sort, quite the opposite in fact. So presumably that meant it was her fault: always the competitive one. Apart from the wild year in her mid-teens, Sarah had always been top of the class, the overachiever, desperate to please, the third of three daughters trying to win the approval of her parents. She had always harboured a suspicion that she was her parents' last shot at having a boy – and when she turned out to be another girl, she faded into the background of the first and second-born, Lucy, who now lived in Glasgow, and Helen, in Nottingham. Sarah was somewhere in there, somewhere in the mix, just never at the front.

She walked slowly with them up to the gates of Grace's school, giving her a kiss and an extra hug before her daughter squirmed away and ran towards her friends in the playground. Sarah stood at the gates, studying the adults in the playground, checking who was coming and going, trying to spot anything out of the ordinary. All seemed normal. After a minute she moved further up the hill to the infant school next door, holding Harry's hand tightly as they walked into the playground. Looking at each car parked on the street, looking for the black BMW 4 x 4 from last night or any other cars that didn't look like they belonged there. She knew many of the parents here, knew their cars even if she didn't know their names.

Four years of coming here every weekday had taught her the rhythm of morning drop-off at school. There was a pattern to it: those who were always early, who were late, who always parked their 4 x 4 up on the kerb, who risked the head teacher's wrath by parking on the zig-zag lines, the ones whose kids ran ahead and those who had to be half-dragged, half-carried to the school gate. There were parents dressed as if ready to hit the boardroom and others who looked as if they'd dressed in the dark in thirty seconds flat. She would notice something out of place, a person who didn't belong – she knew she would. She just needed to keep her eyes peeled.

There. A man in a black suit and long overcoat standing at the far edge of the fence, looking into the playground through dark sunglasses. He looked as if he was trying to remain inconspicuous, trying to blend into the background. Unsmiling, scanning the area. She had never seen him before. She slowed her pace, Harry tugging at her hand, pulling her towards the school. The man was looking for someone in particular, his head moving from side to side as he took in the crowded playground.

He was hiding something. He had something concealed under his coat.

Oh no.

Sarah stopped walking, the breath catching in her throat. Her phone vibrated in her pocket but she ignored it. She gripped Harry's hand tightly, remembering the words of the man she had met the night before.

To make sure you know how serious I am, I'm going to show you some pictures.

Pictures of her house. Her dad's house. The schools her children attended.

But she'd told no one, so why was this man here? It didn't make sense.

Unless it was a warning. *We are watching you. We know where you will be, where your children will be. We know where you are weak.*

'Mummy, come *on*,' Harry said, tugging at her hand again.

The man had not seen them yet. They could still get away.

She was about to turn and walk back to her car when the man stopped scanning the playground. He broke into a smile and waved as a small boy came running up and reached through the bars of the fence. The man produced a small green Tupperware box from under his coat and handed it to the boy.

Not suspicious after all. He was just another school-run dad who'd forgotten to give his son his packed lunch.

OK. She exhaled a heavy breath and felt the relief flood through her. *It's OK. It's nothing to worry about.* She walked with Harry into the playground, stood with him when the bell rang for the children to line up, and went with him into his classroom as she always did. She hugged him for a few seconds longer than usual when it was time to say goodbye. He had that beautiful child smell, sweet and clean and unsullied by the world, that she loved breathing in as she held him close. She was about to say something to him but before she could get the words out he was pulling away from her embrace, trotting off across the classroom to see his friends Esther and Leigh. Sarah lingered a moment longer, not wanting to let him out of her sight. Her fears of a few minutes ago may have been misplaced, but that didn't mean the danger wasn't real.

And Harry was so small, so trusting. So vulnerable.

His reception teacher, Mrs Cass, caught Sarah's eye and smiled. Raised her eyebrows. Sarah knew what the young teacher meant: *Everything is OK. I can take it from here.* Harry adored her, as did all the other children in the class. Sarah took the hint and retreated to the door, taking her place among the other anxious parents watching their babies become reception year schoolchildren.

Mrs Cass clapped her hands and all the children turned to look at her, their faces wide-eyed and eager.

With one last look at her son, Sarah turned and walked back out into the playground.

25

Walking quickly back to her car, Sarah checked the time on her phone – 8.59 – and saw a text from Marie.

Where are you? M x

She typed a quick reply.

On my way. You OK? x

She was driving away from school when the next text message dropped in, and waited until she'd pulled up at some traffic lights before reading it. Traffic was solid all the way to campus and she knew she'd be cutting it fine to make the Tuesday morning staff meeting.

Did you get the email this morning? M x

Sarah didn't like the sound of that. She fired off a quick reply as she sat at the red light.

What email? x

The lights turned green and she put the car in gear, the old Fiesta's engine almost stalling before it shuddered back into life and slowly picked up speed. It was fifteen years old and seemed to develop a new strange noise every week, but Sarah had no spare money to spend on getting it fixed. She was dreading its next MOT.

Traffic was thick all the way to campus but there were no more texts from Marie. With a growing sense of unease, she drove up the hill to the main arts faculty building in search of a parking space. It was never easy finding a space if you had to do the school drop-off first and Tuesdays were always the worst, for some reason. She circled the car park in front of the faculty – a sprawling Georgian manor house had been converted into offices and seminar rooms – looking in vain for one last parking space. But there were none. She gave up and drove back down the hill, checking by the library and the staff club. Still no spaces.

Eventually she parked in the main staff car park and hurried up the hill, on foot this time, towards the arts faculty building. The sky was overcast and the air felt heavy with impending rain. Students bustled by her, heading for lectures, a few of her own undergraduates smiling and saying hello as they passed. There was a turning circle in front of her building, with a Victorian statue of the Roman god Neptune in a fountain at its centre. Someone – a student, presumably – had climbed up the statue and put a traffic cone on Neptune's head. The building's porter, Mr Jennings, was contemplating the water god's new headgear from the bottom of a stepladder propped against the stone rim of the fountain.

'Morning,' he said to her with a nod.

'Morning, Michael,' she replied, a little breathless from her speed-walk.

Hurrying through the main doors, she ran up the stairs to the second floor, dumped her laptop in her office and headed for Lovelock's office. His office space actually consisted of three rooms – the outer office, where his PA sat, his inner office to the right, lined with books from floor to ceiling, and a large conference room.

Jocelyn Steer was in her mid-forties and had been Professor Lovelock's PA for years. Sarah had never got beyond a relationship of basic cordiality with her – she'd tried to be friendly but had come to realise that Jocelyn never cracked a smile for anyone. She considered herself to be the gatekeeper to Lovelock's diary, his office, his university life, and it was a role she executed with the zeal and commitment of a member of the Waffen SS. Idle enquiries, time-wasters and members of the university's administrative staff were to be shut down with ruthless efficiency. The last time they'd seen each other was as Sarah stormed out of Lovelock's office the week before.

Sarah checked her watch again: 9.27. Three minutes to spare.

'Hi, Jocelyn,' she said, walking into Lovelock's outer office.

'Morning,' Jocelyn replied, her tone clipped.

Sarah stopped: even by Jocelyn's standards, this was an unusually cool welcome.

'Is everything OK?'

The older woman pursed her lips.

'It's not my place to say.'

'Not your place to say what?'

Jocelyn drew herself up in her seat, but wouldn't meet Sarah's gaze.

'What happens behind closed doors is none of my business. But you might want to –'

'What does that mean, behind closed doors?'

'In Alan's office. He's a very important man, you know.'

'Yes,' Sarah said, frowning. 'I know that.'

'Perhaps you should think about that the next time you're alone in there with him.'

26

Sarah felt an unpleasant chill crawl up her spine. *What had Jocelyn seen? What conclusions had she jumped to?*

'What?'

Jocelyn tucked her grey cardigan more tightly around herself.

'Sorry,' Sarah said, 'what does that mean, what you just said?'

'I think you know very well what it means.'

'Actually, I don't, but whatever you've heard, whatever he's told you –'

'Anyway,' Jocelyn said, cutting her off, 'I don't want to make you any later than you already are.'

Sarah checked her watch again. She still had a minute.

'What do you mean?'

'They started at nine sharp today.'

Sarah felt panic wash through her like a tide. She noticed for the first time that the conference room door was closed.

'How come? Why?'

'I sent a reminder email this morning, asked colleagues to let one another know.'

'I didn't see any email.'

She checked her phone. She normally looked at email when she first got up, around seven, but she didn't have time – in between getting herself and the kids ready for school – to be constantly checking it before she got to work. Scrolling up, she found the email from Jocelyn. It had arrived at 8.52.

'This gives me eight minutes' notice of the time change,' Sarah said. 'I was still dropping the kids off at school then.'

'Everyone else seemed to be fine with it.'

'Did they all get eight minutes' notice too?'

'The meeting information was circulated last week, as per usual. Professor Lovelock thought it would be helpful to bring the meeting forward slightly to accommodate the dean's other commitments today.'

The dean. *Shit*. The head of the whole faculty. Basically, one of the most important people on campus. Sarah had forgotten he was attending today.

'Departmental meetings are 9.30 every second Tuesday,' Sarah said desperately. 'They're always 9.30 and the meeting information last week was the same as always. Why has it changed today? I've got the school drop-off just before nine.'

'Not everything can be arranged to suit your domestic arrangements, Dr Haywood.'

'I don't expect things to be –' Sarah started, then thought better of it. Her 'domestic arrangements' seemed to be mostly used as a stick to beat her with. She wondered, idly, if they would merit a mention if she were a man. *You know the answer to that one.*

Her life had happened in a different order to most of her colleagues. She had fallen pregnant at twenty-four – she and Nick were being *sort of* careful at the time, without actually believing it would happen to them – then married in a quick registry office ceremony and she finished her PhD a scant three days before going into labour with Grace. She had taken six months out and gone back to work, and when Harry had come along three years later – she had not wanted to have too big a gap between her kids – she had just ploughed on regardless, working hard, juggling work and family and childcare while most of her colleagues were not even contemplating marriage yet, let alone children. Most, like Marie, would put off having kids until they had a permanent position and a semblance of stability in their working lives.

She turned away from Lovelock's secretary and knocked on the conference room door.

All faces turned towards her as she hurried in, and proceedings stopped for a moment. Marie flashed her a nervous smile from across the table.

'Sorry I'm late,' Sarah said. 'Didn't see the email. Sorry.'

The dean of the faculty – a small, round-faced man named Professor Jonathan Clifton – was at the head of the table next to Lovelock. She was well aware that they had studied at Cambridge University together.

'Ah, Dr Haywood,' Clifton said, his voice dripping with sarcasm. 'Good of you to join us today.'

'Sorry,' Sarah said again, digging a notebook and pen out of her bag. She sat in the one remaining seat and Marie passed an agenda to her, a sympathetic expression on her face.

'Shall we continue?' Clifton added sharply.

'Of course,' Sarah said, trying to regain her composure.

Peter Moran, the school manager, gave her a stern look and gestured towards Lovelock.

'To bring you up to speed on what you've missed already, Sarah: we've covered staffing and resourcing, and issues around the January exams. We were just now talking about new funding streams for the school's research – it looks like Alan has uncovered another fabulous opportunity for us.'

'Great,' Sarah said, scanning the agenda.

'It could be a really significant source of funding for the department. And it's in Boston, of all places.'

27

Sarah looked up from the agenda, an alarm bell starting to ring in her head.

'Boston?' she repeated.

'Indeed. A philanthropic organisation with a particular interest in Marlowe's life and works. Only established last year, but they've already given Harvard almost two million dollars for work in this field, so it's a significant find for us. Could be really good for the department.'

Sarah was about to speak when Clifton added: 'Alan has already made some initial enquiries to the fund director.'

She felt her face burning.

'This is Atholl Sanders, right?'

'Correct. I assume Alan's already let you in on it.'

'But that was my –'

Lovelock interrupted in his usual way, his voice booming over hers.

'I wasn't sure you'd remember, Sarah,' he said. 'We haven't discussed it since the conference. Hats off to you for making the most of the complimentary wine at the reception there, by the way. As Head of Department I'm all in favour of my staff members getting maximum value for money. I think you and Marie must have drunk the place dry.'

There was a bark of sycophantic laughter from Webber-Smythe and chuckles from Moran, Clifton and a few of the others around the table. Sarah exchanged a confused look with Marie, who frowned back at her and gave a tiny shake of her head.

'Alan's been in touch with the trust,' Moran said, 'and they've invited him to Boston for four days in January to give a guest lecture and have some further discussions around funding opportunities.'

Sarah felt dizzy with anger. She knew she had to be calm, controlled, but inside she was burning up. The injustice of it was like bile in her throat, threatening to choke her. She took a breath and held Lovelock's gaze.

'I talked to you about it on that Wednesday night at the conference, Alan, in the taxi, remember?'

'I'm surprised you can remember anything about that night, Dr Haywood,' Clifton added with a humourless smile. 'From what Alan tells us, I imagine it was all a bit of a blur.'

Sarah felt the breath hot in her throat. The unfairness of it was overwhelming. For a sudden horrible second she thought she would burst into tears, right here in front of all of them. *No. No. Don't do that. Not that.* She bit her tongue, hard, until the pain made her tears recede. *Don't cry. Don't you bloody dare, Sarah. Don't give them the satisfaction.* But she couldn't contradict him either. Not vehemently, not if she eventually wanted that permanent contract.

'That wasn't quite how it happened,' she said, her voice flat.

Lovelock leaned forward, hands clasped in front of him, a sympathetic smile on his lips.

'The truth is, Sarah, I've been in contact with them for some months.'

Liar, she thought but didn't say. *You're a bloody lying bastard.*

Clifton leaned forward too, his hands palm-up as if he was about to say something blindingly obvious.

'With all due respect, Dr Haywood, they'll want to deal with the head of department, rather than ... ' He gestured at her, seeming to run out of words. 'Rather than a junior member of staff.'

'You're very welcome to join me on the trip, Sarah,' Lovelock added, his voice neutral. 'I know this wonderful little boutique hotel in Beacon Hill – it was Benjamin Franklin's house in the late eighteenth century.'

It seemed to Sarah that all eyes around the table swivelled to focus on her. She felt sick. *You stole my idea and then lied about it. Brazen, just like that. Like it was nothing. Is that what you have to do to get to the top? Cheat and steal and lie, just so you can climb the greasy pole?*

And then: *Be calm. Walk the line.*

'Thanks,' she choked out. 'I'll think about it.' Knowing that she would do nothing of the sort. The prospect of spending four days on a foreign trip with him was totally and utterly out of the question. Even though it would be good for her career, even though this was a rare opportunity to build her network and it would look good on her CV, even though she had found the bloody opportunity herself, there was no way she would put herself in that situation with him. It was just too risky. She couldn't face the prospect of trying to keep him at arm's length for four days straight: the Rules wouldn't work if it was just the two of them. There would be nowhere to hide.

'Good,' Clifton said, looking down at his agenda. 'Let's move on, shall we?'

28

'Professor Clifton?' Sarah said quietly as they filed out of Lovelock's meeting room. 'I don't suppose you've got five minutes, have you?'

The dean of the faculty checked his watch ostentatiously. He was a small man and the large timepiece looked faintly ridiculous on his wrist, as if he'd swiped it from his father's bedside table.

'I have the finance steering committee at 10.45. I can give you three minutes.'

'Great, thanks,' Sarah said. Her anger had boiled down into a hot, hard lump that had burned in her chest for the last hour of the meeting. She had said almost nothing after Lovelock had shut her down on the Atholl Sanders lead, and she knew she couldn't challenge him head-on in a meeting in front of half the school. But she could at least give the facts to the dean, so he could decide for himself.

'What's on your mind, Dr Haywood?'

Sarah looked over her shoulder at a few of their faculty colleagues lingering nearby.

'I wonder if we could we speak in private?'

'As I said, I'm pushed for time but we could walk and talk if you like?' He gestured towards the stairs at the far end of the corridor.

'Of course,' Sarah said as they started walking. She waited a beat until they were out of earshot of the other members of staff. 'I wanted to fill you in about the Atholl Sanders discussion.'

'Ah yes, Alan's latest venture.'

'Not exactly.'

Clifton slowed a little and glanced across, his small beady eyes meeting hers.

'How do you mean, Dr Haywood?'

'That was what I wanted to explain. It was me that did all the legwork on the Atholl Sanders foundation. I found the opportunity originally and I wanted the chance to develop it.'

'I see.'

'Alan seems to have presented it at the meeting just now as *his* idea. But it was actually me that found it – and I wanted to lead on it. It doesn't seem fair, how it's happened.'

Clifton stopped as they reached the bottom of the stairs, his face darkening.

'Dr Haywood, I've known Alan for more than thirty-five years and I can assure you that he would never do anything unethical or improper in the way you seem to be implying.'

'All I'm saying is that he –'

'And I'm certain that he would *never* do anything which might risk damage to his own excellent reputation, or to the reputation of this university.' He fixed Sarah with an unblinking stare. 'I'm absolutely *certain* of it. Do you understand me, Dr Haywood?'

For a second, Sarah was at a loss. Was Clifton just denying it, or did he really not know what Lovelock was like, even after all these years? Was it possible that he couldn't see it, or was he blinded by personal loyalty? By Lovelock's financial value to the university? It was impossible to tell from his inscrutable face.

Either way, it was clear that asking him for a quiet word had been a bad idea.

'Yes, I understand.'

'Was there anything else, Dr Haywood?'

'I just wanted to let you know how things had – had come about. That's all.'

'Right.'

'I'm keen to take on more responsibility in bringing funding in. To help the department.'

Clifton lowered his voice and leaned closer.

'Here's a small suggestion, my dear: trying to undermine your boss is not the way to go about helping the department.' He checked his watch again. 'I really have to get to my next meeting now. Have a good day.'

With that, he turned on his heel and went out into the drizzly November morning. Sarah stared after him, heart beating hard in her chest.

Marie appeared at her side.

'You OK?'

'No,' Sarah said, blowing out a breath. 'No, I'm not OK. I'm bloody furious. I just tried to tell the dean about Alan stealing my idea and he acted like I was lying through my teeth.'

'Original members of the Queen Anne Uni Old Boys' Club, those two.'

Sarah shook her head in disbelief, still watching Clifton's retreating figure.

'Honestly, I give up with this bloody place.'

'Want to get a coffee?'

'Can't. I'm teaching at eleven, straight through until half four. Don't think I'd be very good company, anyway.'

* * *

The anger stayed with her all day, swelling and burning in her chest whenever she thought about what had happened. It was only when she got home with the kids that she let her emotions rise to the surface.

She gave Grace and Harry a digestive biscuit each, put fish fingers and chips in the oven for their tea and went upstairs to the master bedroom. It was times like these that she missed Nick the most, when she wanted to sit down and share a bottle of wine with him, and just talk about everything that was going on in their lives. Work problems, frustrations, funny moments with the kids, small triumphs and troubles ahead. The future. He had been her outlet, her safety valve.

She couldn't get used to his side of the wardrobe being empty.

Sitting on the edge of the bed, she let the tears come. It had been just over a month since he'd gone, but she still had a raw mixture of anger and love when she thought of him. Maybe resignation was starting to creep in, too. She took her mobile out of her handbag. Nick's number rang six times then went to voicemail, so she hung up and dialled again. This time it rang only once before Nick's recorded voice came on.

'Hey! You've reached Nick's phone. Would love to chat but I'm probably on stage, or in an audition, or otherwise tied up. Leave a message at the beep and I promise I'll call you back. Thanks!'

She hung up again and sent a text instead, her hands shaking. *When are you coming home?*

She stared at the phone's screen, willing him to reply. Willing him to tell the truth for once.

The mobile remained obstinately silent in her hand. Jonesy, their ginger tomcat, padded into the bedroom and jumped up on to her lap, purring his deep bass purr. Sarah put the phone down for a minute and scratched him behind his ears. Jonesy blinked his pleasure and raised his head to her hand, kneading her sweater with his big front paws. She picked up the phone again and typed another text.

Are you with Arabella?

She hated herself for asking anything of him – even an answer to a simple question. But she had to know, for the kids and for the practical stuff too, for childcare, for bills and mortgage payments and everything else they usually shared. Would it be another week, a fortnight, a month? Longer?

She selected another name in her address book and sent a third text.

There was a high-pitched scream and, almost simultaneously, a cry from the lounge. Jonesy jumped off her lap and padded under the bed, reappearing a moment later with a dead mouse in his jaws.

'Jonesy! Where did you get that?'

She grabbed for him but he scampered off towards the stairs, taking his prize with him.

Sarah sighed and wiped her eyes with a wad of toilet roll.

There was more shouting and crying as she headed downstairs. Her children were at each end of the sofa in the lounge, crying.

'He kicked me,' said Grace, through her tears.

'She hit me first,' said Harry, sniffling and pointing to his forearm. 'Look, she made a mark.'

Sarah leaned over and studied his arm but could see nothing.

'It hurts,' Harry said in a small voice. '*So* much.'

'He keeps changing the channel,' Grace protested. 'It's my turn to watch *Tracy Beaker* but he keeps putting baby stuff on.'

Sarah switched the TV off and put the remote high up on the bookcase.

'Right, who wants to help me lay the table for tea?'

Both children looked at her as if she'd asked them to swim the Channel.

'Who's going to help?' Sarah repeated. 'Grace?'

Her daughter let out a slumping sigh, and Sarah made a mental note – again – to limit her TV time. Grace seemed to be entering her teenage years five years early.

'Come on, Grace. Tea's nearly ready anyway.'

'Why is it always me?' Grace said, sliding off the sofa and following her mother into the kitchen.

'Because you're my good girl, aren't you? My helper. You know where everything is in the kitchen. Harry's still a bit small, he can't reach the cupboards.'

Grace didn't look convinced.

'When's Daddy coming home?' she said.

The question made Sarah stop. She took a breath, looked away. *Don't let them see you upset.*

'He's doing another play, touring around lots of different places.'

'Cool. But when's he coming home?'

'Soon, Grace. Soon. Can you put the ketchup out on the table for me, please?'

She fed the children their tea, and tidied up the kitchen around them as they ate. The house seemed to be in a constant state of war between her clearing things up and the kids leaving Lego, colouring books, plastic dinosaurs and dolls, building blocks and clothes and the rest of their toy boxes strewn across every available surface.

When the doorbell rang, both kids sat bolt upright like meerkats.

'Daddy!' they shouted simultaneously.

The two of them pushed back their chairs and ran into the hallway. Sarah didn't follow them, knowing it wasn't their father returning, listening instead to their high voices in the hallway as they greeted the visitor; the familiar deep voice in return, telling one how handsome he was and the other that she'd grown, even though it was only a day since he'd seen them last. Her children came trotting back a moment later, sat down and resumed eating their fish fingers.

'Grandad's here,' Grace informed her.

Sarah waited a moment until they were settled back with their tea, then went out into the hallway herself. Out of their view.

Her dad took off his coat and held out his hands to her.

'I got your text. How's my youngest girl doing?'

The look on his face said he knew the answer already. But he asked anyway. He always did. He was the one person she could share anything with – even though she didn't dare tell him about the strange turn her life had taken in the last twenty-four hours.

'Not so good, Dad,' she said quietly. 'Not so good.'

29

A midweek sleepover at Laura's was a welcome chance to talk. Chris was away and Laura wanted the company. After dinner, with the children tucked up in bed, Sarah and her friend lay full-length on the two sofas in Laura's lounge, the fire on low, candles flickering on the hearth. Sarah took a sip of red wine, trying to think of a way to broach the other question that had been ever-present in her thoughts since her meeting with Volkov.

'Can I ask you a question?'

'No, of course not.'

Sarah pulled a face.

'What if you could do something, and no one would ever find out about it? No one except you.'

'Something like what?'

'Anything.'

'And no one would ever know?'

'No one.'

'So I could shag Channing Tatum without his wife finding out?'

'Well, not quite like that. Something – something bad.'

Laura smiled.

'It would be bad, trust me. He'd be *begging* for mercy by the time I'd finished with him.'

Sarah shook her head, smiling back at her friend. She thought for a moment, unsure how to phrase the next question. It was a bit of a risk, she supposed – but not if she stayed hypothetical. Not if the reality of the situation stayed firmly locked away in her head.

'What about something that was, well, not quite legal?'

Laura took a sip of her red wine and put the glass on the table next to her, refilling it from the nearly empty bottle.

'Not involving Channing Tatum?'

'Just forget about Channing for a moment.'

'OK. Something not quite legal. Like punching my twatty next-door neighbour when he makes a really loud drunken phone call at 3.00 a.m. and we can hear every bloody word through the adjoining wall?'

'Something like that.'

'Then yes. I'd smack him into next week if I could get away with it. I've been trying to get my darling husband to do it for months, actually. Or at least knock on the door and ask him to stop being a noisy arse. But Chris normally sleeps right through it.'

'So you'd do it? You'd take a swing at your neighbour?'

'If it was a freebie? God, yes. He's woken us up so many times I've lost count.' She smiled at the thought. 'How do I get away with it, though? Am I invisible, or something?'

'Not invisible, exactly. More . . . untraceable.'

'Interesting. And no one would find out?'

'Exactly.'

'Sort of like the perfect crime?'

'Yes. And perhaps it would be something more serious than just smacking your neighbour.'

'You're starting to worry me a bit now, Sarah.' She cocked her head on one side. 'Are you all right?'

She remembered Volkov's warning.

Tell no one.

'Yeah. I'm fine. Just had a bit too much wine, maybe.'

'Sure?'

Sarah laid her head back against the cushion, staring at the shadows dancing on the ceiling in the candlelight.

'It's just been a bit of a shit few weeks, that's all, what with Nick leaving and getting passed over for promotion again. Things have been getting on top of me lately and every day I pray for a little bit of good news, for something to go my way, instead of constantly getting screwed over. Instead of people *constantly* fucking taking advantage.'

'Like your Professor Lovelock stealing your idea about that funder in Boston and presenting it as his own?'

'He told everyone I was so pissed that night in Edinburgh I wouldn't have remembered what I was saying anyway.' Her voice cracked as she swallowed back a sob. 'Sorry, Loz. You know me – can't cope with people being nice when I'm feeling crap. People being nice just makes me want to burst into tears.'

'I could be horrible to you, if you like?' Laura said, exaggerating her Leeds accent. 'You lousy trollop. You stinky fishwife. You skanky moo.'

Sarah laughed.

'You mardy minger.' Laura threw her a quizzical look. 'How am I doing? How do you feel now? Better?'

'Yes, better, thanks,' Sarah said. 'A bit less like crying, at least.'

There was silence between them for a moment. Laura put her wine glass on the floor and swung her legs off the sofa so she was sitting upright.

'Sarah?'

'Yes?'

'Look at me.'

Sarah turned her head to meet her friend's gaze.

'What is it?'

'You know you can talk to me about anything, don't you? Anything at all. It wouldn't go any further, I wouldn't tell Chris or my mum, or anyone. It would just be between you and me, OK? And it would stay that way.'

'I know, hon. Thanks.'

'So,' Laura said, 'are you going to tell me what's going on?'

30

'Nothing's going on, Loz,' Sarah said.

'Is it about Nick shacking up with Arabella or whatever her name is? Are you going to . . . do something to her?'

Sarah gave a sad smile, shaking her head.

'No.'

'Shame. If there was ever someone deserving a good slap, it's her. Is it Nick, then?'

'Not him. The kids would never forgive me, for one thing. It doesn't matter, Loz, I was just messing about, wishful thinking. Too much wine. Let's talk about something else.'

But Laura didn't want to leave it alone.

'I've got it.' She snapped her fingers and pointed at her friend. 'It's your boss, isn't it? Lovelock?'

Sarah sat up on the sofa and tucked her legs under her, so she could face her friend properly. Laura was one of the very few people who knew everything that had happened with Alan Lovelock. All of the things he had done, and tried to do. All of the details. She had never told her dad – he would worry too much.

'What would you do,' Sarah said, 'if he was your boss?'

'You know what I'd do, love. I've told you a dozen times: I'd be straight down to HR and get him kicked out so fast his feet wouldn't touch the ground.'

'What if HR was useless? And he was untouchable?'

'The "bulletproof prof" thing?'

'Yeah.'

Laura shrugged.

'I suppose ... I suppose I'd gather evidence myself, catch him in the act. I don't know, record him saying stuff. Find other women who have had the same issues. Make a case that they couldn't ignore.'

'And what if all of that had been tried before, and none of it worked? In fact, not only did it not work, but the victims ended up being "managed out" of the university.'

'Dunno. Then I might ask Chris to go to his house and have a chat with him.' She paused to refill her glass with red wine again. 'Failing that, Chris could kick the living shit out of him, see if that got the message across.'

Sarah smiled. Laura's husband, Chris, had been a promising rugby player in his youth and still played for his local side. At six feet four and sixteen stone, he cut an imposing figure. He towered over Nick. Chris was thoroughly lovely, funny and dedicated to his family, but he had a certain physical presence when he walked into a room.

'Seriously?'

'Yes. Actually, no.'

'You wouldn't have Chris sort him out?'

'Oh yeah, I would – but not at his house. In some dark alley somewhere.'

'So . . . what? Violence is the answer?'

'Anyone who says violence never solved anything has forgotten about slavery, Hitler and World War Two.'

'That's a bit deep for ten o'clock on a Wednesday night.'

'You know, Hillary Clinton used to say something about all the attacks she had to put up with while she was running for president. She said: "*When they go low, you go high*".'

'And look what happened to her.'

'*Exactly*. Holding the high ground is no guarantee you're going to win in the end. If your opponent's already in the gutter, sometimes you've got to get down there with him to land a knockout blow. Does Nick know how many times Professor Sex Offender has tried it on with you?'

'He knows most of it. Not the grimmer details, but most of it.'

'And he's never got angry? Never wanted to confront Lovelock or pay him an anonymous visit?'

Sarah shrugged.

'You know Nick. He's a lover, not a fighter – a pacifist. The world's youngest hippy, born into the wrong decade. And anyway, I've always told him to keep his distance in case he messed up my chance of a permanent contract. I always thought the problem would go away when I got some security in my job and I could finally tell Lovelock where to go. And Nick's gone now. I'm not sure he's coming back this time. I'm not sure I'd let him.'

'Listen, how about I talk to Chris? He could pay professor perv a visit, put the wind up him.'

Sarah shook her head.

'That's very kind of you, Loz, but I wouldn't want Chris to get in any bother.'

'It would be the last trouble you'd have from the old bullet-proof prof. Chris would do it, you know. He wouldn't mind.'

'I know. He's a sweetheart.'

'I just hate seeing you like this, Sarah, it makes me feel so helpless.'

The two of them lapsed into silence for a moment. Sarah drained the last of her wine and put her glass on the floor. It was her third of the evening and the soft buzz of alcohol was warming, reassuring, despite all her troubles.

'What if there was another way?' she said, staring into the fire's flickering flames. 'A way where no one got in trouble? Where *you* didn't have to get involved, and neither did Chris or anyone else you know.'

'Like a magic spell or something?'

In Russia they called me volshebnik. *The magician. Because I made things disappear.*

'Kind of like that. But no one would ever know it was you.'

'So there'd be no way it would be traced back to me? No comebacks?'

'No comebacks.'

'So there's absolutely no way I could be connected to it, ever?'

'That's right. Perfect alibi, you would be nowhere near it when it happened, no connection to you at all.'

'Hmm. OK.' She nodded, slowly. 'I like the sound of this.'

'So, would you do it?'

Laura thought for another moment before answering.

'A once in a lifetime chance to do something with no consequences?' She finished the last of her wine. 'You know what? Fuck it. I think I would.'

31

Sarah lay in Laura's spare bed, exhausted and fuzzy-headed from red wine, but unable to sleep. Staring at the glowing red numbers of the clock radio on the bedside table as they clicked onwards, minute by minute.

3.09.

It still felt like a dream. All of it. The little girl, Aleksandra, the scarred man, Volkov and his unbelievable offer. It all seemed to belong to another life, a different person. Not her life. She wanted it to be a choice that someone else had to make, someone else's problem to solve. She floated in that for a minute, halfway between sleep and wakefulness, hoping that it was all just a product of her imagination.

You give me one name. One person. And I will make them disappear.

But it wasn't a dream. It was real. It was her life.

Her choice.

A choice between reason and passion. Between logic and emotion. And when had that ever been a fair fight?

She had not asked for more details, and she realised now that this had been a mistake. What did *disappear* even mean? It could mean all kinds of things. Was it that they were sent away, far away, and never came back? That they were threatened, to make them flee the life they knew, or face the consequences? That they were paid off and set up in a new life somewhere far away?

None of these options seemed very likely. Not as likely as the most obvious answer. The obvious answer being that they vanished . . . permanently.

She picked up her phone to check her emails, as a distraction. There he was again: three emails from Lovelock, two of which were red-flagged as urgent. She went to put the phone back in her bag. Getting a Midnight Mail from him was guaranteed to keep her awake for another few hours.

Her hand brushed against the other phone in her handbag, the little Alcatel flip phone Volkov had given her. Did it even have any charge? She should turn it on and check, just in case. *Bad idea.* Because turning it on would mean she was another step closer to looking at the single number stored in its memory. And then she'd just have to dial the number and say two words:

Alan Lovelock.

And her problems would vanish – if the offer was to be believed.

Laura had nearly persuaded her, almost convinced her, that she should take Volkov's offer – without even realising what she was saying. Almost, but not quite.

Sarah pushed the duvet off and turned on the bedside light, reached down to her handbag again, burrowed inside it until her hand closed around the smooth plastic shape of the mobile she'd been given. What had he called it? A *throwaway* phone. She withdrew it and held it in her palm, the case cool to the touch. It was the only thing she had, the only evidence, that she had not imagined the whole encounter with Volkov and his entourage – this little rectangle of black plastic was proof that it was real, that *he* was real, that his offer was real. She turned it over in her hand, feeling the weight of it. Just a few ounces. Nothing more.

She ran her thumb over the smooth casing of the phone and flipped it open. It looked like the most basic model you could get – tiny screen, old-style keypad, power button, nothing extra, nothing fancy. It reminded her of one of the first phones she had ever owned back in the late 1990s, a no-frills hand-me-down from her sister Helen.

Just switch it on. It probably hasn't got any charge left anyway. Just switch it on to check. Where's the harm in that?

Her thumb hovered over the power button.

No. It was better not to go there, better to leave the phone in the bottom of her handbag, switched off. Dialling that number would mean crossing a line from which there would be no going back. Because what did the word 'disappear' really, honestly mean? It meant setting herself apart from normal society, and the law, and her family, and everything she held dear. She couldn't do that. Instead, she would do what she had always done: grin and bear it and wait for things to get better. Because they always did, in her experience. Almost always. If you stuck it out long enough. It was just a case of perseverance. That was it. Sheer bloody-minded perseverance.

She closed the phone and put it back in her handbag, switching the bedside light off again and telling herself that perseverance would be enough. She would get rid of the throwaway phone. Put it in the dustbin. Bury it in the garden. Drop it into the river. Put all of this behind her, write it off as a strange episode in her life to be locked away somewhere and never spoken of again.

First thing in the morning, she would get rid of it. And once she had done that, she would do what she should have done a long time ago – she would go to Human Resources to make a formal complaint using the proper channels and the proper process. The fact that she was even considering Volkov's offer had convinced her that her issues with Lovelock had to be sorted out. Enough was enough.

32

Sarah sat in the reception area of the Human Resources department, fingers laced tightly together in her lap. She was going over in her head what she was going to say to Robert Webster, the deputy director of HR who oversaw disciplinary issues, complaints and alleged staff misconduct. Webster's glass-panelled office was at the far corner of the large open-plan space, beyond rows of desks that had emptied for lunchtime. His door was shut.

She checked her watch. Five minutes until her appointment.

Still time to back out. You could walk away, make an excuse. Easy as that.

Her phone buzzed in her handbag. A text from Marie.

You free to meet for lunch? Think we should talk again.

Sarah typed a quick reply.

Can't, sorry. Managed to get an appointment at HR today, back at 2.

She'd confided in her friend that morning that she'd had enough, that she was going to go to HR, though she hadn't expected to get a meeting so fast.

Marie had stared at her.

'What exactly are you going to do?'

'Tell them. Tell them everything.'

'About Alan?'

'Yes. I'm going to record the meeting on my phone – and any meeting I have in future with Alan.'

'Are you sure?'

'I can't do it anymore, Marie. I can't carry on like this, I'm at the end of my tether. I've been putting it off, and putting it off again, for so long now that I've started to forget who I am and where I started from. I'm not this person that just sits and takes endless amounts of shit week after week, month after month, just to get where I want to go. That's not who I used to be, but it's who I'm turning into. I don't want to do it anymore.'

'I totally agree, you know I do. We've both had to put up with behaviour that he should have been fired for long ago. We know what it's like to work with it day in, day out, keeping a lid on it all. But if you do this, are you ready for what's going to come after?'

'I don't know. I don't know anything anymore, only that something has to be done about him.'

'But are you ready to go to war with him? Because that's what he'll make it, as soon as he finds out.'

Sarah had felt her throat tightening, the weight of tears behind her eyes. It was always hard to argue with her quietly spoken, studious, hyper-intellectual friend. She had a frustrating habit of seeing everything in a totally logical, practical way.

'I just want to do my job,' Sarah said. 'I don't want a war with anyone.'

'If you do this you're going to get one whether you like it or not. Remember what happened to Gillian Arnold, what he did to her? If you go to war with him, only one of you will be left standing at the end of it. If you rock the boat, we'll all end up losing.'

Sarah had remembered the gaunt face of her predecessor, the angry confrontation in Lovelock's garden at the party. *She* had tried to take him on – and seen her career crash in flames. *But I have to try*, Sarah told herself. *Perhaps I will be the tipping point, the one that makes the university finally sit up and take notice.*

'Whose side are you on?' she found herself saying.

'Yours, of course,' Marie said. 'I'm just not sure this is the way to go about it.'

'There is no other way.'

'There must be, Sarah.'

'No,' she'd said, immovable. 'There isn't.'

Now she checked her watch. It was almost time for her appointment.

Her mouth was dry. She stood up and went to get some water from the cooler across the open-plan office, filling one of the plastic cups and taking a long drink. From here, she could look into a corner of Webster's office through the floor-to-ceiling glass wall because the blinds were only partially closed and she could see him lounging behind his desk, smiling and laughing, fingers laced behind his head.

She refilled her cup from the water cooler, still watching. She'd only met Webster once before, at an induction event when she first joined the university, and remembered him as a rather dour and humourless bureaucrat, a tall, cadaverous man in grey suit and grey tie. But perhaps she'd misjudged him – because now he had his head thrown back, his bark of laughter audible across the open-plan space. He had his jacket off, sleeves rolled up.

Sarah returned to the waiting area and sat down. Checked her watch again. Her meeting was due. *Last chance to back out.*

She unlocked her mobile and selected the Voice Recorder app, switching it on for a few seconds and then listening back to make sure it was working. She was thinking again about what she would say, where she should start, when Webster's door opened abruptly and voices spilled out into the wider office. The deputy director of HR stepped out of his office, still smiling. It looked unnatural on him. He stuck out a hand to his visitor, who did likewise, and they shook vigorously. There was another exchange of words and Webster laughed again. His visitor emerged fully from the office and clapped him on the shoulder.

Sarah felt a cold rush of fear.

It was Lovelock.

33

Sarah watched, frozen to the spot, as her head of department crossed the office towards her. His face showed no surprise at all that she was here.

'Afternoon, Dr Haywood,' he said. His tone was light but his eyes bored into hers. 'Everything all right, I hope?'

'Yes. Fine.'

'I wouldn't have expected to see you here.'

'I have a one o'clock meeting.'

'Really?' A dark smile played across his lips. 'I was just having my regular catch-up with Bob. I always tell him we should do it in between sets at the tennis club but he's much too competitive for that.'

'You play tennis together?'

'Every week.' He took a half-step nearer to her, his voice still booming. 'I'm the captain of the first team, for my sins, and he's my vice-captain.'

'Do you have a lot to talk about?'

He smiled.

'Oh, we talk about all kinds of things. Staffing issues, tricky colleagues, things that need to be nipped in the bud before they can affect the university's reputation.' He leaned closer. 'Bob calls them three-P conversations.'

'What does that mean?'

'Potential problem people. Three Ps, you see?'

His unblinking eyes held hers. Sarah said nothing, feeling the blood drain from her face.

Coming here had been a bad idea.

'People are endlessly fascinating, aren't they?' Lovelock added.

'I suppose so.'

'As your head of department, is there anything I should know about your one o'clock meeting?'

'There's nothing to know, really.' She reached for a convincing lie. 'In fact, I've got to return someone's call now, so I don't know whether I'll be able to make it.'

'If you're going to stand him up, I'll walk you out, shall I?'

He took her by the elbow as if to guide her towards the door. She shook his hand off, taking a step back.

'Don't touch me.'

He leaned closer, towering over her, speaking softly so that only she would hear.

'Think very carefully about what you do next, Sarah. *Very* carefully.' He looped his scarf around his neck and was about to turn away when he caught himself, and turned back to face her. 'By the way, did Jocelyn email you about the meeting?'

'What meeting?'

'This afternoon at 4.30.'

'I've got a catch-up with one of my PhD students.'

'Cancel it or move it.'

'What's the meeting about?'

'It's important. Very important.'

'OK but –'

'I'll see you at 4.30 My office.'

With that, he turned and walked out towards the stairs.

Sarah stared after him, his words still echoing inside her head.

Think very carefully about what you do next, Sarah.

She looked the other way, towards Webster's office, where the door was still half open, the deputy director of HR awaiting her arrival. But could he be trusted? Could she gamble on getting a fair hearing? Or was she following the same path to ruin that others had trodden before her?

Marie's words echoed in her head. *If you go to war with him, only one of you will be left standing at the end of it.*

She hesitated a moment longer, torn between the two options.

Jump, or step back.

Pull the trigger, or walk away.

She picked up her bag and headed out to the stairs.

34

The meeting invitation email was waiting for her when she got back to her desk. There was no agenda attached. *Maybe he's going to tell me he's changed his mind. Then he'll explain that it has all been a mistake. That he is going to give me that long-promised permanent contract after all.*

She was disabused of that notion as soon as she sat down in front of his desk.

'The truth is, Sarah,' Lovelock said after a brief preamble, 'I've been increasingly concerned about your attitude.'

'My attitude?'

'And the quality of your work.'

'I don't understand.' She frowned. 'My students gave me a good rating in the teaching survey. I've run the new masters course this year, I'm getting journal publications . . . I feel like it's been a good year.'

Lovelock raised his eyebrows as if none of this was remotely relevant.

'Before I forget, I wanted to check something.' He indicated her mobile phone, which she'd placed face up on the desk between them. 'You're not recording this conversation, are you?'

'No, I'm not.'

'Because recording a conversation like this would be a breach of HR guidelines, not to mention a significant breach of professional and ethical standards.'

Sarah felt the colour rising to her cheeks.

'I know that.' *You bloody hypocrite*, she thought.

He indicated her phone.

'Do you mind?'

'I'm not recording,' she said again.

'All the same, I'd be more comfortable if you put it away.'

'Fine.' She picked up the phone and tucked it into the side pocket of her handbag. *Jocelyn must have seen me fiddling with it outside while I was waiting for the meeting.*

He gave her his best TV smile.

'Super.'

'You were saying something about my attitude.'

'Look, let's not get too bogged down in details,' he said. 'As head of school I have to look at the bigger picture. It's part of my role, unfortunately.'

He smiled again as if he expected sympathy.

'As you know, we're all operating in a challenging funding environment. What you may not know is that there are some tough decisions coming up for us, and I have to look at all the options.'

'How do you mean, tough decisions?'

'Can't really go into too much detail at the moment, except to say that the Chief Financial Officer is asking all departments in the faculty to make savings. This is, of course, highly confidential and I would expect you to behave accordingly. Keep it just between us.'

'Of course.' With a creeping sense of dread, Sarah started to realise where the conversation might be going. 'How much do we have to save?'

'A significant sum. You don't need to know specifics, but essentially there are various options. One of those options is to reshape the current staff profile. To look at our staffing structures and make sure that we've got an optimal balance across the school: the right numbers of staff at the right levels, meeting the highest standards of academic excellence.'

'You mean people being made redundant?'

'It's likely that will happen to some people, Sarah.' He stood up and came around the desk, bringing another chair over to her. He draped himself over the chair, one arm on its back, sitting sideways so he was facing her. She could smell his sweat, pungent and sharp. 'But that doesn't have to happen to *you*. Not necessarily.'

Sarah shifted away from him in her seat. Her mouth was dry and she had a powerful urge to be anywhere in the world other than this room.

'I don't understand.'

'What I mean is: there will be *casualties* in the restructure. People who will be *moved on*, so to speak. But you don't have to be one of them.'

'Well, that's good. I certainly don't want to be one of them.'

'I'll discuss the changes that are needed with senior colleagues in the department, obviously, but at the end of those discussions, the dean will act on my recommendation – and mine alone. Despite your efforts to besmirch my reputation.'

'What do you mean?'

'You told the dean the Atholl Sanders funding lead was your idea. You went behind my back.'

She felt the heat rising to her face again.

'It *was* my idea.'

He smiled and shook his head.

'Academia is a collaborative enterprise, my dear. The sooner you realise that, the better we'll get along. And the more chance you have of staying in your job.'

'OK.' Sarah realised she was gripping her bag so tightly her knuckles were bone white.

'My word will determine what changes are made in the department.'

'Right. Yes.'

'Who stays and who goes.' His eyes were boring into her, as if he could see inside her head. 'Clearly, temporary staff on fixed-term contracts – like yourself, Sarah – are the most vulnerable and will be near the top of the list. That's just the way of the world, I'm afraid.'

'What are the criteria?'

'I beg your pardon?'

'How are you selecting which staff will be in the firing line?'

'There will be a range of standard measures used.'

'Such as? I have one of the highest teaching ratings in the school. My research is coming on and I've got more years in post than both Charlie and Patrick, I also have more of an admin load than them and I've not had more than one day sick in the last year. I feel as if I should be in quite a good position.'

'Lots of things will be taken into account, Sarah. *Lots* of things. As I said, there will be a range of measures, and I'll use those to make a judgement.' He crossed his legs, his trousers brushing her shin. 'So I need to be sure that we have an understanding.'

Her mind was scrambling to catch up with the meaning of his words.

'W-what kind of understanding?'

He leaned closer. His breath had a sharp unpleasant tang to it. Whisky. Not even five o'clock in the afternoon and he was already on the way to being drunk.

'Think about it, Sarah. Think about what you want. And what *I* want.'

He put a heavy hand on her knee, slid it up towards her thigh. His skin was soft and clammy to the touch. She took his hand and pushed it away.

'Cheeky,' he said. Undeterred, he ran his index finger up and down her leg. Up and down.

Sarah felt herself flinching away. Inside she was screaming, raging, half-blinded with anger and frustration and the sheer bloody injustice of it all. All of the work she had put in, all of the hours, all the nights she'd worked past midnight until she was nodding off over the laptop. All of the days punch-drunk with fatigue, pushing on and keeping going regardless. None of it seemed to matter. None of it would make a difference.

'Please don't do that,' she said, trying desperately to keep her voice steady.

He uncrossed his legs, splaying them open, and put one hand on the bulge at the crotch of his trousers. He rubbed himself idly.

'You can stop the pretence,' he said, his voice thick. 'I know you want it.'

'No. I don't. I really don't.' She pushed his hand away again.

'It's wet, isn't it?'

'What?'

'Your sex.'

For a second she was too stunned to respond, her mouth opened but no words would come out. She shook her head slowly. '*What*?'

'Don't lie, don't tell me it isn't. I can tell you're wet. You're dripping. It's the fear reflex kicking in – fear is erotic. It drives the urge to copulate.'

'No.' She wanted to say something more substantial, but the shock was making all her words collide with each other inside her head. 'You're wrong.'

He leaned forward, sliding his hand up her thigh.

'Just let your inhibitions go.'

'No,' she said again.

He reached up and stroked her cheek with his fingertips. She felt something snap inside her. A line was being crossed.

This had to end.

35

She stood up, backing away from him.

'Get *off* me!'

He sat back in his seat, legs spread wide.

'You know, Sarah, once in a while you should let yourself go. Go with the flow.'

'I'm going to report you.'

'No. You're not.'

'I'm going over to HR right now, to make a formal complaint of bullying and harassment.'

He held up his hands.

'What harassment? I just want a close working relationship with all my staff.'

'That's bullshit and you know it! This has gone far enough.'

'I can't stop you talking to Bob in HR, Sarah. Very best of luck with it.'

'I mean it.'

'I know. And good luck dealing with the counterclaim.'

'What?'

'Good luck dealing with my counterclaim, detailing every incident where you have thrown yourself at me, *begged* me to have sex with you, as part of your plan to sleep your way up the ladder. At the hotel in Edinburgh, for example – hanging around outside my hotel room pestering me to let you in. Or at my party the other week.'

'That's not true,' Sarah said, her voice cracking with the strain of keeping it level. 'That's the *opposite* of the truth. It's complete and utter fiction.'

He shrugged, leaning back in his chair.

'Who can say what the truth is? It's flexible. History is written by the victors, you know that. And I've already given Bob a few hints about what you're like.'

'You know the truth,' she said. 'So do I.'

'The truth is that you said nothing was wrong. You denied that I'd ever made any such advances on you.'

'I never said that!'

'You did. Less than a fortnight ago.'

'You're a liar.'

'On the patio at my party, do you remember? I heard you say it very clearly and so did a dozen witnesses.'

Sarah shook her head as the memory returned, feeling sick. The woman, Gillian Arnold, had asked her about Lovelock in front of all those people. *Has he tried to get you into bed yet?* Sarah had panicked, fallen back on the safe option: to lie. In front of witnesses, she had denied there was any problem at all.

She knew what he was doing. None of the other incidents had been witnessed. There was no direct, substantiated evidence on her side. She could make a claim to HR right now, set that process in motion, but he would throw the accusations right back at her. The university's HR department was feeble enough at the best of times, but faced with two contradictory claims – one of them from the most eminent scholar in the entire university – they would seek the path of least resistance. At best, a crappy compromise that satisfied neither complainant. Worse still, months of protracted meetings and conciliation and discussions with HR, with Lovelock, ending with some kind of fudge that avoided any kind of decisive, constructive action.

And, undoubtedly, her career would be doubly screwed.

She wanted the earth to swallow her up.

'This is bullshit,' she said through clenched teeth.

'Think about it, Sarah. I'm a reasonable man – I can be a nice chap, if you're nice to me.'

'What does that mean, exactly?'

'I think you know.' He put his legs together again and patted his lap. 'You know very well what it means. And you know what else? I know you want it, I see it in your eyes.'

She stared at him, feeling the hatred rise in her throat. There were a thousand words she wanted to hurl at him. Sharp words, deadly like knives. Brutal words that would cut him open from neck to navel. But the only thing she could think to say was pathetic and she hated that she couldn't do better than stating the blindingly obvious.

'I'm married, Alan. So are you.'

'Don't allow yourself to be strangled by bourgeois conventions of monogamy. Your husband clearly doesn't, from what I've heard. Why don't you just give in to it?'

So there it was. A week ago she had been looking forward to getting her foot on the next rung of the career ladder. A permanent job. Security for her kids. Stability for them all. Now that was gone for another year. In fact, she might not even have a job at all.

Unless she gave Lovelock what he wanted.

36

Sarah sat motionless in her car in the dark, slanting shadows of the car park. Her head was ringing with anger, her throat raw and fists clenched tight on the steering wheel. Her eyes stung but she was so angry she couldn't even cry anymore. That *bastard*. Every time you thought he'd hit rock bottom, he always found a way of stooping even lower. He had spent the best part of two years harassing her, groping her and pressuring her to sleep with him. Unsubtle flirting had deteriorated into unwanted advances and physical contact. But now he seemed to have decided that if she wouldn't give in, if she wouldn't just lie down and let him take what he wanted, then he would simply get rid of her. Have her declared surplus to departmental requirements.

Since the age of sixteen she had worked harder than everyone else, hard enough so she could make her own luck, to ensure she had options. She'd always worked longer hours than colleagues, sacrificing hobbies and free time along the way, to give herself the best chance of following her dream. Falling pregnant at twenty-four had been an accidental exception to that particular rule, but it had only made her more determined to be in charge of her own destiny.

And now this.

All your work – all the hours and months and years – counts for nothing. Literally nothing. All your studying, all the exams, the PhD, the interviews, the sleepless nights and short-term contracts, the struggles, the sacrifice, the traumas and little triumphs along the way. They amount to nothing. Zero. Nada. Because he *holds all the cards.*

She was in an impossible situation, and there was no way out. No good solution.

Or maybe there was.

She remembered that she'd not stopped the Voice Recorder app on her mobile phone, when she tucked it into the side pocket of her handbag. She took it out, unlocked it, and sure enough there was a digital time counter on the home screen – forty-one minutes and rising – showing that it was still going. Just as Laura had suggested.

I've got him, she thought. *My God, I've got him. No way they can argue with this.*

She sat up in the driver's seat, a flush of adrenaline quickening her pulse, and stopped the recording. It appeared in the menu as Rec002. *Whatever you do, don't delete it by accident. Upload it to the laptop as soon as you get home. Maybe write out a transcript too, get it all down in black and white.* She hit the play icon and heard a series of rustling sounds, picturing herself as she'd switched it on in Lovelock's outer office just before the meeting. Sitting there while he'd kept her waiting, the distant tap-tap-tap of his PA Jocelyn Steer typing in the background. Sarah put her ear closer to the microphone. A hiss of static and a brief exchange with Jocelyn as she'd gone through to the inner office, phone in hand; a knock on his door, more clicking and rustling sounds. Lovelock's voice starting the meeting, the usual preamble before he got to the real reason why he'd asked her in.

'The truth is, Sarah, I've been increasingly concerned about your attitude.'

The recorder had picked up every word. It was faint, but it was clearly him.

Sarah's heart began to beat a rapid rhythm against her ribcage, and all she could think was: *I've got him.* Finally, she had some evidence. She needed to think, to work out the best way to play this, but first she would listen to the whole encounter again. She put the speaker a little closer to her ear as the audio file continued to play, Lovelock's voice with an edge to it now.

'. . . because recording a conversation like this would be a breach of HR guidelines, not to mention a significant breach of professional and ethical standards.'

'I know that.'

'Do you mind?'

'I'm not recording.'

'All the same, I'd be more comfortable if you put it away.'

'Fine.'

There was more rustling, so loud that Sarah recoiled from the sudden noise in her ear, and then –

And then nothing.

She checked the display on the screen to make sure the timer was still going. The clock ticked onwards as the audio played. A hiss of white noise. She turned the volume up to maximum and put her ear right to the speaker. More white noise. There was still something, but way off in the background, very vague and distant. Nothing recognisable as him and her. Barely recognisable as human voices at all. She let it run for another few minutes, hoping that it might become clearer. Knowing that it wouldn't.

It was no good. She must have muffled the microphone when she tucked the phone into her handbag. She hurled the mobile onto the passenger seat, slamming her palms on the steering wheel with a shout of pure frustration.

'Shit! Shit! Shit!'

The recording was no good after all. It would just be her word against his again, with no evidence to back up her version of events. The sense of powerlessness was overwhelming. A plunging black hole that pulled her deeper and deeper. One she knew she could never escape.

As she sat in the cold darkness of her car, staring through her half-misted windscreen at a blank brick wall, her white-knuckled hands on the steering wheel, she thought back to another conversation. A conversation with a powerful stranger. It was in this very car park, three days ago, that three men had lain in wait for her. Blank-eyed men who had most likely done things she could only guess at.

In her head, she heard him again. She could almost smell the smoke from his cigar.

Here is my offer. You give me one name. One person. And I will make them disappear.

It was madness. Plain and simple. An unbelievable offer from a stranger.

I will make them disappear.

What would her life be like, if he was no longer in it? Would she still have that feeling of creeping dread, deep in her stomach, when she was driving to work in the morning? Of course not. Would she have a fair chance to move onwards and upwards, to have some security in her life, to provide a stable future for her children? Yes. Would the world be a better place, without Lovelock in it? Plenty of people who knew him, who *really* knew him, knew the answer to that question.

She dug into her handbag, feeling in the front pocket for the small phone Volkov had given her. She hadn't got around to throwing it away. Now she pulled it out and held it in her hand for a moment. She'd still not switched it on since she'd been given it. Staring at it for a full minute, her thumb brushed back and forth across the smooth dark cover. She flipped it open and held down the power button, some part of her brain hoping that it might be out of battery and she would not have to make this decision. So she would not have the option.

Because every step was a step nearer.

The phone's screen glowed into life, illuminating the car's dark interior. There was no unlock code, just the default start screen, a standard range of apps displayed. Sarah stared at it for a moment, the breath hot in her throat. She had the feeling she was standing on a high window ledge, looking down.

Vertigo is not actually the fear of heights. Vertigo is the fear that when you are standing on the edge, you won't be able to resist the urge to step off.

She hit the orange 'Contacts' icon at the bottom of the screen.

Lovelock created this situation. Not you. He passed you over for promotion again, and it was that anger – that rage – that boiled over when you saw the little girl on Wellington Avenue. Lovelock made it happen. He put you in an impossible situation. He set all of this in motion.

There was only one number in the phone's memory, a mobile. The name was simply listed as 'AAA'. Her thumb hovered over the green 'call' icon for a few seconds, then away again. She pressed the back button, retreated to the home screen, and hit the power button again. The screen went black.

She held the small mobile in her hands. Only a few ounces, but it felt as heavy as a rock: the power of life and death in her right hand.

The power to reclaim some control over her own destiny.

She checked her watch: 5.26. There was just over an hour left before the Russian's seventy-two-hour deadline passed. Soon the offer would disappear – forever.

She pressed the power button again, watched the screen glow to life for the second time, and selected the address book. Stared at the mobile number again. It was probably all nonsense anyway – just another man on a power trip. People just didn't do this sort of thing. It didn't happen in real life.

But what other options did she have? Simply lie down, and let her boss ruin her life? Sack her, force her to move her family again, ruin her career? Or give him what he wanted?

No. There had to be another way. A way in which she didn't have to submit. Didn't have to be humiliated. Didn't have to lose.

Perhaps sometimes in life, an impossible situation required an unthinkable solution.

She pressed the green icon and put the phone to her ear.

37

Sleep wouldn't come.

She took a full dose of her pills but her brain was wired, replaying the conversation in her head, the enormity of what she had done pressing in from every direction. She turned over again and again, looking at the clock radio each time she moved onto her right side. Seeing how few minutes had passed since she last checked the display. The white heat of her anger from earlier in the evening had subsided into a low throbbing in her temples, a headache that just wouldn't quit.

The phone call crowded out every other thought.

She saw it now for what it was: a deal with the Devil. And she knew only too well how that had gone for Dr Faustus. He had enjoyed his twenty-four years of good fortune and success and adulation, but it had ended – as he knew it would when he signed his name in blood – with the Devil coming for his soul.

The phone call had been a moment of madness. There was no doubt that Lovelock was a man who used his power to prey on others, presenting one face to the world and an entirely differ-ent one in private. A highly intelligent, devious sexual predator who probably had a list of victims going back decades. But it couldn't be right, to do what Volkov had offered her. No matter what Lovelock had done or would do in the future, it couldn't be right. Could it?

She wavered back and forth like this all night, finally slipping into a shallow restless doze as dawn approached. She dreamed of Volkov, but there were knives where his hands should be. Wicked curving blades that tapered to a shining point. She dreamed of Lovelock sitting at her kitchen table, his skin grey and his eye sockets empty red holes. When he spoke, maggots crawled out from between his lips.

She woke with a start, her heart fluttering against her ribcage, one thought overpowering all others.

Oh God. What have I done?

The full enormity of what she might have set in motion settled on her at 4.41 a.m. And by the time dawn had spread its cold, grey light into the room, she knew what she had to do. She put on her dressing gown and slippers and crept out of the bedroom, careful not to disturb the children as she crossed the landing. Harry was a light sleeper and would stir at any sign of movement in the house, coming to find his mother wherever she was. And once he was up, he was up for the day. What she had to do now, she needed to concentrate for.

Walking on the balls of her feet as quietly as she could, she went downstairs to the kitchen. Jonesy was sitting on the kitchen worktop and greeted her with a slow-blinking stare. She pulled the kitchen door closed behind her, searching in her handbag for the little black Alcatel phone. Switched it on and watched the screen light up.

She felt heavy-headed from lack of sleep. But she forced herself to concentrate, to think about what she would say, how she would phrase it. She needed to be clear and unequivocal. *It was a very kind offer but I'm afraid I've made a mistake. I've had more time to think about it and I'd like to withdraw my request. Please disregard what I said last night. Very sorry to have wasted your time, but I hope you understand. I hope your daughter is able to forget what happened to her, just as I hope to forget it.*

Jonesy jumped up onto her lap and began kneading her dressing gown, purring deeply. Sarah dialled the number for the second time in twelve hours and put the phone to her ear.

A few seconds of silence, followed by a woman's electronic voice.

'I'm sorry, this number is not available. Please check and try again.' *Click*. Nothing.

She frowned and dialled again, only to get the same recorded message. *This can't be right.* Panic rising in her throat, she checked the phone's contact list and call history again: one number, one call, 29 seconds long at 5.27 p.m. yesterday. Her call, as she sat in the car park at work shaking with fury.

She felt her face growing hot. With a trembling hand, she stabbed the number a third time. The electronic voice came on again. It was no good: the number was disconnected.

Whatever she had set in motion could not now be stopped.

38

Sarah made a strong coffee, chewing her thumbnail anxiously as the kettle boiled, and opened her laptop on the kitchen table. She should still have an hour or so before Harry woke up. She would find out who the mysterious Russian was, and contact him somehow, explain that it had been a mistake. That she wanted to withdraw the name she had given last night. She'd half-convinced herself already that it was a good sign the phone number no longer worked: perhaps all that meant was that it had been a con trick right from the start. Just an ego trip, a bit of a joke at the gullible Englishwoman's expense – and she had fallen for it.

But she still wanted to find out who the stranger was, to be certain. And how hard would it be to find the identity of such a rich man? He must have a sizeable footprint on the web, if he was as wealthy as he appeared to be. He certainly had a base in London, she knew that from the night they had taken her. But where was it, and how did he make his money?

She googled 'Volkov', even though he'd said it wasn't his real name. There were lots of hits; famous and not so famous.

None that looked like him. She put his name into Google Translate.

Volkov meant 'wolf'.

Next, she googled 'Russian businessmen London'. More than 450,000 results came up. She spent fifteen minutes combing through the links on the first five pages, but found nothing that rang any bells. She might not know his name, but she knew what he looked like, so she switched to the image results. A seemingly endless drop of pictures dominated by shots of Roman Abramovich and Boris Berezovsky. She started at the top, working her way down the page, carefully scanning every face to see if it was familiar. A couple of hundred images down she found one that resembled the mysterious Russian. She clicked on it to blow it up, a side profile taken outside on a windy day by the looks of it. All the caption revealed was a name: Andrei Ivanov. Was it him? There was a resemblance in the shape of the chin, the hairline. It wasn't a particularly good photograph.

She opened another tab and googled the name. The top result was a Wikipedia page:

Andrei Ivanov, billionaire businessman and owner of a string of hotels in Russia, Europe and South America. Believed by some to have links to organised crime and connections at a high level within the Russian government. Ivanov was shot dead, along with his bodyguard, in the stairwell of an apartment building in Moscow's Rublyovka district on 12 January 2014. He was believed to have been targeted by a business rival over a long-running disagreement. His killer has never been found.

No good. This man had been dead for several years. Sarah looked at the photo on the screen again. Now that she studied it more closely, it was obvious that the eyes were wrong. Too deep-set. And he looked to be in his early forties, whereas the man she had met must have been in his mid-fifties.

She went back to scrolling through pictures, taking her time so she didn't miss anything. But after another fifteen minutes, she had still drawn a blank. This was useless. She needed a name.

She thought back to Monday night, when Volkov's men had taken her from the campus. Hooded and laid flat on the back seat of the BMW, she had tried to estimate the amount of time that had gone by. Counting minutes in her head she had got to fourteen, give or take. Call it twelve. At an average urban speed of twenty miles an hour, twelve minutes of driving gave a potential driving distance of four miles from campus. Basically, this created a circle across north London, from Barnet on one side to Edmonton on the other, from Palmers Green in the south to the M25 in the north. Maybe six or seven miles from one side to the other.

Just a population of about two million people, then.

And what if her calculation was wrong? If the time was too high, or her guestimate of speed too low? Then she'd be way off.

She was about to try another Google search when Harry appeared in the kitchen doorway, hair sticking up at all angles and eyes still heavy with sleep. Without a word, he held his arms out to her and she picked him up, setting him in her lap for a cuddle. They sat like that for a long time, hugging in silence, Sarah breathing in his sweet little boy smell, cotton sheets and talcum powder and baby shampoo from last night's bath. For that one moment she forgot everything, closing her eyes and letting all her worries fall away in the warmth of her son's embrace. She rocked him gently in her lap, as she'd done when he was a baby. She kissed the top of his head as it rested on her chest, blond hair still tousled from sleep.

Then everything came rushing back at her, the knowledge of what she might have done.

She opened her eyes again and shut the laptop with her free hand.

Harry looked up at her.

'Is it Saturday yet, Mummy?'

'Not yet, darling. Soon.'

'So is it a school day?'

'Yes. Come on, let's get you ready, shall we?'

Half an hour later, while Grace and Harry ate their breakfast, she dug the little Alcatel phone out of her handbag and switched it on again. Checked the recent calls log in case someone had tried to ring her back when she was in the shower.

There was still just one dialled number, one call out, at 5.27 p.m. yesterday. Then three failed calls to the same number this morning.

The decision was made, it seemed. She tried to focus on what a future would be like without Lovelock in it, feeling herself buffeted by emotions from every side. Remorse. Anxiety. Fear. A tiny, guilty sliver of relief, too. But it still didn't seem real, not at all.

Her thoughts were interrupted by Grace's inquisitive voice.

'Have you got a new phone, Mummy?' her daughter asked.

'Oh, this? No. I'm . . . looking after it for a friend.'

She hit the phone's power button and the screen went black again.

'Can I have a go on it?'

'It's almost out of battery,' Sarah said, putting it back at the bottom of her handbag.

'Can I have a iPhone, Mummy?'

'Not yet, Gracie, when you're a bit older. Perhaps when you go to big school.'

'Olivia Bellamy in my class has got a phone already.'

'Really?'

Olivia bloody Bellamy has everything, Sarah thought, not for the first time.

'It's an iPhone 7. She brought it in last week but Mrs Brooke got cross and took it away and she had to go and collect it with her mum at the end of school.'

Sarah had a brief vision of Grace's headteacher, the formidable Mrs Brooke, giving a stern talking-to to Olivia's mother.

'Good for Mrs Brooke, I say.'

'She's on Instagram. She's got one hundred followers.'

'Mrs Brooke?'

'No, silly!' Grace pulled a face. 'Olivia.'

'That's really for teenagers, I think. And grown-ups.'

Harry piped up, leaning across the kitchen table.

'Can I have an ice phone, Mummy?'

'A what, darling?'

'An ice phone, like Olivia.'

Grace snorted.

'Not an *ice* phone, an iPhone. Idiot.'

Harry pouted at his mother.

'Mummy, she called me idiot.'

'Don't be horrible to your brother, Grace.'

'He is, though.'

Harry reached over and pulled one of his sister's pigtails, snatching his hand back before she could grab it.

'Now you're going to get it!' Grace said, moving around to retaliate.

'Mum!' Harry wailed.

Sarah stretched her arms out on both sides, like a policeman directing traffic, catching one child in each hand and holding them at arm's length. Nick was gone. It was down to her alone to keep the peace.

'That's enough, both of you. Grace, go and clean your teeth. Harry, finish your cereal please. We have to go in five minutes.'

Grace harrumphed and stomped off towards the stairs. Harry took one tiny mouthful of his Rice Krispies and pushed the bowl away, jumping off his chair and hurrying back to the lounge for five more minutes of Lego. *Just a normal day*, Sarah thought as she watched him go. A normal morning. Get the kids dressed, breakfast, brush teeth, school drop-off, commute, work.

Except it wasn't normal. Because of one phone call.

39

The guilt gnawed at her as Friday wore on.

Her appetite seemed to have disappeared and she found it increasingly difficult to concentrate. She had a growing sense of things happening just beyond her eyeline, of wheels in motion, but all of it was outside her control. A runaway train with no brakes. And with the number on the mobile disconnected she had no way of changing its course. It was no problem being busy all the time, to take her mind off it, but whenever her mind had a few moments to wander, she found herself thinking about Volkov. While she was sitting in a meeting, or at her desk, or waiting for the kettle to boil in the little staff kitchen, her mind would slip back to the moment she had made that phone call, sitting alone in her car in the dark.

And then she would have the sick, plunging feeling in her stomach again. As if a china vase had slipped out of her hands and she knew it would shatter into a thousand pieces as soon as it hit the cold hard ground. Watching it fall, as if in slow motion.

One phone call. Less than half a minute. Perhaps this would be the moment that divided her old life from the new, moving her from innocence to guilt. The moment her life jumped the tracks and took off in a whole new direction.

Or was it all just a bluff, an elaborate ruse, a rich man's power trip at her expense?

Because nothing had happened. At least, not yet. She'd not known what to expect, she hadn't asked the person who answered the phone what would happen or how long it would take – if anything happened at all. Life simply went on, seemingly undisturbed.

Not knowing was driving her crazy.

There was something else, too, a feeling almost like she was being watched at work by an unseen observer. As if Lovelock was constantly one step ahead of her. He'd known she was going to HR. He'd known she was going to record their last meeting, and that she'd spoken to the dean about the Atholl Sanders opportunity. But how did he know so much? She couldn't pin it down, it was as if –

'Dr Haywood?'

Sarah came out of her reverie.

'Sorry, what?'

Peter Moran, the school manager, was staring at her across the polished oak table.

'I was asking if you had anything to add to Charlotte's suggestion?'

Charlotte Hanson, the media relations manager assigned to their faculty, smiled at her expectantly. Sarah gazed around the table. Everyone seemed to be looking at her.

'Oh, er, nothing,' Sarah said. 'Not at the moment.'

Charlotte brushed her blonde curls behind her ear.

'I was just suggesting some social media activity around the 450th anniversary of Marlowe's birth. Some blogs and so forth, maybe a piece for *The Conversation*? Pitching you out to the media for some interviews, see who might be interested?'

'Yes, that sounds good.' Sarah tried to recover her thoughts. 'Really good. I'll pick up with you tomorrow if that's OK.'

'We'd also like to do some preparation with Professor Lovelock in advance of his book coming out in the spring,' Charlotte added. 'I know he'll be doing lots with the BBC but we'd also like to get everything lined up at this end as well.'

Sarah nodded but all she could think was: *His book won't be coming out in the spring, because he will be long gone by then. He will have disappeared. Or perhaps it will be published posthumously.*

'Of course,' she said. 'Yes. Good idea.'

She hurried back to her office after the meeting wound up, keen to be away from people for an hour or so before her next lecture.

Her office phone rang as soon as she'd sat back at her desk and she jumped, startled. It was Jocelyn Steer, Lovelock's PA.

'Sarah, do you have five minutes?'

'Err, sure.'

'Super. Two things: just want to remind you that there is an extra departmental meeting this coming Monday and could you pop through to Alan's office?'

She tried and failed to come up with an excuse to dodge the request. Jocelyn could see her electronic diary on Outlook so

Sarah couldn't claim to have an imminent teaching commitment without being caught out in a lie.

'Of course,' she said instead. 'When?'

'Right away would be good. Thanks so much.' She hung up.

Her heart sinking, Sarah stood and gathered herself. *Does he know something? About what I did? Or maybe this is the day he tells me he's cut my post as part of the restructure.* She stood in front of her desk for a moment, trying to work out which was the worse of the two options. Both were disastrous in their own separate ways, but surely the latter was much more likely than the former?

Eventually she put on her jacket and went slowly through to Lovelock's office. He was sitting on the edge of his desk, waiting for her.

'Ah, Sarah. Thanks for coming through. Close the door, will you?'

She pushed it shut behind her but stayed near to it, keeping as much distance as possible between the two of them. He gestured towards the chaise longue along the side wall between two floor-to-ceiling bookcases. It was covered with dark red leather and looked like an antique family heirloom, its upholstery faded with age.

'Why don't you have a seat?'

'I'm OK, thanks.'

'You make me nervous standing there by the door.' He grinned wolfishly at her. 'Come on, women prefer it on the couch, or so I'm told.'

He gestured again at the chaise longue, and she went over and perched on the end furthest from him. He crossed his legs, angling his body towards her.

'So: the departmental restructure. I wonder if you've had anymore thoughts on it.'

She was amazed, even after working with him for three years, that he could behave in the way he did and then – a day later – act as if nothing had happened. As if he hadn't made lewd remarks or harassed her or put his hands on her. It was a kind of selective amnesia, she thought, mixed with a colossal belief in his own irresistibility.

'I didn't think it was down to me.'

He stood up and moved over to her on the chaise longue, perching on the end with his right leg dangling. He was wearing slippers, she noticed, suede moccasins that seemed thoroughly out of place at work.

'Oh, I wouldn't want you to have that impression. You can certainly influence the outcome of what's decided.'

I'm pretty sure I've influenced the outcome, she thought. *But not in a way you're going to like.*

He carried on talking, gesturing, moving closer, but she couldn't hear his words. They were simply noise, drowned out by the volume of thoughts in her head.

He knows. He knows.

Don't be ridiculous. Of course he doesn't. It was a stupid idea. There was no way he could know about her contact with Volkov. *But what if he does? What if he knows there is a blade hanging over his head, ready to swing?*

His smell was stronger now, a sharp body odour. He'd once told Sarah that a man's natural pheromones should not be masked with chemicals, and consequently his office always had a very specific smell to it. *Smells like a tomcat's jockstrap*, Marie had once said. It had been funny at the time but it wasn't now. She leaned away slightly and tried to breathe as lightly as possible.

She looked at him and tried to feel bad for what she had done. Tried to stoke up her guilt again, to find some strands of remorse for this thing that she had set in motion.

But it wouldn't come.

Another thought struck her with a force so strong she caught her breath.

Unless I tell him.

Is that the right thing to do? Warn him that he is in danger?

But he would never believe her. And there wasn't a way of saying it which didn't sound completely mad. As fast as it had arrived, she banished the thought.

What's done is done. Sow the wind, reap the whirlwind.

Instead, as Lovelock edged further into her personal space, one thought drowned out all the rest: *maybe this will be the last time I'll have to go through this. The last time.*

Because you're a dead man walking, Alan.

He was still talking.

'The clock is ticking, Sarah. Tick-tock. Decisions will be made, one way or the other.' He shifted towards her in the seat, resting his arm along the back until his fingertips brushed her shoulder. 'You'll either be part of the new structure, or you won't. It's up to you. But changes are going to be made – soon. Changes are coming.'

You bet they are, she thought.

Ten minutes later she stumbled out of his office. Angry and embarrassed, again. Flushed and fearful. She'd lost count of the number of times it had happened now. Maybe a dozen. Maybe more. But today was different. Because maybe today would be the last time.

Jocelyn Steer's eyes followed her as she hurried away down the corridor.

40

Saturday passed in a flurry of housework and playing with the children, of taxiing them to swimming lessons and friends' parties, of cooking and cleaning and washing. She wanted to be busy, to be doing something to take her mind off the events of the previous week, and she was glad when she was able to slump exhausted in front of a film after the children had gone to bed.

On Sunday morning, Sarah prepared lunch while the children painted at the kitchen table, aprons plastered with colour. Harry seemed to have got more of the poster paint on himself than on the paper in front of him, but he was happy enough, his face a picture of concentration. Grace was running through a long and complicated falling-out between her friends that had come to a head at a birthday party the previous day.

'Chloe was mean to Millie,' her daughter explained, 'and then Francesca said that she'd been invited to Chloe's birthday party and she didn't want Tara to go, and if she did go then she wouldn't, so then Chloe said that Tara couldn't go after all and then Millie told Alisha that she didn't want to go if Tara wasn't going and that Chloe's mum was mean and horrible and a chav.'

'Uh-huh.'

'But I think it was all Francesca's fault really. *She's* the one who started it.'

'Mmm. Yes.'

'What do you think, Mummy?'

'I think you should all just be friends, darling, and try hard to be nice to each other.'

'Even Francesca?'

'Yes. Even Francesca.'

Grace harrumphed as if this was a ridiculous answer and returned to her painting.

She planned to take the children to Alexandra Park in the afternoon, but only if the rain held off. The TV was on mute in the kitchen, switched to the lunchtime news bulletin. With both children painting happily, she leaned back against the worktop with her coffee to wait for the local weather forecast. The image switched from the national news to BBC London for the regional bulletin. She turned the sound up.

'Our top story today,' the well-coiffured presenter announced. 'Police are investigating the death of a man whose body was recovered from the River Lee in the early hours of this morning. Detectives have cordoned off a stretch of the bank of the river in Edmonton, as forensic teams comb the area for clues. Liz Storey has more.'

All the strength seemed to go from Sarah's legs. She put her cup down heavily, spilling coffee across the counter. The cup rolled off and smashed onto the floor, Grace squealing in alarm.

Sarah ignored the mess and the noise, grabbing the remote and turning the TV's sound up.

The pictures on the screen cut to a smartly dressed young reporter standing on the bank of a river. Behind her was a lock, water rushing over, where a policeman in a high-vis jacket stood by blue and white crime scene tape strung between two trees at the water's edge.

The reporter looked into the camera and it seemed to Sarah that she was staring straight at her.

'The body – believed to be that of a man in his mid-fifties – was found by a dog walker this morning but appears to have been in the water for at least a day.' The picture cut away to another shot of the crime scene tape, two police cars backed up near to the scene and evidence technicians in white coveralls going back and forth. 'Police are treating the death as suspicious but are still working to identify the dead man at this stage. Unconfirmed reports suggest that the victim may have been mutilated. The coroner has been informed and an inquest is due to be opened in the coming days. This is Liz Storey, BBC London News, reporting from Pickett's Lock on the River Lee.'

Sarah froze.

Oh God oh God. How did they get to him so fast?

She knew the area. She'd taken Harry to a summer birthday party at a five-a-side football centre just down the road from there. It wasn't far from Wood Green.

Her hand shaking, she opened her laptop and called up Google Maps, scrolling until she found the river and the lock. *There*. A thin horizontal line that marked where the concrete structure spanned the river from side to side. That was the spot where the BBC reporter had been standing moments ago for her live report. She zoomed out slowly, the map bringing in more and more names as the scale increased. Her heart was beating so hard she thought she might faint, or be sick. She zoomed out a little more and scrolled slightly north before she found what she was looking for.

The village of Cropwell Bassett.

The lock was about three miles from Lovelock's house.

A man in his fifties.

Police treating the death as suspicious.

Unconfirmed reports suggest the victim may have been mutilated.

Sarah felt a tidal wave of horror mixed with a tiny pinprick of . . . What, exactly? Not relief. Not that. It was the weirdest feeling.

She covered her hand with her mouth as a voice whispered in her head. Asking the same question, over and over again.

What have you done?

What have you done?

She felt sick.

The body was the right age, right gender and found in the right area. The identity was not confirmed yet, but that would surely come in a day or two. And then all hell would be let loose.

She had been stupid and naive to believe Volkov. He had lied to her, had promised that he could make someone disappear and never be seen again. Had promised that Lovelock would vanish off the face of the earth.

And now a body had turned up in the river three miles from his house.

41

Be calm, she told herself. *Focus*. Now this thing is done, this debt has been paid – whether you wanted it to happen or not. Now you have to be smart, to do what is necessary to make sure that this act of violence never, *ever*, attaches itself to you or your family. It must not even come close.

She had to think clearly. Gripping the edge of the kitchen worktop, knuckles white, she stared out of the window. What now? What was the first thing she should do, right away? The first priority had to be getting rid of any evidence, anything at all that connected her to Volkov. She realised with a start that she still had the mobile phone that he had given her. She had meant to throw it away, but she'd forgotten. Deep down she had never really thought anything would happen.

But now it had.

She found the little Alcatel phone in the bottom of her handbag and turned it over in her hand, still not believing what she had unleashed with a single phone call. How many ripples would flow out from that call? How far would they reach?

She opened it and switched it on. The battery still had 58 per cent charge.

She selected Contacts and dialled the number again, just in case it had been reconnected, hope rising in her chest that perhaps she could still do something to change the course of whatever it was she had begun.

The line was dead. Just like before.

The number was useless, but for some reason she didn't want to lose it forever. She found a Post-it note, scribbled Volkov's number on it, and tucked the note into her purse.

The phone had to go. But where? The dustbin wasn't due to be emptied for another ten days. That was no good. It had to be away from here, away from her home and her children. Somewhere it would never be found.

She put the phone in a plastic bag, fetched a handful of heavy stones from the garden and dropped them in, before tying the top of the bag in a rough knot.

Wait. What about fingerprints?

She went into the utility room by the back door and fetched her gardening gloves from the cupboard under the little sink, pulling them on. She undid the plastic bag, tearing it in the process, and took the phone out again. How was this done? She had seen it on TV but had no idea whether it worked in reality or not. She took a wet wipe from the packet next to the washing machine and wiped the phone down thoroughly, handling it only with her gloved hands. When she was content she'd wiped every part of it, she dried it with a towel from the washing basket and tucked it back into the plastic bag. Wrapping the bag tightly with a length of Sellotape, she wedged it into her handbag. There was something else she should do, she felt sure of it, but she couldn't quite put her finger on it. What was it? What else connected her to these men? There was no time to think about it now. Every minute this phone was in her possession, she was connected to a dead man in the river.

Not just any man.

Her boss.

She put her coat on and returned to her children in the kitchen, who were still happily painting at the table. It was a scene of such happy normality, such a contrast from the darkness gathering around her, that she had to stop in the doorway and catch her breath for a moment. She covered her mouth with her hand, wishing she could capture this moment and stay in it forever.

Whatever else she did, she had to protect these two little ones from the darkness. Even if she failed at everything else, she had to succeed at that.

'Come on, you two, let's wash our hands now so we can get coats and shoes on,' she said as brightly as she could. 'We're going to feed the ducks.'

Harry jumped off his chair.

'Yes! Ducks!'

Grace wrinkled her nose.

'Do we have to?'

'Yes, Grace, we all need some fresh air and the ducks need some lunch. The sun's going to come out later. Come on.'

'Can we get a McFlurry after?'

'I don't know, Grace, we'll see.'

'Does that mean yes?'

Harry latched on to Sarah's leg and looked up at her with his big blue eyes.

'Maccyflurry! Maccyflurry!'

Sarah couldn't remember everything being a negotiation when she was younger. She remembered getting what she was given by her parents, and being mostly happy with that. But now it seemed that every straightforward instruction she gave had the potential to turn into a bargain to be struck or a treat to be had. On any other day it might have niggled at her, but today she was glad of the distraction.

She smiled at her daughter.

'It means we'll see, Grace. Now put your coat and shoes on, those poor little ducks will be starving.'

They drove through Saturday traffic, through Crouch End and Highgate, parked on the edge of Hampstead Heath and walked to the first footbridge over the bathing pond, the children running ahead so they could be first across the water to the little jetty where the ducks gathered.

The sky was dark and the air heavy with impending thunder.

The children reached the jetty and Sarah watched from the bridge as a dozen hungry ducks made a beeline for them across the water. Grace was in charge of the bag of bird seed, and she had given her brother a handful. With his small fingers, he was taking one seed at a time and throwing it to the ducks quacking around his feet, laughing as they circled him.

Sarah stopped halfway across the bridge. At the centre, where the water beneath would be deepest.

With both kids absorbed in what they were doing, she looked around quickly. No one behind her. No one coming towards her. There was a dog walker on the far bank, but he was facing the other way. A jogger in a bright pink windbreaker was coming towards her on this side of the pond. Sarah waited, watching the bright pink out of the corner of her eye. The jogger got to the bridge and kept on running, her back to Sarah as she drew further away.

OK. Now.

She took the folded-over plastic bag out of her handbag, moved up next to the railings and put her hand through the gap. Opening her hand, she let the bag fall, watching as it fell quickly and hit the choppy water with a flat *crack*.

Grace looked up at the noise.

Suddenly she thought: *That was the other thing I was supposed to do. The SIM card. Oh shit, I didn't take the SIM card out.*

Too late now.

She watched as the air in the bag billowed upwards as it settled on top of the water. For a horrible moment, Sarah thought perhaps it wouldn't sink at all. But then the bag rolled over, the Tesco logo visible for a second, before it sank beneath the grey surface of the pond.

In the distance there was a low rolling growl of thunder, and it started to rain.

42

'Sorry, am I last again?' Sarah said, putting her bag down and digging in it for her agenda. She had only made the departmental staff meeting with minutes to spare.

'Not quite,' Peter Moran said. 'Alan's not here yet.'

'Did his first meeting overrun?'

'No, he had nothing in the diary before this, according to Jocelyn.'

Sarah felt her heart drop into her shoes. She'd spent most of yesterday afternoon and evening scouring the local news websites, listening to radio bulletins, trying to find out more about the body that had been pulled from the river. But no identity had been released yet and she had tried hard to convince herself that it was not Lovelock after all, that it was just a coincidence: this was just some other poor unfortunate who had met an untimely end.

And yet . . . she'd never known Lovelock to be late for a staff meeting – not once in the two years she'd been in his department. His baritone voice dominated departmental meetings – it tended to dominate every meeting she'd ever had with him – so his absence would leave a large hole in the proceedings. He was normally at his desk for eight at the latest, firing off emails and Skyping with collaborating academics in time zones far away.

Today, it was a few minutes before 9.30 and the chair at the head of the conference room table – his chair – was still empty.

Perhaps today is the day after all, she thought. Conflicting emotions clashed inside her. The creeping sense of foreboding that had been growing for days rose up to full height, blocking out everything else. Her breakfast – what little she had managed to force down – rolled in her stomach. People were making small talk around her, but in Sarah's head, all she could hear were the words of the TV reporter from yesterday morning.

. . . the body – believed to be that of a man in his fifties – was found by a dog walker this morning . . .

Moran handed her an agenda.

. . . appears to have been in the water for at least a day . . .

'Are you all right, Sarah? You look a bit pale.'

'Has anyone heard from him?'

. . . Police are treating the death as suspicious . . .

'Not yet.'

'Has Jocelyn tried ringing him?'

'No answer, apparently.'

. . . are still working to identify the dead man at this stage.

'Perhaps we should give him a bit longer?'

Moran gave a non-committal grunt and picked up his mobile. Checked it for messages before putting it down again.

Marie gave her a sympathetic look from across the table, eyebrows raised as if to say *Are you OK?*

Sarah nodded and gave her a tight smile. She felt sick.

Moran cleared his throat.

'Let's get started, shall we? I'm sure Alan will be joining us shortly. Any other apologies for absence?'

He scanned the faces around the table.

'Looks like it's just Alan,' someone said.

'OK . . . ' Moran made a note. 'First item for discussion: the mid-session January exams.'

Sarah tried to concentrate on what Moran was saying, but it was impossible. Lovelock was *never* late. After a few minutes she reached down and took her phone from her purse. Holding it in her lap, and trying not to get Moran's attention, she googled the news story about the body that had been found in the river. Maybe they had identified him already. If they had, his name would soon be out there in the media, and on social media.

Maybe she would have to be the one to tell everyone what had happened. That his body had been identified.

That he was dead.

No. She didn't think she could pull that off in a way that looked natural. Her voice was bound to give her away. Better to carry on as if everything was normal, and let it filter out in the usual way. It would probably be all around the department – all around the university – in a matter of hours.

Act normal, she thought. As if it's just another weekday morning.

Act as if your deal with the devil didn't just pay off.

She hit refresh again but her phone wouldn't reload the web page – there were signal black spots in some parts of the building and Lovelock's office was one of them. She locked it again and put it back in her handbag.

Someone else could break the news, it would be better that way. Maybe Jocelyn was on the phone now. Maybe the police were waiting in the outer office, two grim-faced detectives and a police car parked right out front where all the students would see it. Maybe they would handcuff her, frogmarch her out of the building in front of everyone. She thought about how she would need to look when she heard. Shock, disbelief. She should watch to see how the others reacted and then do what they did. *Be natural.* Easier said than done.

The door from the outer office opened sharply.

All heads turned towards it as Alan Lovelock bustled in, bringing the smells of rain and sweat and cold November air into the room with him.

43

Sarah spent the rest of the day riding a wave of relief so powerful it made her dizzy. She struggled to concentrate on anything beyond the simple knowledge that she could get her old life back. *It had all been a misunderstanding. Or a con trick, or something.* Despite what Volkov had said, he'd not made anyone disappear after all. Because here was Alan Lovelock, just as before.

She would get her life back. Her old life. She tried not to think about the flip side. The fact that this meant *all* of her old life – including the fact that he was still here. Still her boss.

As day turned into evening, the initial feeling of relief at seeing Lovelock still alive was slowly replaced with the leaden knowledge that he was, well … the same. That nothing was going to change. He would block her promotion and threaten her with the sack and harass her whenever he could get away with it. She was still powerless to stop him. She was back in the same hole she had been in last week, last month, last year. Back to square one.

* * *

Sitting in her office the next morning, Sarah read the story on the BBC *News* online for the third time.

Police have named the man whose body was found in the River Lee on Sunday as 56-year-old Brian Garnett.

Mr Garnett, of no fixed address, had been missing for more than a week and was last seen at a homeless shelter in Walthamstow. His body was found at Pickett's Lock and is believed to have been in the water for several days.

An inquest is due to be opened by the coroner tomorrow. Police have appealed for information to establish Mr Garnett's whereabouts in the days before his death.

Detective Sergeant Emma Sharpe said: 'I would urge anyone who knew Brian, or who saw him at any point in the last two weeks, to come forward so that we can piece together his last movements. He was known at a number of homeless shelters in north London and may have been drinking on the day he went missing.'

She googled the local weekly paper, the *Gazette*, which had a little more detail and some quotes of the usual 'You don't expect that around here' variety from dog walkers and the local councillor for the area. According to the *Gazette*, there were suggestions that Mr Garnett had suffered with drug and alcohol problems for many years, and that he may have fallen into the river while under the influence of one or both. There was no mention of the body being mutilated, as the original TV report on Sunday had stated.

Feeling more than a little foolish, she closed the browser tab and sat for a moment. Behind it was another tab, www.jobs.ac.uk, the place to go for jobs in academia. There was nothing doing at Belfast or Edinburgh Universities, the other two UK centres for study in her specialist field. There was a job that she could potentially go for at Bristol University, but it was another fixed-term contract, outside her area of expertise, a step backwards in career terms.

And it was one hundred miles away.

And the kids were in good schools now.

And she was just barely scraping by on one salary, never mind the expense of moving.

She wasn't going anywhere.

She closed all the remaining browser tabs to reveal her email inbox, heavy with unread messages from the last couple of days. *Focusing on work is difficult when you've asked someone to make your boss disappear off the face of the earth.*

She saw now that the whole thing had been ridiculous, a weird glimpse into a parallel universe that existed alongside her own. A universe with its own laws and rules, its own violent code of honour, its own balance of revenge and reward. Its own broken promises, too.

Of course, there had been relief when Lovelock had appeared. But the relief had quickly been squashed by the leaden reality that she was firmly back in her rut, fighting a battle against impossible odds. A battle she couldn't win.

She went back to marking a stack of first-year essays on sixteenth-century poet Edmund Spenser, a contemporary of Christopher Marlowe's in Tudor London. Uncapping her red pen with a sigh, she began to annotate the essay in front of her – which would be vastly improved if the student could spell

Spenser's name correctly, she thought. That would be a good start, but it seemed that even the brightest of her undergraduates didn't pay much attention to spelling. Autocorrect had a lot to answer for.

Peter Moran appeared at the door of her office, one hand gripping the door frame. He was red-faced and looked out of breath.

'Have you seen Alan today?'

'No. Is he not in his office?'

Moran frowned as if this was a stupid question.

'Obviously not, hence me asking you.'

'I've not seen him – but I've had my head down marking these papers, to be honest.'

'He's due to give a presentation to the Vice Chancellor and executive board this morning.'

'He's probably on his way there now?'

'It was supposed to start fifteen minutes ago. It's not like him to be late, not for something as important as that. The VC's kicked off and everyone's running around like headless chickens trying to find out where the hell Alan's got to.'

A feeling of dread began to crawl up Sarah's spine. She made an effort to keep her voice level.

'Maybe he's had car trouble again? Like he had the other day?'

'He would have rung in to let us know – it's too important a presentation. I've tried calling him but his mobile is switched off.'

Moran went to the next office along the corridor. She heard him ask the same question but she couldn't hear the reply. She sat, frozen, at her desk.

Be calm, she told herself. *It's another false alarm, just like the body in the river. It'll be fine, probably his car again, or an issue at home. Maybe a bout of flu. That's it – he's probably ill, laid up at home with a temperature.*

But her instincts told her otherwise. The Vice Chancellor was the most important man on campus, the head of the whole university, and Lovelock would not have missed a meeting with him unless he was – *unless he was what?* Deep down, she knew that this was it – this was the real deal. He was gone.

She went outside to the little walled garden behind the arts faculty building. It was empty. The students never came here and it was usually quiet outside lunchtime. She found a bench and sat down, trying to make sense of her emotions, to work out how she felt about the latest news.

It's happened. This time they've done it.

She took a deep breath, then another. *In through the mouth, out through the nose.* She sat up straighter, looking around to see if anyone was watching.

This is what you wanted. This is your doing.

It was important that she acted normally, to give the outward impression that she had no idea where Alan Lovelock might have disappeared to.

After all, there's no way it can be connected to me.

Is there?

44

The days passed in a blur. Sarah kept her office door shut and avoided close contact with colleagues as far as possible, but still overheard the gossip in corridors as staff speculated on where Lovelock had gone and what might have happened to him. Naturally, it had become the most talked-about subject in the department, and speculation was rife – even the students were starting to cotton on that something was not right.

Slowly, the facts – which seemed to be few and far between – began to emerge from the spiderweb of gossip and guesswork that had become part of every conversation. Lovelock had left his house at the usual time on Tuesday morning, and his wife insisted that he seemed his normal self. But he never arrived at the university. Somewhere between home and work, he had gone missing – and forty-eight hours later he'd still not been seen. His car had disappeared too and his mobile was either switched off or out of battery.

To all intents and purposes, he had vanished off the face of the earth.

Sarah's stomach clenched every time she heard a colleague talking about it. At night she lay awake for hours, the same thought on a loop, over and over.

You did this. You did this. You did this.

On Thursday morning there was a strange, charged atmosphere in the faculty when she returned from lectures. Sarah sensed it straight away: a tension in the air, office doors open, whispered conversations, people looking over their shoulders. No one was at their desk, everyone was up, talking quietly, checking phones, huddled in small groups. She slowed as she passed Lovelock's open office door. Jocelyn Steer appeared to be the one exception, typing steadily at her desk, her face the usual mask of frosty indifference.

Sarah could already feel her stomach tightening as she bumped into Marie at the top of the stairs. Her friend looked agitated.

'What's happened?' Sarah said. 'What's going on?'

Marie checked over her shoulder and leaned in close, speaking quietly.

'Big meeting with all the top bods – directors of HR, communications, security and legal. They've been in there for an hour already.'

Sarah groped for the right response, the *innocent* response, that would sound right in the circumstances.

'About what?'

'Are you for real?' Marie snapped. 'What do you think everyone's talking about? Alan, of course.'

'Is he back? Has he been in touch?'

'Don't think the top brass would be meeting like this if everything was OK, do you?'

'I don't know. Maybe they've had some news from –' *From the police*, she was going to say, but caught herself just in time.

'News from who?' Marie said.

'I don't know. His wife?'

As she was about to say something else, Jonathan Clifton emerged from one of the meeting rooms deep in conversation with a heavy white-haired man in his early sixties. Sarah recognised him vaguely from stories on the university's internal news service – a pro-vice chancellor, one of six who sat at the university's top table, the Executive Management Board. Peter Moran, the school manager, and a handful of others followed close behind. All of them wore harried, tight expressions.

Sarah and Marie exchanged a glance and hurried down the corridor into the common room, where more faculty staff were gathered, clutching mugs of tea and coffee.

'What's going on?' Marie said.

All eyes in the small group turned to Diana Carver, a junior lecturer in the department, who was standing next to the kettle.

'They found his car, apparently. Alan's car.'

'What?' Sarah said, before she could stop herself. 'Where?'

'His Merc. The police found it parked up at some reservoir in Enfield, back of an industrial estate.'

'Oh my God,' Marie said quietly.

'I've googled it,' someone else said, two-finger scrolling on his phone screen. 'It's sort of halfway between here and his house. Bit of a detour, but it's kind of on his route into work.'

'He disappeared on his way to campus, didn't he?' Marie said.

'Yeah,' Carver said, nodding slowly. 'Tuesday morning.'

Sarah interrupted, trying to keep her voice even.

'But he wasn't . . . ' She tailed off, her mouth dry. 'He wasn't with the car?'

'No sign of him.'

'Maybe he's in the reservoir,' someone said, almost in a whisper.

They were all silent for a moment, contemplating possibilities.

Sarah's mind raced in a different direction.

Was this deliberate? A ploy to throw police off the scent? Was that it? Was the Mercedes all they would ever find of him?

'Are they searching the reservoir?' Marie said finally. 'With divers?'

'Don't know,' Carver said. 'There's nothing on the news about it, I've checked.'

'Bloody hell,' said another voice. 'Doesn't look good, though, does it?'

'How do you know about the car being found?' Sarah said.

Carver shrugged.

'My sister-in-law's a secretary in the registrar's office, which is about as secure as a leaky sieve. It's all kicking off up there, apparently, the usual headless-chickens routine. Hence the meeting here with a pro-vice chancellor and all those managers.'

'Are they going to make a formal announcement about it?'

'Too early for that, I'd say.' Carver glanced towards the open door. 'But if he doesn't turn up soon, the shit's really going to hit the fan.'

45

Sarah was secretly glad when Friday came. It was an Inset day at the children's schools and she'd booked it off to look after them. She was glad to be away from work, away from her colleagues, away from the gossip about Alan Lovelock.

Her mobile rang while she was making lunch for the children, a landline number that was not recognised. It was Peter Moran, his voice high and tight.

'Sarah? Can you talk?'

'Yes, I'm just about to –'

'The police are here. They want to speak to you.'

'Me? Why?'

'It's about Alan.'

Sarah felt her heart sink.

'Have they found him?'

He ignored her question.

'Can you come in?'

'Well, yes, I suppose I could after we've –'

'In the next half an hour would be good.'

'What's happened, Peter?'

'Just be quick, I want them to finish up as soon as possible. The students are already asking questions about the police cars outside.'

He hung up before Sarah could ask anything else.

She sat for a minute, staring at the wall, waiting for her racing heart to slow a little.

Think about what you're going to say. Think about what an innocent person would say.

She rang her dad, but he wasn't answering his mobile. He wasn't picking up the landline either. Then she remembered: he played bowls on a Friday.

She checked her handbag and quickly packed a separate day bag with the kids' water bottles, colouring books, pens, tissues, wet wipes, a couple of brunch bars and three bananas. Her hands gripped the wheel tightly as she drove, the children unusually subdued in the back of the car.

In her office, she set Harry up with his colouring book and pens, and gave Grace her book and mobile, selecting the Crossy Road app that she liked to play on.

'How long will you be, Mummy?' her daughter asked.

'Not long. Ten minutes. I'll be just next door, talking to the policewoman.'

'What are you talking to her about?'

'Just some work things.'

'Are you in trouble?'

'No, Gracie.' She made herself smile. 'I'm not in trouble.'

Harry slammed down his colouring pen on the desk with a *smack* and let his head roll back.

'I'm bored,' he said.

'Already?'

'Booooooooored . . . '

'We've not even been here two minutes.'

Her son let his body go floppy, sliding off the seat and onto the floor, where he proceeded to roll around saying the same word over and over again.

'Bored bored *bored*.'

Sarah lifted him to his feet, brushed him down, her mind reaching for something that might hold his attention for a quarter of an hour. She looked around, and her eyes settled on the old-fashioned blackboard in the corner of her office, a relic from when the building had been occupied by the maths department in a previous decade.

'Look, Harry, I'll let you draw on the blackboard – you can be like the teacher at school. There's even a little step you can stand on.'

She handed him a long, thick stick of white chalk.

Harry trotted over to the blackboard and picked up a second piece of chalk, grinning, with one in each hand.

'I can be the teacher,' he said. 'The teacher of all the receptions.'

Sarah turned to Grace. 'You're in charge. Look after your brother.'

'Do I have to?' Grace complained. 'He's annoying.'

'Yes. I'll be in the next room along if you need me for anything. Otherwise stay in here, OK?'

Grace nodded reluctantly and Sarah backed out, pulling the door shut behind her.

Sarah entered the vacant office next door, which had been commandeered by a couple of detectives for the afternoon as they spoke with members of staff. The policewoman smiled and held out a hand. She was in her late thirties, athletic and tall – close to six feet, Sarah guessed – with shoulder-length blond hair.

'I'm Detective Inspector Rayner.' She indicated her colleague, a slim black man at least ten years her junior with short-cropped hair and a neat beard. 'And this is Detective Sergeant Neal.'

Sarah shook both their hands in turn.

'Nice to meet you.'

'Have a seat. Thanks for coming in on your day off. Would you mind shutting the door behind you?'

Sarah did as she was told.

'It was no problem to come in, really.'

'Are those your kids next door?'

'Yes,' Sarah smiled. 'Grace is eight and Harry's five.'

DI Rayner smiled back.

'I bet they keep you on your toes.'

'You can say that again. I just wish I had half their energy.'

The detective leaned forward slightly in her chair.

'So: we're investigating the whereabouts of one of your colleagues, Alan Lovelock. You're probably aware that he's missing.'

'Yes, I've heard. Terrible.'

'We're talking to a number of members of staff here to find out if anyone has been in contact with him. The inquiry is still at an early stage, but our understanding is that for Professor Lovelock to be out of contact for this long is extremely uncharacteristic behaviour.'

'Yes. Yes it is.'

'Let me run you through a few of the details.' DI Rayner flipped back a few pages in her notebook. 'He hasn't been seen since leaving the house at about 7.45 on Tuesday morning. His wife was understandably concerned and called us that night, after not hearing from him all day. His car was found by the

King George's Reservoir near Enfield Lock on Wednesday evening. I've been looking at this since about Thursday lunchtime, and, so far, I've found no activity on his phone, his bank account, his email, his social media accounts. Nothing at all, in fact, since Tuesday morning, which means he's now been missing more than seventy-two hours.'

Sarah shivered. She felt cold and hot at the same time.

'Yes. We're all very worried. His poor wife must be in a terrible state.' As she spoke Sarah could feel her face flushing.

Stop talking. Just stop.

DI Rayner's eyes narrowed slightly.

'Are you feeling all right?' the detective asked.

'Yes. Fine.'

'You're sweating.'

'Just had a bit of a rush-around morning with the kids – it's an Inset day at their schools – then coming in here, you know.' She crossed her arms. 'It's been a bit of a mad day.'

'I see. I'd like you to think carefully about the last three days – have you had any contact, anything at all, with Professor Lovelock in a professional capacity?'

'No. Nothing.'

DS Neal scribbled something in his notebook.

'And how about,' DI Rayner added, 'in a personal capacity?'

'I'm sorry?'

'Outside of work. Personal.'

'Why would I have –'

'Yes or no?'

Sarah felt the sweat on her palms and laced her fingers together.

'No. Of course not.'

'Are you sure?'

'Yes. Positive.'

DI Rayner leaned forward, fixing Sarah with unblinking blue eyes.

'So it's not the case that you were involved with Professor Lovelock outside of work?'

46

'*What*?' Sarah said, not sure she'd heard correctly.

'I asked if you were personally involved with Alan Lovelock.'

'No!' Sarah answered rather more forcefully than she had intended. 'Absolutely not.'

DI Rayner exchanged a glance with her partner.

'So,' DS Neal said, picking up the questioning, 'how would you describe your relationship with him?'

'Relationship?'

'Your working relationship.'

Sarah hesitated, searching for the right words. She turned the wedding ring on her finger.

'Normal, I suppose.'

'Define normal.'

'He's my line manager.'

'Do you know each other socially, as well?'

'No, not really.'

DS Neal flipped back a page in his notebook.

'But you went to a party at his house a few weeks ago.'

'He invited me. He invites lots of colleagues from the department.'

'Have you ever been romantically involved with him?'

Sarah felt the colour rising to her cheeks again.

'*Romantically*? No. Never!' She knew as soon as she'd said it that the words had come out too fast. 'I already told you that.'

'Has he ever propositioned you?'

Sarah paused for a second. The questions were heading in a direction she hadn't anticipated. But she had to play it safe, make sure they had no inkling of motive. The lie made her palms itch, but it was just easier to lie. Smarter.

'No.'

'And what about the other way around?'

'I'm sorry, what?'

'Have you ever propositioned him?'

'Absolutely not!' she said.

'Have you ever had sex with him?'

'No! Who said that?'

DS Neal shrugged.

'Just one of those questions we have to ask, I'm afraid.'

'I'm married,' Sarah said.

DI Rayner leaned forward in her chair.

'Some of our enquiries suggest that Professor Lovelock may have been having a relationship, or relationships, outside his marriage,' she said carefully. 'One of our lines of enquiry is to work out whether he may have fallen foul of an angry spouse. Someone who caught him messing around with their wife, got angry, decided to take revenge.'

'Do you really think that could be a possibility?'

'What about your husband, Sarah? Has he met Professor Lovelock?'

'He's . . . they might have met once or twice, briefly. Not really properly.'

'Is he the jealous type?'

She shook her head, frowning at the question.

'No. And anyway he's – he's not around at the moment.'

'You're separated?'

'We're just having . . . a little time apart.'

'What's prompted that, if you don't mind me asking?'

'I do mind. And it's not relevant to this at all.'

'But it could be relevant if your husband perceived that there was a relationship going on behind his back, and that he perceived your boss –'

'There wasn't.'

'I'm sorry?'

'There wasn't a relationship. Whoever told you that is mistaken.'

Jocelyn Steer, she thought.

'Past tense?' the detective said.

'I'm sorry?'

'You said there *wasn't* a relationship. Past tense.'

'I just meant it wasn't – *isn't* – something that's ever happened.'

'Did Professor Lovelock want it to happen?'

Again, she hesitated.

'No.'

'Are you sure about that?'

'Yes.'

'Still, we may want to talk to your husband at some point.' The detective turned over the page of her notebook. 'One last thing, and then we'll let you get on with your day: can you think of any reason that Professor Lovelock might have had to harm himself?'

Sarah made an act of thinking for a moment, then shook her head.

'Not that I can think of, no.'

'Did he seem down or depressed in any way, the last few times you saw him?'

'No. But he probably wouldn't have confided in me anyway.'

'OK.' The DI made another note. 'Thanks, Sarah. Those are all the questions we have for now. If anything occurs to you that you think might help, please get in touch, OK?' She handed Sarah her card.

Sarah took it and saw herself out, waiting until she was safely in the corridor and the door was shut behind her to allow herself a small sigh of relief.

They don't seem to know anything, not really. They don't know about Volkov. They don't know about his offer. They don't know about any of it.

They don't know what's happened to Alan.

Unless –

Unless they know more than they're letting on.

47

Sarah unlocked the door to her office and was confronted with clouds of white dust hanging in the air. There was a fine layer of white on every surface and the blackboard was completely covered with chalk drawings of stick men, aeroplanes, tanks and houses and smears of white from one side to the other. Harry and Grace turned to look at her, grinning guiltily. Both had a blackboard rubber in each hand and were covered from head to foot in white chalk dust. Harry began enthusiastically banging the board rubbers together and more plumes of dust billowed around them.

'Look, Mummy!' Harry said, beaming. 'We made smoke!'

Grace waited a beat, watching to see if her mum got angry and shouted at her brother. When Sarah did neither of those things, she banged her own rubbers together to create more clouds of the white powder.

'Smoke!' Grace repeated.

'This is fun!' Harry said, beaming, his hair, skin and eyebrows coated in a fine layer of chalk dust. As was his sister, the desk, her chair, the filing cabinet, piles of books on the floor and most of the other surfaces in the office.

'That's enough now,' she said distractedly. 'Stop playing, we have to go.'

She began to brush him down, creating more clouds of chalk dust which settled in ever thicker layers on every exposed surface, and her own clothes. She quickly realised that she was simply transferring the white powder from one place to another.

'Bloody brilliant,' she said under her breath. 'This is all I need.'

'Bloody brilliant!' Harry repeated, grinning.

'Come on, you two. We're going.'

She gathered up all the colouring books, pens, *Star Wars* toys, pencils and cereal bars she had brought with her, plus the children's coats and jumpers and shoved them all into her backpack, ushering her children out of her office, downstairs and outside to the main car park at the front of the building.

A police patrol car was parked in the turning circle next to the statue of Neptune there, with a dozen students nearby taking pictures of it, posing for selfies and talking in excited tones. *No doubt posting on Snapchat, Instagram, Twitter and everywhere else*, Sarah thought. She wondered how long it would be before the secret got out about the university's prized professor. Not long, judging by the amount of interest being generated by the police car. Since vanishing on Tuesday he had missed five lectures, and she knew student speculation on social media was already spreading like a virus. And, like a virus, it would soon be out there in the wider population – if it wasn't already.

She headed for her car – parked illegally in a disabled spot – holding each child by the hand so they couldn't run off. Grace moved to get in.

'Wait a minute,' Sarah said.

'What?' her daughter replied, pre-teenage outrage in her voice.

'We need to get some of that chalk off you first.'

'What chalk?' Grace said through white-filmed lips.

'Just wait a minute.'

She went to put her bags in the car and when she turned back – barely a few seconds later – Harry was crying and Grace was looking away from him, arms crossed, a look of studied disinterest on her face.

'What's going on?' Sarah said.

Harry lunged for his sister. She sidestepped him and his momentum sent him sprawling to the pavement.

He jumped up and came at her again. As Sarah reached out to hold him back, she dropped her handbag, the contents spilling across the asphalt.

'What's going on? Why are you fighting again?'

'He put chalk on me,' Grace said.

'You're already *covered* in chalk.'

Harry sniffed and stuck out his bottom lip. A tear made a clean line down his chalk-covered face.

'She pinched me, Mummy.'

'That's enough, both of you. I've enough to deal with, never mind you two behaving like a couple of bloody toddlers.'

'You *swore*, Mummy,' Grace said accusingly.

She knelt next to them, gathering up the spilled contents of her handbag while brushing more of the white dust from her children and trying to make sure they didn't come to blows again.

'Do you want a hand?' A friendly voice beside her.

She looked up and saw a tall, dark-haired man with a backpack over one shoulder. Not young enough to be an undergraduate, Sarah thought, but he didn't look quite old enough to be a member of staff either. He had the look of a rugby player, broad and wide-shouldered, and was dressed more smartly than the average student.

He handed her a couple of lipsticks that had fallen from her handbag.

Sarah took them from him, grateful for the help.

'Thanks, I appreciate it.'

'No problem.'

He lingered a moment longer, as if plucking up the courage to say something further.

'You work with Prof Lovelock, don't you?'

Sarah felt an immediate stab of concern at the mention of his name.

'We're in the same department, yes.'

'Thought so.' The man smiled broadly. 'My girlfriend has him on Wednesdays: says it's the best lecture she's ever had. But he didn't turn up this week and the word is, he's missed everything else as well.'

'The word from who?'

'It's all over Twitter. Is he ill, or something?'

'No, don't think so.'

The man raised an eyebrow.

'Woah. So the rumours are true, then?'

48

Sarah put the last few things back into her handbag before zipping it up.

'What rumours?'

'People are saying on Twitter that he's been suspended. Criminal misconduct.'

If only, Sarah thought.

'Don't think it's that, either.'

The man looked down at her with dark, confident eyes.

'Really? So, he's not ill and not suspended. Done a runner then, has he?'

A slim, dark-haired woman appeared at the man's side. Sarah knew her from somewhere but she couldn't quite place her. She had an iPhone in her hand and was wearing an exquisitely cut black trouser suit over a crisp white blouse. Sarah read the name on the university ID card hanging around her neck on a lanyard. *Lisa Gallagher, Press Office.*

'Hi,' she said briskly to the tall man. 'Are you a student?'

'Yeah. Postgraduate. Politics.'

'Long way from your faculty, aren't you?'

'I was just on my way back to my hall of residence.'

'Really? Which hall?'

'Sorry, I've got to be off now.'

'I know you, don't I?'

'No, I don't think so.'

'Yes, I do. You're Ollie Bailey. *Daily Mail*, isn't it? Or is it the *Evening Standard*?'

The man looked at her, seeming to contemplate his options. After a moment he smiled and held up a hand in mock surrender.

'*Mail*,' he said finally. 'So where is he?'

'Where is who?'

'Alan Lovelock. Your star professor?'

'Give me a card and I'll send you our statement.'

Bailey produced a small notepad from his back pocket and scribbled some notes in shorthand.

'Already got your official line: doesn't say very much. But there is a police investigation going on, right?'

'I'll send you the university's formal statement,' Gallagher repeated. 'In the next hour.'

'Is it true that he's been picked up as part of Operation Yewtree?'

'You can go now.'

'Is it true?'

'Bye bye.'

'I don't have to go anywhere. This is public property.'

'Wrong. I'd be quite happy to have my colleagues from Security escort you off campus, if you like.'

He shrugged, and turned to Sarah again.

'It was nice to meet you, Dr Haywood.'

As he walked away, Sarah looked down and realised she had her own staff card on a lanyard around her neck, her name and title on display.

'He's a reporter?' Sarah said, feeling the flush of embarrassment rising to her cheeks.

'In the broadest sense of the word.' She turned to face Sarah. 'You're staff, aren't you? What did you tell him?'

'Well, just that Alan isn't ill.' She felt herself going red again. 'And that he wasn't suspended.'

Gallagher frowned, fixing Sarah with her blue-green eyes.

'How do you know that?'

Sarah opened her car and began strapping Harry into his seat.

'Well, I've just been interviewed by two detectives.'

'What else did you say to Bailey?'

'Only that Alan and I were colleagues, and that he hadn't been around for a few days. People are speculating about it on Twitter.'

'Don't say anything else. To *anyone*. All right?'

Sarah was struck by a horrible thought.

'Is he going to quote me?'

'Wouldn't surprise me.'

'Tomorrow?'

'Or tonight, if it's online.'

'But I didn't give him permission.'

'This is the *Mail* we're talking about.'

Sarah finished strapping Harry into his car seat and closed the door.

'I'm sorry, I didn't realise. I was distracted with the kids, and we just got chatting.'

Gilligan handed her a business card.

'If you have any other approaches from media, refer them straight to me. All my numbers are on the card.'

'Of course.' She tucked the card into her handbag. 'I didn't realise that Alan would be such big news. I'm sorry.'

'As soon as there's blood in the water, the sharks start to circle.'

Sarah felt her heart clench.

'Blood? Is he – is he hurt?'

'It's just a figure of speech – I'm sure he's fine. What I mean is, when the nation's favourite professor goes AWOL, it's bound to get attention from the more prurient sections of the media. Sniffing for a story.'

'I really am very sorry about this. I just didn't realise he was a journalist, he didn't introduce himself.'

Gilligan checked her phone's display briefly and put it in her jacket.

'Just remember: any other media ask you for comment, refer them *straight* to me. No exceptions. This situation with Professor Lovelock has all the makings of a real, gold-plated shitshow, and we don't want to make it any worse than it already is, do we?'

49

Sarah woke with a piercing white wine hangover on Saturday morning and it took a minute – as it did every morning now – before reality settled on her again. The briefest of moments while she floated out of pre-dawn sleep, before she'd even opened her eyes, when she wasn't aware of anything – not Volkov, or the scarred man or Alan Lovelock. Not the phone call that had sealed her boss's fate.

Then it all came crashing back in, all at once. And from that point on, every minute she was awake, thoughts of him were within touching distance all day long.

That was how it was now.

She made the children's breakfast and spent the best part of two hours combing news websites and social media for any hint, any clue, that the police were closer to finding Lovelock – or his body. Sure enough, the *Daily Mail* had run a story on their website about his mysterious disappearance from the campus of Queen Anne University, quoting various unnamed sources alongside the university's official response which said very little apart from the fact that they were cooperating fully with police and their thoughts were with Lovelock's family 'at this difficult time'. The story carried the byline of Ollie Bailey, the reporter who had buttonholed her the day before, and she had frozen for a moment when she thought he might have singled her out to quote her by name.

She breathed a sigh of relief. He'd used her quote, but not named her – referring to her as 'a close academic colleague'.

At ten, she took the children to Harry's football match where her dad joined them to cheer his team on as they went down to a 12–1 defeat. Harry and her dad stayed at home after lunch while she took Grace on a girls' shopping trip to The Mall in Wood Green.

By four, Sarah was flagging and the pair sat down in a Costa Coffee. While Grace fussed with the marshmallows on her hot chocolate, Sarah sipped a cappuccino and did a quick search on her phone for any updates on Lovelock. The *Evening Standard* had done a version of the story, lifting the *Mail* piece virtually word for word, and the local paper, the *Gazette*, had done the same with the addition of a little local colour. The only update seemed to be the addition of some older pictures of Lovelock, and a 'no comment' response from his wife.

She put her phone down and cradled the last of the cappuccino in both hands, savouring the strong earthy taste and the instant hit of caffeine. She studied her surroundings for the first time as Grace played with her new stationery set. It was a normal Saturday afternoon, with normal people doing normal things: a table of teenage girls giggling over their phones; a pensioner reading the paper; a young dad with a baby in a pram; a woman opposite a man in a wheelchair at the table across from them, the woman laughing a light, high-pitched laugh.

Sarah frowned, the sound was out of context, out of place. Wrong, somehow. The woman's laugh was both familiar and unfamiliar at the same time. She looked more closely at her. Late forties, smartly dressed in a woollen jacket and jeans, straight hair falling to her shoulders. Sarah knew her, but the context was wrong. She looked different. Everything about her was different.

The woman laughed again as she stood up and put her coat on, and this time the man in the wheelchair laughed with her.

Sarah studied her, not quite believing how different she looked out of work. She also couldn't ever recall hearing her laugh before, or even seeing her smile.

'Jocelyn?'

Jocelyn Steer turned, the smile still on her lips.

'Oh – hello there, Sarah.'

'I almost didn't recognise you.'

'I'll take that as a compliment.'

'I mean you look so – so different.'

And she did. At work she always dressed in muted greys and blacks, cardigans and long dresses, hair tied back, no make-up. No smiles – and definitely no laughter.

'My work clothes are rather different to my normal wardrobe.' She motioned to the man in the wheelchair. 'This is my husband, Andrew, by the way.'

'Nice to meet you,' Sarah said.

Andrew smiled and nodded, but said nothing. Sarah introduced them to Grace, and Jocelyn shook the little girl's hand with a wide smile.

'I didn't mean to be rude,' Sarah said. 'It's just a bit of a surprise, that's all.'

'Don't worry about it. Really.'

It wasn't just Jocelyn's appearance that confused Sarah. It was her mood as well – how upbeat she was.

'How are you doing? With – with everything that's going on at work?'

'I'm fine. You?'

'I suppose so.'

Jocelyn leaned down to help button her husband's coat.

'Listen, we were just on our way home. Do you want to walk back to the Tube with us, if you're heading that way?'

They walked up the hill towards Wood Green underground station in the gathering darkness. The air was cold and smelt of winter, the streets busy with people as shoppers headed home and early Saturday drinkers came out. Sarah held Grace's hand tightly while Jocelyn pushed her husband in his wheelchair, manoeuvring him expertly through the crowd.

'I want to apologise for the other week, by the way,' Jocelyn said. 'That Monday meeting.'

'When I was late?'

'The thing I said about you being alone with him in his office. I think it might have come out the wrong way, how I said it. I'm sorry.'

'So you didn't tell the police I was in a relationship with him?'

'No! Of course not. I hate how he treats people, how he's treated you. I hate what he gets away with.'

'And you didn't tell him I tried to record my last meeting with him?'

Jocelyn looked taken aback.

'Me? No. I had no idea.'

They walked a little further through the crowds.

'If you hate the way he is, why don't you just leave?' Sarah said.

Jocelyn shrugged.

'I can't afford the upheaval of looking for another job, not with everything else we've got going on at home and me being the breadwinner now. Alan upgraded me right to the top of the next pay scale a couple of years ago, so I earn more there than I could elsewhere.' Her eyes dropped to the wheelchair and she gave a sad smile. 'And he's told me more than once that he wouldn't give me a reference if I quit, or it would be an atrocious one. Alan has a habit of – shall we say – making it difficult for people to leave.'

'I noticed,' Sarah said.

'I know where the bodies are buried, so to speak, and he knows I know it, too. It's kind of an unspoken thing between us.'

'He wants to keep you close because of what you've seen and heard?'

'Yes. So I worked out a way to survive: I play a role. I play the frosty, frumpy bitch and keep absolutely everyone at arm's length. Including Alan.'

'Has he tried it on with you, too?'

'Once, when I first started. Then I figured out my own set of rules. My camouflage. You have your Rules, and I have mine.'

'You know about the Rules?'

She shrugged.

'I keep my ears open.'

'You don't seem too upset about what's happened. Him going missing, I mean.'

'Oh, he'll turn up. He always comes out on top, one way or the other.'

'And if he doesn't?'

They stopped walking at the mouth of the Tube station and Jocelyn leaned towards her, voice low.

'Let's just say I don't think it would be a terrible tragedy. But what do you make of it all?'

'Me?' Sarah said, searching for the right sentiment. 'Obviously, I hope he's OK, same as everyone else.'

Jocelyn studied her for a moment.

'Of course. The same as everyone else.'

Sarah put out her hand and they shook.

'It was nice to meet you. I mean the *real* you.'

'You too.' Jocelyn gripped her hand, her face hard again – a hint of her work persona. 'If you mention any of this, I'll deny it all, of course.'

'Of course.'

'But if not, perhaps we could do it again some time?'

They exchanged mobile numbers and went their separate ways.

50

Caroline Lovelock's pale face greeted her when she got home. Sarah was making tea for the children with the TV news in the background, mulling over her encounter with Jocelyn Steer. She set pasta on to boil and took two tins of tuna from the cupboard, still struggling to get over how different Jocelyn looked outside work. How different she *was*, in reality. How badly she had misjudged her. She chopped a red pepper and an onion, stirring the pasta sauce on the hob.

On the wall-mounted TV, the national news finished and switched into the regional bulletin for BBC London.

'Our top story tonight,' the presenter said. 'The wife of TV academic Alan Lovelock appeals for his safe return.'

Sarah turned and dropped the cutlery she was holding with a clatter, grabbing for the remote as the presenter continued, a picture of Lovelock appearing in the top left corner of the screen.

'Detectives say they are becoming increasingly concerned for the safety of the popular TV professor after he failed to arrive at work on Tuesday morning. Caroline Lovelock, his wife, appeared at a police press conference this afternoon. Our reporter Anna Forsythe has the story.'

The picture switched to a crowded room, a table festooned with microphones, bright lights shining on four people behind the table. DI Rayner was there, with another senior officer in uniform, and a woman that Sarah didn't recognise at the other end. At the centre of the table sat Caroline Lovelock in a dark jacket and cream blouse. She looked calm and composed, despite the forest of microphones angled towards her face.

'It's been four days since Professor Alan Lovelock was last seen,' the voiceover intoned. 'And the Metropolitan Police are now stepping up their search in what they say is becoming an increasingly high priority case. Caroline Lovelock had this to say today.'

The picture switched to a tighter shot of Caroline Lovelock, a large Metropolitan Police logo plastered on the blue background behind her. She picked up a piece of paper from the desk and began to read.

'Alan, if you're watching this, I just want you to know that we're all worried about you, and we want you home safe as soon as possible. Please just get in touch, either with me or with the Metropolitan Police, to let us know that you're safe. Or if anyone knows anything about where Alan might be, please pass on your information to the police.'

She finished talking, put down the piece of paper, and stared straight into the camera. She looked intensely uncomfortable but seemed determined not to cry, not to break down in front of the nation's media.

I did this, Sarah thought to herself, feeling an icy chill at the back of her neck. *I made this happen. I put her in that chair, in that room, with those people.*

I've made her a widow.

She wanted to look away but couldn't tear her eyes from the screen, from Caroline Lovelock's unblinking brown eyes staring back at her, the guilt pressing in on her from every direction threatening to squeeze the air from her lungs. Not for the first time she thought of *Doctor Faustus*, the Elizabethan tragedy she had spent so many hours of her professional life reading, dissecting, analysing. He had sold his soul to the Devil in exchange for earthly success, money, power, knowledge, sealing the deal in a contract written in his own blood. And after twenty-four years the Devil had returned, to drag his soul to Hell for the rest of eternity.

Stop it. That's nothing to do with you. With your situation.

Faustus is just a story, just words on a page.

The image on the screen cut away to a shot of Lovelock's house, taken from the end of the drive. The reporter was still talking, wrapping up her story, but Sarah couldn't hear anything she was saying.

'I'm sorry,' she whispered.

But what's done is done.

'Sorry for what?' Grace appeared at her side.

Sarah jumped.

'Gracie! You nearly gave me a heart attack.'

'What are you sorry about, Mummy?'

'Oh, nothing. It's gone now.'

Grace looked at the cutlery scattered on the floor, at the pasta starting to boil dry and the unopened tins of tuna.

'Is tea ready, Mummy? I'm starving.'

51

By Monday, the story was everywhere.

The cafeteria was packed and it seemed to Sarah that everywhere she looked, all the students eating lunch on the long bench seats were talking about one thing: Professor Alan Lovelock, who had now been missing for almost a week. The lads behind her in the queue had spent the last five minutes trading theories back and forth that they'd seen circulating on social media: either he had been suspended, or arrested, or was on a crystal meth binge in Las Vegas. Or maybe all three, one of the students said with a trace of admiration in his voice.

'Maybe he's been kidnapped by ISIS,' his mate said with a laugh.

Sarah suppressed a shiver and kept her eyes focused straight ahead. She finally got to the till, paid for her ham salad sandwich and joined Laura at a small table at the back of the cafeteria. Monday was nominally Laura's 'working from home' day, but when Sarah asked her to meet on campus for lunch and an urgent chat she'd agreed straight away.

Sarah sat down opposite her friend and began to unwrap her sandwich.

'Thanks for coming out.'

Laura leaned forward over her fish and chips. It always amazed Sarah that she could eat the way she did and stay so slim.

'No problemo,' Laura said. 'So, what do you think?'

'About what?' Sarah said.

'You know: about what's happened to your boss? Where the hell's he gone? It's in *all* the papers.'

'How should I know?'

Laura shrugged, spearing a chip with her fork.

'I'm not saying *you* know, just wondering what you think? I saw his wife on telly on Saturday doing that appeal. So what's the goss?'

'It's just a big mystery. No one really knows anything.'

'Aren't you curious?'

Sarah took a bite of her sandwich and chewed, to give her time to think. The sandwich was thin, bland and almost completely tasteless.

'Of course. We all are,' she said, still chewing. Her mobile pinged with a new text message and she flinched, turning the phone face down on the table.

'So what's management saying?'

Sarah shrugged.

'The dean's playing his cards very close to his chest. It's like they've all taken a vow of silence. Either that or they just don't know.'

'You think?' Laura speared a piece of battered cod and put it in her mouth. 'Of course they know. They're just not saying.'

'What makes you say that?'

'Someone *always* knows.'

Sarah took another small bite of her sandwich.

'Perhaps.'

'Aren't you enjoying it, though?'

'What? No. What do you mean?'

'I mean the creepy bastard not being around?'

'I suppose.'

'Sarah, are you OK? You're not worried about Lovelock, are you?'

Sarah stopped chewing.

'Why would I be worried?'

'No idea. I just thought you'd be doing cartwheels, with him being gone.'

'I'm a bit old for cartwheels.'

Laura checked over her shoulder and leaned forward, dropping her voice so that no one else would hear.

'Do you think he's dead?'

Sarah felt a needle of fear in her chest. She took another small bite of her sandwich, the taste like ashes in her mouth.

How long until people figure it out? Even without a body, sooner or later it would be obvious.

'What?'

'Perhaps he's dead? One of those people who just goes to the Scottish Highlands with a bottle of Jack Daniel's and a hundred paracetamol, and decides to take them all and lie down on a mountain top.'

If only, Sarah thought.

'It doesn't seem like the kind of thing he would do.'

'More's the pity,' Laura said quietly.

'You shouldn't say things like that. Not when he's missing.'

'He'd be doing the world a favour.'

'Don't say that,' Sarah said.

'True though, isn't it? You had the worst of him, you're one of those who bore the brunt of it for the last two years. Everyone knows it.'

'Everyone?' Sarah repeated. She could feel her nerves jangling, feel the heat rising in her throat.

'It's true, isn't it? What about that chat we had at mine, the other week? About doing something really bad that no one would ever find out about? Don't tell me you never wished he'd just fall under a bus.'

Sarah shook her head.

'No. And you mustn't tell anyone else that, either.'

'Why?'

'*Just don't*, OK?'

Laura froze, her fork halfway to her mouth. She returned it to her plate.

'Hang on a minute, do you think they suspect you of being involved in him going AWOL?'

'They will if people keep on saying that I was one of his victims.'

'But you were, love.'

Sarah slammed her palm down on the table, the sound of it surprising them both.

'I know. But the police will see that as motive!'

A little circle of silence spread out around them as other students and staff in the cafeteria turned towards the noise. When they saw that it was not going to blow up, they turned back to their food.

Sarah rubbed her forehead with her fingers, telling herself to calm down.

'The police are looking for suspects with a motive. They'll include me in that group if they think I had a reason to harm Alan.' She slumped back in her chair. 'Or if they think I could have asked someone else to harm him.'

'Sorry, love, I didn't mean to upset you. But that's mad, isn't it? You having a motive?'

'The police might not think it's mad.'

'I don't think you should worry about it. It's not like you *are* involved, is it?'

Sarah studied her friend for a second, trying to work out whether she knew more than she was letting on. *Of course she doesn't. I'm being paranoid. Aren't I?*

'No,' she said finally. 'But the police may put two and two together and make five.'

'Wouldn't be the first time.'

'Listen,' Sarah said, 'I need to ask you a favour.'

'Of course. Anything.'

'When I was at yours the other night, for the sleepover with the kids, I asked you that hypothetical question about whether you'd do something if you knew you'd get away with it. You know, like maybe something illegal.'

'Yeah, I remember.'

'I'd really appreciate it if that stayed just between the two of us.'

'OK.'

'In view of what we've just discussed about the police jumping to conclusions.'

'Right. Of course.'

'Can you do that?'

'Sure. But you didn't . . . ' She trailed off.

'No, of course I didn't. But if the police hear about that conversation, God knows where they'll go with it.'

'I understand.' Laura made a zipping motion across her mouth. 'Lips sealed.'

'Thanks, you're a star.' Sarah made a show of looking at her watch, then stood and dropped her half-eaten sandwich into a nearby bin.

'Listen, I've got to head back up to the office. Thanks for coming over.'

Laura picked up a last chip from the plate and bit it in half.

'I'll walk out to the car park with you.'

Sarah distractedly checked her mobile as they walked out into the atrium. A text message from an unrecognised number had arrived a few minutes ago. She clicked on it.

I know what you did.

52

Everything seemed to grow quiet around her. Distant. She stopped walking, staring at the text message on her phone. Just five words. But with the potential to destroy everything.

I know what you did.

There was a lurching, plummeting sensation in her stomach as if she was in freefall.

'Sarah? Are you all right?'

She couldn't respond. Her throat was suddenly so tight she couldn't form the words.

Laura moved nearer, as if to look at the screen of the mobile.

'Is it something from Nick?'

Sarah just about managed to hit the phone's *home* button to make the message disappear before Laura saw the words.

'It's nothing,' she choked out, shoving the phone into her bag.

'Are you sure? You look a bit freaked out. Are you OK?'

'I have to go.'

'Can I help, Sarah?'

'I really have to be getting back.'

They walked back to the department, Sarah batting away her friend's questions with short answers.

Back at her desk, she took out her phone and looked at the text message again, a chill creeping over her skin.

I know what you did.

The sender was just displayed as a number. Her phone's address book didn't recognise it. So who was it from? Who would send a message like this? Perhaps one of Lovelock's friends or colleagues from the faculty? It suddenly occurred to Sarah that there was a much more likely candidate: Caroline Lovelock, his wife. She remembered seeing her on the TV news a couple of days ago, staring straight into the camera. She remembered the icy glare she had given her and Marie at the party a few weeks before. What was it Gillian Arnold had told her that night? *'I was even getting abusive texts and emails from Caroline, his wife. Can you believe that? Like it was all my fault . . . '*

Could it be that Caroline somehow suspected Sarah was involved in her husband's disappearance? Her half-eaten lunch rolled in her stomach and she fought back a wave of nausea and guilt, thinking about what his wife – widow? – must have been going through these past six days. Taking three deep breaths, she typed a careful reply.

Who are you?

Pressed send.

She continued staring at the screen, willing the message to be a mistake, a misdirected text meant for someone else. It was easily done – one wrong digit was all it would take.

But somehow, she doubted it.

I know what you did.

But what did they know? What *exactly* did they know? And more importantly, how?

She needed answers. But her phone remained obstinately silent.

With shaking hands, she typed another short text.

Who is this?

No reply.

She sat, staring at the screen, waiting for a reply to drop in. When she couldn't wait any longer she got up and went to the window with the sudden idea that perhaps the sender was out there, right now, staring up at her.

She scanned the scene in the car park below. The usual ambling students clustered in small groups, chatting on their way to lectures or the union.

There was no sign of Lovelock's wife, or anyone else who looked out of place.

Still standing by the window, she held the mobile in front of her and called up the text message again. With only the faintest idea of what she would say, she selected the mobile number and pressed dial.

She had to know who this person was, how they'd got her contact details.

It couldn't be Caroline Lovelock, could it? There was no way she could know, was there?

One way or another, she had to know. The number rang three times and then, with a click, it was answered.

They picked up.

Sarah held her breath, straining to hear a voice, anything.

Across the electronic distance came a faint sound of breathing. She pressed the phone harder to her ear, straining to hear the person at the other end.

'Hello?' Sarah said. 'Who is this?'

The breathing diminished into silence at the other end of the line.

'Who is this?' she said again, her voice rising.

With a *click* in her ear, the line went dead.

53

Sarah phoned in sick the next day, unable to face the prospect of work. With the kids at school, she was alone in the house.

Alone with her thoughts.

She thought about driving out to Lovelock's house to speak to Caroline face to face, rather than sitting here, waiting for her to send another threatening text. But as soon as it entered her head, she recognised that it was a very bad idea – for lots of reasons. She jumped as her mobile pinged with a text message. Heart in her mouth, she unlocked the phone. Fear turned to frustration when she saw the message was from Nick.

We should talk. Are kids OK? And you? xxx

Nick had been gone more than six weeks now and had not returned her last two messages. She put the phone down, thinking she might reply, she might not – but she certainly wasn't going to respond straight away. She would let him stew for a little while, until she had worked out how she felt about her husband. Whether she wanted him back – now or ever.

She started as her phone beeped again, the sound piercing in the midday quiet of her childless house. Clearly Nick couldn't cope with her silence. Now he'd made contact, she knew he would keep texting her until she replied. She grabbed the phone and unlocked the screen, resigned to the prospect of a lengthy back and forth with her husband.

It was another text from the unknown number.

Perhaps everyone should know what you did.

She stared at the words, the breath catching in her throat. Her hands shaking, she typed the same question she had asked the day before.

Who is this?

The reply was almost immediate. But as before, it ignored her question entirely.

Your house. 1 p.m. today.

She dropped the phone and covered her mouth. That was less than twenty minutes from now.

Whoever it was, they were coming to her house.

Another text message landed as she picked the mobile up off the floor.

Share this with anyone and I will go to the police instead.

She dialled 999 anyway, her thumb hovering over the green call button.

But what was she supposed to say?

Well, officer, someone offered to kill my boss, and now his wife – at least I think it's his wife – is threatening to expose what I did. And she's coming to my house in fifteen minutes. Can you send an officer round please?

It was ridiculous. Of course she couldn't ring the police.

She called her dad's number instead, listened to it ringing and ringing before it went to voicemail. She hung up and rang him again, this time waiting for the voicemail message to end.

'Dad? It's Sarah. Can you ring me when you get this please? It's urgent, really important. Thanks.'

She hung up and ran into the hallway, slotting the chain into place on the front door.

She's coming to the house.

She checked the windows front and back to make sure there was no one already there, watching her. She went into the lounge, then the kitchen, then upstairs to the front bedroom to look out onto the street. Back downstairs into the lounge, sitting on the edge of the sofa staring at the big clock above the fireplace.

Be prepared. For anything.

She went back into the kitchen and pulled the sharpest blade out of the knife block, a black-handled boning knife; holding it in her hand for a moment then sliding it back into the block. She withdrew it again and took it into the lounge, looking for a place to conceal it, somewhere out of sight.

There. She placed it on top of the bookcase where it couldn't be seen but where she could reach it if she stretched her arm up.

She fetched the Stanley knife from the toolbox and gripped the cold steel handle, pushing the blade out with a click-click-click until an inch of sharp steel was exposed. It was a brand new blade but she still tested it against the ball of her thumb, nicking herself in the process. Blood oozed into the wound and she sucked it away, the taste coppery in her mouth. She retracted the blade back into the handle and put the Stanley knife on top of the stack of cookbooks in the kitchen, high enough so the kids wouldn't be able to reach. Repeated the process with the poker from the fireplace, which she laid on the floor next to her bed.

But it was no good. The walls were closing in on her.

There had to be a better way to do this. She didn't have to sit here, stuck in a web and waiting for the spider to return. She grabbed her coat and scarf and a beanie hat that belonged to Nick, scooped her car keys out of the bowl in the hall, and with a final check out of the window she undid the chain and opened the front door. Another quick check up and down the road – all clear – as the front door slammed shut behind her. She jumped into her car and reversed it out before parking it on the other side of the street, three doors down from her own house. Put on the hat, coat and scarf, and hunkered down low in her seat.

12.57.

Three minutes until the appointed time.

Her phone buzzed with an incoming call.

'Sarah?' her dad said. 'I got your message, is everything all right?'

'It's fine, it's all – all under control.'

'Are you at home? Do you want me to come over?'

She scanned up and down the street again. Still quiet. From where she sat, she could see anyone who arrived at her house before they saw her. And if she had to, she could just drive away before they even knew she was watching. She pulled the beanie hat a little lower on her head.

'No, I'm OK. But could you do me a favour? Could you get the kids from school and have them at yours this afternoon?'

'Of course, love. They can have tea at mine if you like, and then I'll bring them over before bedtime.'

'Perfect.'

'You sure you're OK?'

'Yes. Thanks, Dad.'

They said their goodbyes and hung up.

Mrs Lowry, one of her neighbours, was coming down the street with her little terrier, Buster. Sarah looked down, pretending to be checking her phone, trying hard not to catch her eye. But she was a second too late. She sensed Mrs Lowry slow and stop next to her car.

Sarah finally looked up at her, buzzing the window down.

'Hello, Jean,' she said briskly.

'Hello there, dear.' Mrs Lowry was bent over her walking stick and bundled up against the November wind. 'Is everything all right?'

'Just going to nip to the shops in a minute.'

'Oh.' She peered over Sarah's shoulder to see if anyone was in the back of the car with her. 'Children at school?'

'Yes, I'm on pickup duty later.'

'Awfully cold to be sitting out here in your car, though.'

'I needed some fresh air,' Sarah said, willing her elderly neighbour to take the hint. The longer she stood there, the more attention she would draw to Sarah's presence on the street. 'But you should get indoors, Buster looks absolutely perished.'

The truth was, Buster always looked perished. He didn't seem to have enough fur to cover himself and was always shivering, winter or summer. His whiskery little face was pinched and nervous.

Go, Sarah thought again. *If someone pulls up now you will be the first thing they look at. You, then me.*

Mrs Lowry didn't take the hint.

'How's that cat of yours?'

'Jonesy?'

'The ginger one. He was in my garden again the other day, doing his business in my flower bed. Gave Buster a terrible fright, he did.'

'Oh. Sorry about that. I'll check the fence later.' She turned the keys in the ignition as if she was going to leave, the Fiesta's engine coughing into life. 'I best get that shopping done.'

'Right you are, dear. See you, then.'

Sarah put her seat belt on and watched in her wing mirror as the old woman shuffled slowly up the street, Buster shivering by her side, before turning into her drive. She buzzed the window up again and settled back down in her seat, sliding low and pulling the cap down to shade her eyes. The mid-afternoon sky was heavy with clouds and she hoped that she would be harder to spot by whoever it was that wanted to pay her a visit.

After a minute had passed, she turned off the ignition and checked her phone again. No more messages. It was already 1.04: the mystery caller was late.

She adjusted the rear-view mirror so she would be able to see anyone driving up the street behind her.

A police car turned into the far end of the road and drove towards her.

What the hell? What are they doing here?

The patrol car continued its slow progress up the road, two uniformed officers sitting in the front. Were they looking at houses? The one in the passenger seat seemed to be, his head swivelling left and right. Sarah looked down at her phone's dark screen again, feeling utterly conspicuous. She slid a little further down in her seat again, desperate to avoid eye contact with either of the policemen.

She sensed the car slowing as it approached. It was almost on her. *Was it going to stop? What if they were here when the mystery visitor arrived? Would they think she had called 999?* She stared at her lap, willing the patrol car to keep going and carry on up the road. Then it was past her. She kept an eye on it in the wing mirror as it receded towards the junction, indicated, and turned onto Abbey Drive.

Sarah let out a huge sigh of relief and leaned back against the headrest, closing her eyes for a second.

Calm down. You've already spoken to the police, and you got through it just fine. There is nothing to connect you to this act, no evidence that the mystery caller could possibly know about. You just need to see who it is first, then you can make a judgement about what to do next.

If they ever show up.

She jumped at a sharp knocking on the glass, opening her eyes to see a face looming beside her. It took her a second of pure incredulity, a hammer blow of shock, to realise who she was looking at.

Alan Lovelock.

PART III

54

Lovelock followed her into the house, putting the chain on the front door and turning the key in the lock. He went after her into the lounge, ducking slightly to avoid hitting his head on the door frame, and pulled the curtains in the bay window.

The room was plunged into shadow and Sarah instinctively turned the light on.

'No,' he said. 'Leave it off. Sit on the sofa.'

'It's so wonderful that you're safe, Alan,' she said, with as much conviction as she could muster. 'We were all really worried about you.'

He dismissed her remark with the wave of a hand and sat down opposite her in Nick's favourite armchair, long legs crossed, long-fingered hands splayed over the armrests. Even in the darkness, his eyes were unnaturally bright. They looked different, somehow, shining with something Sarah had never seen there before.

'You know what I loathe most in the world, Sarah?'

'I don't know.'

'Stupidity,' he said slowly. 'Especially from a woman. And do you know the one thing I value above all else?'

'Recognition?'

'*Information*. With the right information you can do almost anything. You can make other people *do* almost anything. Say, for the sake of argument, I knew you were involved in my kidnapping and false imprisonment.'

Sarah felt as if she had plunged into ice-cold water. She suppressed a shiver.

'That's not true.'

'That you were not only aware of it, but had somehow made it happen.'

'No! You're wrong.'

Lovelock laughed, a harsh barking sound in the gloom of the dark sitting room.

'You know what you have failed to ask me, since I sent you those text messages?'

She shook her head.

He took his phone out, unlocked it and scrolled up a list of messages.

'This nice new phone was provided by the police chaps while I got myself on my feet again. Seeing as my own phone is lost and they wanted to be able to reach me quickly. Aren't they thoughtful? I used it to tell you that I knew what you had done. You replied to ask who I was – twice – but you didn't ask what any other person would have asked. You didn't ask what my message actually meant. You didn't ask *what it was that you were supposed to have done*. And why was that? Because you already knew.'

'Alan, I know you must have had a really difficult –'

'And then when I saw the look on your face out on the street just now, I knew. Everyone else who's seen me since yesterday morning has been smiling, laughing, delighted, relieved. My poor wife burst into tears when they told her I had been found. But your reaction was utterly unique – you didn't do any of those things: you looked like you'd seen a ghost, like Macbeth staring at Duncan's headless corpse in the banqueting hall. As if you'd seen a revenant spirit returning from the dead. Because, as far as you were concerned, I *was* dead.'

Sarah shook her head, trying to think of something to say to contradict him.

'No, that's not –'

'No one else actually thought the worst, you know. Mostly they assumed I'd gone off with some young postgraduate for a few days of boozing and shagging. A few thought I'd had some sort of breakdown. But none of them thought I was actually dead. Except you.'

'I didn't think you were dead.'

Lovelock stood up slowly, until he towered over her in the centre of the shadowy living room. He took off his dark tweed jacket, dropped it on the floor and unbuttoned his shirt cuffs.

'Of course you did. And I thought, why would my little Sarah be looking at me like a man returning from beyond the grave? Why would that be? Unless she knew something that all the others didn't. Unless she knew something that even the police didn't know.' He sat down on the sofa next to her, his hand resting casually on her knee. 'Unless she had something to do with the scarred man.'

She flinched at his mention of Volkov's henchman.

'I don't know who that is.'

'Don't bother with a denial – it's written all over your face. Honestly, I think I know you better than you know yourself.' He reached out to tuck a stray strand of hair behind her ear before she could flinch away. 'By the way, you're a terrible liar. I don't know how you persuaded this tattooed Russian to do it, what you did for him, but I know you were involved. Where did you meet him? In a bar? Was he offering his services on the Internet?'

'I've told you, I don't know who you're talking about.'

'How much did you pay him? Or are you fucking him, is that it?'

'I've never –'

'That's it, isn't it? You're fucking this man with the scar across his head. You know, when he kidnapped me, he said something which didn't make sense at the time. After they'd bound and gagged me, just as he was closing the boot of his car. He looked down at me and said something in Russian. I can only assume he thought I wouldn't understand.'

Lovelock moved closer to her along the sofa.

'Unfortunately for you – and him – I spent a year at Moscow State University in my younger days and I still have a basic grasp of the language. Don't you want to know what he said?'

'What?'

'*Milaya molodaya vrach zhelaet Vam vsego nailuchshego.* Which means: "The pretty little doctor sends you her very best wishes".' His eyes narrowed. 'So who do you think he might have meant? The pretty little doctor?'

'I've no idea.' Her heart was thudding so hard in her chest that it was painful. 'It could be anyone, any number of people.'

He shook his head, slowly.

'I don't think so. Not when I thought about the timing of all this, and your reaction to my text messages and then to my miraculous return from the grave. And now you're completely and utterly unable to give anything even close to a convincing denial. That just about clinches it.'

'So – so what are you going to do?'

'Well, the police caught this Russian thug with me in the boot of his car, so one assumes that there is no danger from him anymore. Caught red-handed, you could say. He will have a trial, and he will go to jail – perhaps he'll give them your name, perhaps not. But I do know one thing: I've spent a lot of time talking to the police in the last thirty-six hours. And you know what?' He held his thumb and forefinger a hair's breadth apart. 'They are *this close* to arresting you, Sarah.'

55

Her fear was razor sharp, like a splinter of ice in her spine.

'Arresting *me*? What do you mean?'

'The only reason they haven't is because I've not told them about the Russian's remark yet. I haven't told them about the "pretty little doctor" he mentioned as his parting shot. But I *will* tell the police – unless you start to play fair with me.'

Play fair. She had always been fascinated by the euphemisms people used to disguise their behaviour. She let her eyes wander to the top of the bookcase, where the black-handled carving knife lay just out of sight. Two steps across the room and she could reach up and grab it, and before he knew what was going on she could bury it in his chest up to the hilt, slide it in between his ribs, she could claim self-defence and –

No. That was madness. She had wished him dead once already and that had landed her here, catapulting her from one impossible situation to another.

'It's not true,' she said. 'I don't know what you're talking about.'

'If you think I'm bluffing, how about I just tell the police what I know?'

She couldn't look at him.

'Why would you do that?'

'It's just like whist, my dear. You played your king, and now I'm playing my ace. You lose.'

She fought to keep the fear out of her voice. *Don't let him hear that.* But it was impossible.

'I'm sorry for what happened to you but I have no idea what –'

'Enough! We're going to have a new relationship, you and me. A relationship where you stop saying *no* and start saying *yes*.' He leaned closer, grabbing her arm.

She flinched away but his other hand gripped her shoulder hard, keeping her frozen in place.

Stay calm, just stay calm, don't let this happen, don't let him do this –

'Alan, you're hurting me. *Please*.'

His breathing was heavy, his neck flushed red.

She almost cried out as he gripped her breast, pinching the nipple hard between his thumb and forefinger. Abruptly he released his grip and grabbed her hand, putting her palm on the crotch of his trousers. Holding it there, pushing it against the hardness of his erection.

'You like that?' he said, his voice thick. 'Good. Very good.'

Her voice was small and breathless and she hated the sound of it in her own ears.

'Please – please don't hurt me.'

Dad, I need you. Nick. Laura. Someone, anyone.

Please help me.

Please.

Lovelock leaned forward until his mouth was inches from her ear, his breath hot and damp against the side of her face. The sour stench of whisky.

'You made this personal. *You* did that. You upped the stakes. So even when you beg me to stop, I'm not going to.'

And then he was kissing her roughly, his stubble scratching against her cheek, pushing her back into the sofa, his thin lips slavering against her neck and ear as she turned away. His hand on her breast again, clutching, pinching painfully at the skin beneath her blouse. The sharp tang of his sweat was almost overpowering. She felt his bulk pressing in on her and tried to squirm away from him, fearing her heart would burst it was pounding so hard. The fear had turned from a distant abstract worry about the police to a bright blinding terror of what was about to happen.

So this is it. This is the destination. He's going to rape me in my own home, right here on my sofa.

She tried to remember what you were supposed to do to survive a situation like this. *Comply. Don't antagonise. Stay calm. Don't fight.*

'Alan, not here, not –'

'Shut up. *Shut up*. You don't talk anymore. *I* do the talking. I'm going to tell you how things are going to work between us from now on. Starting today, you are going to do *what* you are told, *when* you are told.'

He kissed her again, stubble rasping her neck, his big hands pushing her back into the sofa. His hands on her, all over her, grabbing and squeezing, pushing her legs apart and gripping her thighs so hard she knew she would find bruises later. Sarah felt the world slowing down around her, everything zeroing into this one point of focus. She was frozen to the spot, her limbs heavy and her heart slamming against her ribcage.

Shutting her eyes, she turned away from him, desperate to avoid the incipient violence she could feel heavy in his hands.

Stay calm. Don't antagonise. His rage is one spark away from an explosion.

She became aware, suddenly, of a skittering noise on the wooden parquet floor. And that he had stopped kissing her.

She opened her eyes.

Jonesy, her ginger tomcat, was crouched in the corner, growling. For a moment she thought he was growling at them, but then he turned and she saw he had something large and grey in his mouth. A fat-breasted pigeon hung limp in his jaws, one wing splayed at an unnatural angle. Jonesy continued to growl, lowering his head to the floor. Blood dripped from the bird's feathers.

Lovelock released his grip on her and Sarah quickly moved away from him down the sofa.

Jonesy dropped the injured bird to the floor.

Immediately, the pigeon burst back into life and launched itself towards the curtained window in a mad frenzy of flapping, wingbeats slashing at the furniture, grey feathers flying everywhere. Lovelock cried out in alarm and threw his hands up to protect his face as the pigeon hit the curtain, wings flapping furiously, then came away again before settling on the curtain pole at the top of the window.

Jonesy went to the foot of the curtain, his growl deep in his chest.

Thank you, you big daft cat, Sarah thought. *Thank you, Jonesy. Now please let this be an end to this situation. Please let it break the spell.*

Lovelock moved to the door as if he was going to leave. Sarah was about to say a silent prayer of thanks when he grabbed her roughly by the wrist.

'Upstairs,' he hissed. 'Where's the master bedroom?'

Hopes dashed, she felt her knees buckle, the weakness returning as she desperately tried to think of a way of diverting him, distracting him, to stop this. She had to delay him, put him off. She had to come up with something, anything, to avoid what was about to happen.

'*Bedroom*,' he said again, only this time it wasn't a question but an order. He began dragging her towards the stairs.

Think.

'Not now,' Sarah said, her voice cracking. She was a heartbeat away from collapsing in tears.

'What?'

'The kids are going to be home with my dad any minute.'

He snorted.

'Well then, my dear, we'd better be quick.'

He reached the first step, dragging her behind him.

'Please, Alan, I'm begging you. Not here, not in my house where my children might walk in at any moment.'

'What?'

'Just not in my house, *please*. Let's go somewhere we won't be disturbed. Let's go to your house, I'll come with you.'

He stopped on the second step, looking at his watch.

'Caroline's at home this afternoon.'

Say something, anything, to stop this going further.

'I mean, not today but how about an evening? At your house.'

He considered this for a moment.

'Caroline's going to see her mother this weekend. We'd have the house all to ourselves.'

'Saturday, then?'

He smiled, slowly, a wolfish grin revealing his teeth. Nodded to himself.

'Yes. A weekly arrangement, with an inaugural event on Saturday evening. Then once a week, every week, you'll come to my office. We'll lock the door, I'll sit back and you'll get down on your knees and go to work.' He leaned forward so his face was inches from hers, his reeking breath in her nostrils. 'Or on your back. Perhaps on your front. Perhaps all three. Every week, until I get bored of you.'

There was a tremendous crash and caterwauling from the lounge and a moment later Jonesy reappeared, the flapping pigeon clamped firmly in his mouth again. Lovelock aimed a vicious kick at him but the tomcat was too quick, running in between them and up the stairs, leaving a trail of dark blood drops on the beige carpet.

'Saturday evening,' Lovelock said finally, releasing her from his grip.

He slammed the door on his way out.

56

Sarah wasn't sure how long she stayed behind the locked bathroom door. She washed and washed her face again and again, trying to get his smell off her, to get his stink out of her nostrils. Her head was pounding and her throat painful from held-back sobs – but she knew that if she started crying, she wouldn't be able to stop.

She stripped off her cardigan and blouse, throwing them in the washing basket, before finally unlocking the bathroom door and heading to her bedroom to find something clean to wear. It was only then she saw the mess that Jonesy had left on the landing. The remains of the pigeon – most of the wings, head and feathers, with dark trails of blood and God knew what else – were scattered across the faded carpet.

'Shit!' she shouted to the empty house. 'Shit! Shit!'

She found a plastic bag, put her hand inside it and gathered up the parts of the bird that her tomcat had not eaten, before turning the bag inside out and tying it closed. Then she filled a bucket with water and detergent and knelt on her hands and knees on the landing, scrubbing and scrubbing at the mess with a sponge, trying to get rid of the blood and guts and only succeeding in soaking the worn beige stair carpet a deep brown. Still she continued scrubbing and wringing out and soaking and scrubbing because it gave her hands something to do.

She knew, at the back of her mind, that she was doing what she always tried to do when troubles threatened to overcome her: stay busy, keep her mind occupied so that it wouldn't dwell on the worst of it. Find a distraction and push everything else away.

But today it wasn't working.

Because she could still smell his acrid sweat in the hall and in the lounge and on the stairs.

She could still feel the scratch of his stubble on her cheeks and neck.

And she had the same thought going round and around inside her head, the same image burned onto her retinas: Lovelock leaning towards her, with his bloodshot eyes and broken-vein cheeks, holding his thumb and forefinger half an inch apart.

The police are this close *to arresting you, Sarah.*

Was it true? Was he just bullshitting her? And more importantly, could she run the risk of finding out one way or the other? Could she call his bluff?

I tried to make things better. But I ended up making them ten times worse.

He knows I was involved. Never mind keeping my job, I will be lucky to stay out of prison. My family is at risk now more than ever. And to top it all – the cherry on the cake – somehow I've made Alan into the victim, I've made it so that people will feel sorry for him.

After what had happened this afternoon, if it had been any other man, any other situation, the answer would be obvious: go to the police. Make a complaint. Press charges.

But not him.

Not now.

Because if he had been bulletproof before, now he was totally untouchable.

The thought of it, of proper police help being out of reach, brought her up short. She'd never felt more alone in her life, more completely and utterly wretched. She stopped scrubbing at the carpet and collapsed into the corner of the landing.

She felt the tears come again, and this time she didn't try to stop them.

She sobbed, crying with all her breath and all her heart, in a way she had not done since her mother died, knees tucked up to her chin, her face pressed against the door frame, her body shaking with racking sobs as she thought of all she had lost and what she had left to lose, feeling something finally break inside her. She cried until her throat was choked raw and her chest ached.

She cried until she had no tears left.

She had no idea how long she stayed there. After a while, when she saw the sky outside darkening towards dusk, she went slowly and carefully downstairs. Her limbs ached, her head throbbed, her cheeks were salty with tears. She felt sick and exhausted, filled with a despair she had never known before. Catching sight of herself in the hall mirror, she didn't recognise the wild-eyed stranger who stared back. Suddenly she wanted desperately to shield the children from all of this, to make sure they didn't see her in this state. She didn't want them to be in the place where Lovelock had been, or anywhere near it. Not before she erased every trace of him from the house.

She was the firewall between her children and everything that was wrong with the world. She would protect them.

She texted her dad.

Can the kids stay at yours tonight, and you take them to school tomorrow? x

The reply came back almost straight away.

Of course. Are you OK? x

She was so tired she couldn't even come up with a convincing lie.

Yes. Just need to sort a few things out here. Got a ton of marking to get through. Going to have a nap and then get down to it. See you tomorrow. Kiss the kids for me. x

It didn't sound plausible, even to her. She knew he'd ring at some point to check she was really all right. But she didn't want him to see her like this. She didn't want *anyone* to see her like this.

Five minutes later, he did call. And then again, five minutes after that.

She didn't answer.

57

He was there. He was coming for her. And there was no door, no way out. He was in the hall, she was sitting in the armchair – but it was in the living room of his house, and they were alone, there was no one to help her. She couldn't move as he loomed over her, he reached down and put a hand between her –

Sarah woke with a start.

She was on the floor of her lounge, a blanket wrapped loosely around her. It was past midnight. The central heating had gone off, the house grown cold around her. Her cheeks were wet; she had been crying in her sleep. Around her, scattered like leaves in the autumn wind, was a whirlwind of mess: papers, books, a broken wine glass and an empty bottle of wine lying on its side, clothes strewn around, her old diaries, laptop half-open on its back. Sheets of lined paper covered with wild scribbled handwriting she barely recognised as her own. A broken picture frame full of cracked glass, photo albums of the kids open at favourite pages. Her PhD thesis, bound in thick hardback, lying open and discarded in the corner.

Her head was pounding, her limbs leaden. She felt about a hundred years old. She thought she ought to eat something but her appetite had disappeared weeks ago and had never really come back.

She opened another bottle of wine and took her phone out to compose a text to Nick.

I need you. I need to talk to you. When are you coming back? S x

Three times she typed out a different version of the same message, and three times she deleted it before sending. Eventually she threw her phone to the floor in frustration.

It occurred to her, not for the first time, that maybe this was how it was going to be now. That she had had the best of him – their best years together – and that was all he had to give. They had been through so much together, made two beautiful children, shared a life together. But maybe he was part of her past now, rather than her future.

Maybe he would never come back.

The thought had reduced her to tears many times in the last six weeks, but now the tears wouldn't come. Instead of sadness, she felt resignation. A line being drawn. He had let her down in every possible way, and there was no point crying over something she couldn't change. Not anymore.

She drank more wine and roamed the house, feet dragging, drawing all the curtains and double-checking the doors and windows were locked. She took all the knives out of the kitchen drawers and lined them up on the worktop, largest to smallest. In the cupboard under the stairs she rummaged around until she found Nick's little-used toolbox, going through it until she found a few more weapons to add to her arsenal. Eventually she sat on the sofa with the bottle of wine, staring into the dark fireplace. She saw his face in the darkness. Lovelock.

She wasn't sure how long she spent like that. Hours, maybe.

It was not yet dawn when she went wearily up to the bathroom and opened the cabinet over the sink. On the top shelf were the boxes of Temazepam pills she had been prescribed the year before, when the situation with Lovelock had started to affect her sleep.

From experience, she knew two were usually enough to make her drowsy. She'd never taken more than that.

She pulled out all the remaining strips of blister-packed tablets and counted what was left. Three strips were still nearly full: forty-one tablets in all. How did you swallow that many? Were they best swallowed all at once, in handfuls, or two at a time? Or was it best to break open the little plastic capsules and pour all the white powder into a tablespoon and take it that way? Maybe mix the powder up into a glass of water? No, they were probably better taken two at a time, she thought, then you could keep track of how many you'd had. That was the way to do it. That would give you the best chance of keeping them down long enough for the dose to do its work. Fill a pint glass of water, lay them out beside you, and keep on taking them two at a time. Two by two by two. Then just lie down and let it happen.

No more Lovelock. No more police. No more fear.

Once a week, every week. I'll sit back and you'll get down on your knees.

She filled a tall glass of water from the tap and turned the blister packs over in her hand, punching out each of the tablets in turn. Holding them in her palm: forty-one little orange torpedoes with enough power to make everything go away. They didn't look like much when they were all piled together like that. She found a clean flannel and laid them out on it, pushing the tablets into pairs. Two by two by two. That was the way to do it. She took her phone out of her dressing gown pocket, checked that it was switched off.

The first grey slivers of dawn were creeping through the bathroom window.

She swallowed two of the tablets with a mouthful of water. Then flushed the rest down the toilet.

Closing the cabinet door, she stared at herself in the mirror until she couldn't stand it any longer. Then shuffled to her bedroom on heavy legs and collapsed onto the bed, just managing to pull the duvet up to her neck before she drifted off.

She was still there, curled into an exhausted sleep, when her father let himself in a few hours later.

58

Her dad brought tea to where Sarah slumped on the sofa, staring blankly at the muted TV. She felt empty, hollowed out with crying. The exhaustion lay over her like a shroud.

'Are the kids OK?'

'They're fine. I just dropped them at school.'

'Thanks, Dad.'

He perched on the end of the sofa, handing her the steaming mug.

'Sarah, do you remember when you were seven and you hid all of your Barbie dolls around the house because your sisters kept going into your bedroom and taking them?'

'We had so many fallouts over those stupid dolls.'

'You were so pleased with yourself that you'd managed to get the better of them for once. A week later I came home from work one day and you were crying your eyes out, because you'd forgotten where you'd hidden them. Do you remember?'

She smiled faintly at the memory.

'I remember writing a list of all their hiding places in invisible ink. Then I lost the piece of paper.'

'I had to hunt those dolls down for you. Searched the whole house from top to bottom but I found them all, didn't I?'

'Every single one.'

He patted her ankle gently.

'Sarah?'

'Yes?'

'I have something to show you.'

'What is it?'

'Come on. Let's get you up and on your feet now.'

He turned off the TV and she levered herself up off the sofa with a grunt. She followed her dad through to the kitchen, where he gestured at the table. Arrayed on it, in a line, were the weapons she had hidden around the house: carving knife, poker, Stanley knife.

'You seem to have mislaid a few things around the place, love.'

Sarah swallowed, feeling tears spring to her eyes.

'For protection.'

'Protection from whom?'

'I can't really explain. I'm sorry.'

He considered this for a moment, seeming to decide not to push her for an answer.

'All right. But will you tell me whether I found everything this time?'

'Yes. It was just those three.'

'And what if Harry or Grace had found one of these ... *implements* before me?' he said gently.

'I put them up high so they wouldn't be able to reach. I made sure they couldn't get to them.'

'Hmm.' He nodded, slowly. 'Sit down a minute, Sarah.'

She did as she was told and took the seat opposite her dad, wondering whether to tell him the truth. The *whole* truth. She wondered how she could explain about the weapons she had left around the house, about the man she feared would return and what he might do. The feeling of utter wretched helplessness, when *he* had been in her house for the first time.

She wrapped both hands around her mug of tea and took a sip. It was hot and sweet; she didn't normally take sugar but she was glad of it this time.

'Thanks.'

'I'm worried about you, Sarah.'

She said nothing.

'I think it's time you told me what's going on.'

Sarah shook her head, remembering Volkov's words. *Tell no one.*

'I can't.'

'Can't or won't?'

'I wish I could, Dad. I really do.'

The silence between them stretched out for a minute, until finally he took the seat next to her and simply hugged her. They sat like that for a while before she let him go, and they both settled back into their chairs.

Her dad took a long drink of his tea.

'You know, this is probably going to come as a bit of a surprise, but after your mother died I did something very bad.'

Sarah looked at him, waiting to see if he was joking.

'What?' she shrugged. 'What did you do?'

'I've never told anyone this before, so you must promise not to tell.'

'I promise.'

'Especially not your sisters.'

'Of course.'

'Or Laura, or any of your other friends, or colleagues at work.'

She frowned, unnerved at what might be coming.

'OK,' she said slowly.

'All right. After your mother died, I ... ' He hesitated, but only for a second. 'I spent six months planning to kill a man.'

59

Sarah coughed and almost spilt her drink.

'*What?* No you didn't. What are you talking about?'

'It's the truth.'

'Don't be silly, Dad. You were never going to kill anyone.'

'Lee Goodyer.'

She looked up sharply. Her father hadn't spoken of the accident in years. He talked about his late wife – Sarah's mother – frequently, but not about the circumstances of her death. Not anymore. And she'd never, *ever*, heard him utter the name of the man who had taken him from her: Lee Goodyer, a thirty-two-year-old salesman whose haste to get to his next appointment had ended in tragedy. Goodyer had overtaken a lorry dangerously, recklessly, on an A-road to make up a few minutes in his journey. Sarah's mother, coming the other way, had been forced to swerve to avoid him. She had overcorrected and driven straight into another lorry coming the other way.

She had died instantly.

A jury found Goodyer guilty of causing death by dangerous driving and the judge sentenced him to four years in prison.

'Two years, he served – with good behaviour,' Roger said bitterly. 'Two bloody years for taking a life. It wasn't enough, it wasn't *nearly* enough. So as soon as he was sent down, I started thinking about what I was going to do.'

'You withdrew from us completely. I thought you were grieving.'

'I *was* grieving. But I was channelling it into planning.'

She shook her head, still struggling to believe what he was admitting to. This was her father, after all, who had spent his whole career in maritime insurance and had never received so much as a speeding fine.

'God Almighty, Dad. What were you going to do?'

'I had a few different plans – all of which involved me probably getting caught, but I didn't care at that point. The worst had already happened to me, so why would it matter if I got caught? You have to understand – I was so angry, it felt like anger was all I had left after your mum died.'

'You had us. Lucy and Helen and me.'

'I know, I know. I was stupid. But you and your sisters were grown women, you weren't dependent on us anymore. Me and your mum were married for thirty-three years and he took her life for the sake of a few minutes. He got two years of soft time in prison, and then out to enjoy the rest of his life. I wanted him to pay. Properly.'

Sarah looked at her dad, the best man she had ever known, and saw then that his eyes were full of tears. She leaned over and hugged him again, rubbing his back as if soothing a child.

'What made you change your mind?'

He leaned back from the embrace and smiled, a tear spilling down his cheek.

'You did.'

Sarah frowned, digging in her pocket for a tissue and handing it to him.

'Did I? How on earth did I manage that?'

'Perhaps not you, exactly. Grace.'

'But she wasn't even born when Mum died.'

'The first time I saw Gracie in the hospital, the first time I held her,' he said, wiping his eyes, 'I knew there was a choice to be made. If I went to take revenge on that man there was a good chance that I would be caught and I would go to prison. I would miss her growing up – she might never know who I was. All the plans I'd made about what I was going to do to Goodyer, all the lists and maps and photographs and background information, I threw it all in the fireplace and burned it that night. Then I got stinking drunk. And in the morning I brought the two of you home from the hospital.'

'You weren't serious about doing something to Lee Goodyer when he was released?'

'I was, absolutely. But it was Grace who saved me. *You* saved me.' He smiled. 'By giving me my first grandchild, even though it might have been a bit earlier than you'd planned.'

Sarah shook her head.

'I can't save anyone. I can't even save myself.' She looked up at him, her kind, gentle father, seeing him in a new light. 'Why didn't you ever tell me that story before?'

He shrugged.

'I've never told anyone.'

'And do you still want revenge?'

'I did, for years after. But Grace kept me on the straight and narrow. And then Harry.'

'What about now?'

'The thing is, I thought it would make me feel better, taking revenge on Goodyer. Hurting him. Maybe even killing him. But it wouldn't have turned the clock back to when your mum was still alive. I knew that I had to let the anger go, otherwise, in the end, it was just going to burn me up.'

'Why are you telling me this?'

'Because I had to learn to move forward, to deal with life as it was – rather than how I wanted it to be.' He pointed at her. 'So do you. And now you know my secret, it's time for you to tell me yours.'

60

'I can't tell you,' she said. 'I just can't.'

'I've told you my secret. I can't believe it could be anything worse than me planning to avenge your mother.'

Sarah laughed, but there was no humour in it.

'You might be surprised, Dad.'

'At my age, darling, nothing surprises me anymore.'

'People could get hurt if I tell you.'

He pointed again at the array of weapons laid out on the kitchen table.

'It looks to me like someone is going to get hurt anyway.'

'I mean the kids. The kids could get hurt.'

Roger sat up straighter.

'Are you being threatened? Are Harry and Grace in danger?'

'Not if I keep the secret safe.'

'What secret? What are you talking about? It sounds to me like we should call the police.'

She put a hand on his arm.

'No, Dad! No. Not the police.'

'So tell me.'

She looked at him, at her lovely dad, the concern on his face. The love in his eyes. And she felt the tears come again, pricking her eyes before she surrendered to them, until she was sobbing, chest heaving, weeks and months of emotion pouring out of her.

'I've made a mess of everything, Dad,' she said between sobs. 'It's all gone wrong, and it's all my fault.'

Her dad hugged her tightly.

'What's gone wrong, Sarah?'

'Everything.'

He waited a beat, then said quietly: 'All I know is that you can't carry on how you've been for the last few weeks. And *this*,' he gestured at the weapons again, 'is no way to live your life. So why don't you tell me, Sarah?'

'You have to promise not to tell anyone else. Ever. Not Helen or Lucy, not my friends, no one at work – and definitely not the police.'

'I promise.'

'Swear. On your grandchildren's lives.'

He considered this for a long moment. Nodded, finally.

'I swear not to tell.'

She leaned her head on his shoulder.

'I did a bad thing, Dad. A very bad thing. And now everything is unravelling. It's all getting more and more messed up, and I don't know how to stop it.'

They sat down at the kitchen table and she told him the whole story: Lovelock's behaviour over the past two years, the Rules and how impossible it had become to work with him. She told him about his refusal to promote her and his plans to restructure her out of the department, about Volkov and his offer and what had transpired since the phone call two weeks previously.

He didn't interrupt her, he just let her talk. Finally, when she had finished, she saw that there were tears in his eyes, too. In more than three decades, she had hardly ever seen him really angry – she could remember perhaps two or three times in all those years. He was the practical one, the level-headed one, the insurance broker who had a logical response to everything.

But he was angry now. It was coming off him in waves.

'Jesus Christ alive, Sarah. I feel like I want to go and kill the bastard myself.'

He hardly ever swore, either.

Sarah handed him a tissue and took another for herself.

'I don't know what to do, Dad. I can't make it right and I can't make it go away. It just keeps getting worse and worse.'

'Why didn't you tell me any of this sooner? I could have helped.'

'You'd have worried, and I didn't want that. I wanted you to be proud of me, of what I'd achieved.'

'I *am* proud of you. More proud than you'll ever know.'

'I just want to fix things. I want to know how to put things right.'

Roger was quiet for a moment, his hand resting on Sarah's in the middle of the table. Then he stood up and made them both another cup of tea.

'We'll work something out,' he said finally. He came around the table and gave her another hug. 'But first of all we have to establish what your options are. Give me a few hours to think about it.'

61

Sarah followed DI Rayner through a maze of corridors at Wood Green Police Station until they arrived at a single unmarked door, blank apart from an electronic keypad. The detective hit a series of numbers and the lock clicked. She turned the handle and pushed the door open. Sarah followed her in.

DI Rayner had called to ask if she would come into the station on her way into work. *Just for twenty minutes or so*, she said, without telling Sarah why she needed to be there. They sat facing each other now across a grey metal table in a sparsely furnished white room.

'Thanks for coming in at short notice,' the detective said. 'Hopefully you know by now that your colleague has been found safe and well.'

'Yes, I've heard,' Sarah said, making herself smile. 'Great news.'

'Are you all right? You look a bit pale.'

'Of course. Just relieved. We all thought that Alan was ... well, we thought something might have happened to him.'

'Like what?'

Sarah was surprised by her question.

'I don't know ... I suppose, when no one had heard from him, we assumed the worst.'

'Any particular reason for that?'

'No, not really. But it was unlike him to be out of contact.'

The detective studied her for a second before continuing.

'As I said, this is confidential so I would appreciate your discretion. But we have some information that suggests Professor Lovelock may have been targeted by a Russian crime syndicate. For reasons unknown – at the moment.'

'I see,' Sarah said, a chill creeping over her skin. 'What makes you think that?'

'Let me show you.' DI Rayner led her over to the long window on the far wall, and Sarah saw now that it was a viewing panel into an adjoining room. 'Have you ever seen this man before?'

The scarred man sat on the other side of the glass.

Sarah stared at him. He looked calm. He had no jacket and his sleeves were rolled up, revealing an uneven pattern of heavily inked tattoos up both forearms, a combination of religious symbols and other things that Sarah didn't recognise.

A scramble of questions sent her pulse racing.

What do they know? What might he have already told them?

Above them all, Lovelock's taunt from the day before: *The police are* this close *to arresting you, Sarah.*

The detective shifted beside her.

'Dr Haywood?'

As Sarah watched, the scarred man turned slowly in his chair and seemed to stare directly at her. Sarah looked quickly away.

'Can he see us?'

'No. Mirrored glass. Soundproofing too. We're talking to various people in your department to see if anyone saw this individual on campus in the last few weeks.'

Sarah took a breath, working hard to keep her voice level. *Think.*

'Who is he?'

'At the moment we don't know. He wasn't carrying any ID when he was arrested – just a bundle of cash – and we've got absolutely no hits in the database against his fingerprints and DNA. However, we have some intelligence that suggests he may be involved in Russian organised crime. The tattoos would also indicate that. It's possible this person was following Professor Lovelock's movements in the days leading up to his abduction. So it seems likely there's a link, either some*thing* or some*one,* that connects the professor with the suspect here. We just don't know what or who that is yet. Do you recognise him?'

She made a conscious effort to look back at the scarred man, as if today was the first time she'd set eyes on him. He was staring at the opposite wall again now, face expressionless.

Just because you saw him proves nothing.

'Yes, I think so. He's the man I saw a few weeks ago. I made a report at the time.'

DI Rayner flicked through a file in her hand.

'You were concerned about him being a stalker.'

'Yes.'

The detective gestured to the man on the other side of the one-way mirror.

'You're sure?'

'I think so. What's he done?'

'Well, it may be that the man you saw wasn't actually stalking you, but Professor Lovelock.'

'So he's involved with what happened to Alan?'

'Yes. Confidentially, of course.'

'Of course.' Sarah put a palm under her chin. 'Wow. How did you catch him?'

'It was just a fluke, really. He was stopped by a traffic officer for using a mobile phone at the wheel of his car. So this PC pulls him over, and while he's giving him a talking to, he hears noises coming from the rear of the vehicle. Opens up the boot and finds your colleague lying there, tied up, blindfolded and gagged. This was five days after he'd gone missing, and we're not really sure yet why he was being held captive. It's possible there was going to be a ransom demand at some point – we don't know at this stage.'

'How awful,' Sarah said, trying to sound shocked. 'And what has he said about it?'

'The suspect? Nothing, so far, he just sits there like a stone. But he will, eventually.' She flipped to a new page in her notebook. 'So, would you say Professor Lovelock had any enemies?'

'Enemies?' Sarah repeated.

'People who would wish him harm.'

'He'll have rivals in an academic sense, I suppose – people who he might compete with for research grants and so on. And there are a few people within the academic community who might not have nice things to say about him. But not really enemies.'

'Do you think any of those academic rivals might wish he was no longer around?'

Sarah pretended to think for a moment, before shaking her head.

'I wouldn't have thought so. Is there any evidence of that?'

'We're looking into it. Also at some other potential lines of enquiry, including kidnap for ransom, bearing in mind the professor's significant personal and family wealth. But it seems there's no one with a bad word to say about him.'

Perhaps you should talk to Gillian Arnold.

'I'm sure that's true.'

Sarah felt the detective's eyes on her.

'Now, I also understand that you had a public falling out with Professor Lovelock recently. Some potential new research funding in the US?'

'It wasn't a falling out. Just a little bit of a disagreement.'

'But you were very unhappy with the way he handled it?'

'I wouldn't say that. I –'

'You accused him of being a cheat and a liar. Made a complaint to his line manager.'

'I never said that!'

'Words to that effect? That's what I've been told.'

'It's not true.'

'You're quite sure about that?'

Sarah took a deep breath, and let it out slowly. In the back of her mind, something clicked into place – two, three, four pieces of information coming together and slotting into each other like jigsaw pieces. Now she could see the whole, she was amazed she'd never spotted it before.

My God. Oh. My. God. How did it take me so long to figure this out?

DI Rayner leaned forward.

'Dr Haywood?' she prompted. 'You're quite sure?'

'Sorry – yes, I was a bit disappointed. I hoped he would let me take it forward on my own, but in the end, he picked it up.'

'You must have been angry, though.'

'Initially. But it wasn't a big deal. The whole department will benefit if he can bring in that grant, it will be good for all of us, for the whole university.' A thought occurred to her with sudden urgency. 'Should I have a solicitor with me for this?'

'Entirely up to you,' DI Rayner said, taking a sip of her tea. 'None of your colleagues have felt it necessary up to this point, but you can if you wish. This is not formal questioning, we're just trying to find out where the link is between this gentleman with the scar, and your university. Actually, while we're on that subject, there's something else.'

'What's that?'

'A phone call.'

62

Sarah felt a pressure in her chest.

'When they stopped the suspect,' DI Rayner continued, 'they took the car back to our pound for a full search and forensic sweep. The boot where your colleague was found was completely lined in disposable plastic – presumably to limit deposition of the victim's DNA – but they didn't find anything else useful in the car itself. However, we *did* manage to locate useful evidence based on the arresting officer's report.'

'Evidence of what?'

'The arresting officer reported that the suspect was chewing vigorously when he was first approached. Both mobiles in his possession were subsequently found to be minus their SIM cards.'

'He'd eaten them?'

'Chewed them up and swallowed them. But we were able to recover the pieces – you don't want to know how. Latest generation SIM cards are much more resilient than you might think. Our lab guys have been able to extract some of the data from one of the SIM cards, and we've done some analysis on the calls and texts, where calls came from, the number of the caller, and so on.'

Sarah shivered involuntarily. Was the police officer just playing with her now?

They know it's you. They know it's you!

'This number only received one call,' DI Rayner continued. 'Just one. A twenty-nine second call routed via a mobile phone mast on the east side of your university campus. Five days before Professor Lovelock was abducted.'

She told herself to be calm.

'Oh. From whom?'

'Another pay-as-you-go phone. We've not found it yet, but we're tracking the number now and we'll be straight onto it as soon as it's used again.'

Sarah had a flash of memory, the mobile wrapped in a plastic bag and weighted down with stones, sinking beneath the surface of the pond on Hampstead Heath while her children fed the ducks.

Keeping her voice level, she said: 'Can't you track down the owner through the mobile phone company, or something?'

'It's not quite as easy as that with a pay-as-you-go. But it means we have a direct link between the suspect's phone and your university campus.'

Sarah felt her stomach churning. Her mouth was dry. She licked her lips.

'That's good, isn't it? That there's progress, I mean.'

'It could be the link that we're looking for: it seems highly unusual that the suspect would have contact with someone at the university for any other reason. Hence my question about whether Prof Lovelock had any enemies.'

'We do have thousands of students and staff on campus during term time, though.'

'Whereabouts is your building on the campus?'

'My office?'

'Yes.'

'The arts faculty. North side of the campus.'

'But you sometimes park on the east side?'

'I'm sorry?'

'You sometimes park on the east side of the campus. By the engineering building.'

Sarah took a breath.

'Sometimes. Often there's no space left near my office by the time I get in. Engineering has the biggest car park.'

'That's where this mobile call was made from. At 5.27 p.m. – end of the working day. Perhaps by someone going to their car on the way home.'

'Right.'

'We're reviewing CCTV footage from three cameras on that side of the campus. See what that might tell us.'

'How big an area would that mobile phone mast cover?'

The detective shrugged.

'A decent radius, maybe half the campus and the houses across the ring road on the other side, too.'

'So lots of people.'

'All the same, it's one line of our enquiry. Does the following phone number sound familiar to you?'

She read off an eleven-digit number, twice, looking up in between to check her reaction.

Sarah shook her head, trying to do so in an unhurried, genuine way.

'I don't know many people's numbers off by heart, but that one doesn't sound familiar.'

With a sickening lurch of adrenaline she remembered that she had written Volkov's number down on a Post-it note before she dumped the mobile phone in the river. That Post-it was still in an inside pocket of her purse, stuck to a book of second-class stamps. And her purse was in her handbag, which was now on the edge of the table, about a foot from the detective's left hand.

Sarah made a show of looking at her watch.

'I'm sorry, I've really got to go, I have to give a seminar at ten. Is that all right?'

'Of course,' DI Rayner said, holding her gaze. 'Thanks for coming in at short notice. If you remember anything at all, something you think might be relevant, give me a call. Anything you think we should know.'

Sarah nodded and stood up, hoping her unsteady legs wouldn't betray her on the way out.

63

After the seminar Sarah retreated to her office, sitting still and quiet with the door closed and locked and the lights off, so no one would come knocking on the door trying to bother her. Her lunch – a cheese sandwich – sat untouched on the desk beside her. She had no appetite anyway. She just wanted to be alone, to have some time to think about her situation. About what to do next. All she could think of was the conversation with her father the night before, his calm, methodical, rational dissection of her options. It had been a relief to share the burden with him, to share her secret, but now she knew she had to choose which way to –

There was a light knocking on her office door, followed by a woman's muffled voice.

'Sarah?'

She froze, hoping the person would give up and go away.

'Are you in there? It's Marie.'

Sarah sat perfectly still.

The knocking came again, louder this time, followed by the voice.

'I know you're in there.'

Sarah sighed, got up and unlocked the door.

Marie stood in the corridor, a Tupperware box in one hand and her mobile in the other.

'Hi,' she said. 'Lunch?'

'Just going to have it at my desk, I think.'

'Mind if I join you?'

'Why not?' Sarah opened the door wider and Marie took a seat on a folding chair wedged into the corner, between two stacks of books. Sarah shut the door behind her and went back to her desk.

'Are you OK?' Marie said. 'You look a bit zoned out. Dark in here. Is your bulb gone?'

'Just a headache. Didn't get much sleep last night, that's all.'

'Is Harry having that nightmare again?'

'Nightmare?'

'The one about the giant hamster?'

It took a moment for Sarah to remember what her colleague was talking about: a week-long period over the summer when Harry had woken at least three times a night, every night, insisting there was a giant hamster under his bed.

'Oh, yes,' she lied. 'That one.'

Marie took the lid off her Tupperware box.

'So, what do you make of it all?'

'Of what?'

'Alan.'

Sarah shifted uncomfortably in her seat. *What did Marie know? What did she suspect?*

'How do you mean?'

'What's wrong with him?'

Sarah tried to force a smile, but it wouldn't come.

'How long have you got?'

Marie snorted, spearing a forkful of vegan pasta.

'I know, right? But I mean since he came back from . . . that thing that happened to him.'

'The kidnapping.'

'He's different somehow. The same, but different.'

'You mean worse than he was before?'

Marie nodded.

'It's like he's . . . cracked a bit, gone over the edge. If you ask me, he's come back to work too soon.'

'He's been cracked for a long time, Marie. It's just that most people never saw it.'

'I know, but he seems more *mad* than before. Wired, as if it's turned all of his worst characteristics up to eleven and he can't work out how to dial them back down again.'

Sarah picked up her sandwich, considered it for a moment. Put it back down again.

'It's bound to affect you, I suppose, if some random Russian abducts you and throws you in the boot of his car.'

Marie frowned.

'He was Russian, was he?'

Sarah felt a jolt of alarm. *Be careful, very careful.*

'That's what the police said.'

'Not to me, they didn't.' She pointed her fork at Sarah. 'How come you always have the best gossip, Dr Haywood?'

'Can't remember where I heard it from, actually.'

'Wherever the bad guy was from, I think the experience has tipped Alan over the edge.' She chewed thoughtfully. 'Perhaps it's post-traumatic stress disorder?'

'Perhaps.'

'It would be great if he got signed off for a month or two, wouldn't it?'

Sarah gave a wry smile.

'Probably doesn't help that he's drinking even earlier in the day now.' Marie spoke through a mouthful of pasta. 'What else did the police say when they talked to you?'

Sarah felt her stomach clench with fear. *Be careful.*

'Same as they said to everyone else, I suppose.'

'Have you heard the latest? Alan's been saying the police are close to arresting someone else in connection with the kidnapping. An accomplice.'

Sarah swallowed hard and turned away, pretending to check her phone.

'Really?' she managed.

'Apparently, it's just a matter of time – so he says, anyway. You know what I think?'

'What's that?'

'I don't think they'll have to look far for an accomplice.'

'What?' Sarah felt the heat starting to rise to her face. 'What do you mean?'

'Not random, is it?'

'I've no idea what you're talking about.'

'His wife. Caroline. She's got fed up with him trying to screw everything that moved, and decided to teach him a lesson. It's always the husband – or the wife, in this case.'

'Could be,' Sarah said quietly.

'Or maybe Gillian Arnold – she has plenty of motive.'

'That's true enough.'

Marie put the last piece of penne pasta into her mouth and held her fork up like a conductor.

'You know, I was rather hoping that the whole experience would have given him enough of a shock to bring him down a peg or two. I don't know, encourage him to take a step back, make him into a better person, somehow. But it hasn't, has it?'

'No, it's made him worse. Much worse.' She paused, just for a second. 'It must make you wonder, Marie.'

Marie looked up, confused.

'Make me wonder what?'

'Whether he's still going to honour his side of the deal.'

64

Marie crossed her arms over her chest.

'What do you mean?'

'The deal you made with Lovelock. When exactly did you decide you were going to stitch me up?'

'I don't – I'm not sure what you mean, Sarah.'

'You know, something you said that day I went to report Lovelock to HR has been bugging me for a while, but I couldn't work out why. You said *if I rocked the boat, we'd all end up losing.*'

Marie shifted uncomfortably in her seat.

'I don't remember saying that.'

'Oh, you did. I was too wrapped up in my own anger at the time to think it was anything other than sisterly solidarity. But then I started thinking about it in bed one night, and I couldn't work out what you meant. Why would we *all* end up losing?'

'Sarah –'

'And then I realised it wasn't about solidarity at all, was it? It was pure self-interest. You thought you'd be tarred with the same brush as me: guilt by association. And it might have jeopardised the deal you'd made with him.'

'Honestly, Sarah, I don't know what you're talking about. We're friends, aren't we?'

Sarah held a hand up.

'Hang on a minute, I'm not finished. Lovelock knew that me and you were friends. He said we were "thick as thieves" that night in Edinburgh. He'd probably assume that if I made a formal complaint, you'd encouraged me, and that would scupper your chances of getting the promotion he'd promised you. Better if we all just sat back quietly, nice and compliant, and let him put through the paperwork without anyone raising a formal complaint and the whole process grinding to a halt.'

Even in the gloom of her unlit office, Sarah could see the flush creeping into Marie's cheeks. She pressed on, a calm fury in her voice.

'I couldn't work out where he was getting his information from. I complained to Clifton about Alan stealing my idea on that new funding in Boston, and the next day Alan knew about it.'

'Clifton probably told him,' Marie said in a small voice. 'They're old friends.'

'No, I don't think it would even have occurred to him to pass that on. Departmental spats like that are much too small fry for him. But you were there, right after I spoke to Clifton. You appeared out of nowhere. You were eavesdropping on our conversation, weren't you?'

Marie shook her head, but said nothing.

'I'd told you I was going to go to HR,' Sarah continued. 'But Lovelock got in there before me, to lay the groundwork for presenting me as a problem. He was literally in with Webster when I arrived to go into my meeting with him. Presumably telling him I was mad, unstable, prone to all of the crap that he threw at Gillian Arnold. When Alan called me in later that afternoon, he was a step ahead of me again – he knew I would try to record the meeting. Something I told you I was planning to do. Did you tell the police I was in a relationship with Alan, too?'

Marie didn't reply.

'Jesus Christ,' Sarah said. 'I can't believe you've turned me over like this. What about the Rules? We bloody came up with them *together*.'

'I know.'

'So what made you do it?'

Marie paused, her shoulders slumped. She spoke without looking up from the floor.

'He told me there was a restructure coming, that my job was at risk because I was on a temporary contract. That I'd be one of the first in the firing line. This was a few weeks ago, around the time he had his party.'

'He told me that too.'

'He said I could put myself in a good position if I helped him, if I gave him certain information. Kept an eye on a few people.'

'Including me.'

Marie looked up and nodded.

'He had you down as a troublemaker.'

'Because I wouldn't sleep with him?'

'He had you pegged as someone to put in their place, one way or another.'

'So you made a deal with him.'

'I didn't want to. But it's my career.'

'It's my bloody career too!'

Marie flinched at Sarah's anger.

'But you've got your kids and your nice house, and all of that. I haven't. I've just got this – my career. I've given everything to it, and he said he was going to take it away, that I had to make a choice. And when we saw Gillian Arnold at his party I knew that I didn't want to end up like her. Anything but that.'

'Gillian didn't do anything wrong.'

'Yes, she did – she tried to take him on. Seeing her taught me there was no way to go up against him and win. I tried to tell you that, tried to keep you from starting a fight you couldn't win. But you wouldn't listen.'

There was silence between them for a moment as Marie stood, gathering up her bag and coat and moving to the door.

Sarah shook her head. After her flash of anger, she was suddenly bone-tired. Tired of deceit and betrayal, tired of trying to keep track of who could be trusted. More than anything else, she was sad for her friend. Sad that she had been pushed into this position. Sad that they were lost to each other now.

There was only one more question to ask.

'Marie,' Sarah said wearily. 'Did you have sex with him as well?'

'It wasn't –'

'You know what?' Sarah interrupted, holding up a hand. 'Don't answer that, I don't want to know. Just go.'

Marie went out into the corridor and pulled the door quietly shut behind her.

65

Roger clasped his hands together on the old oak kitchen table and leaned towards his youngest daughter. Sarah had come home mid-afternoon, Grace and Harry were at after-school club and the house had been restored to a semblance of order after the mess Sarah had made of it.

'Right,' Roger said. 'I've been doing some thinking, since we spoke about your situation.'

'OK,' she said slowly.

'It seems to me there is only one question that matters now, Sarah.'

'Just the one? I have about a million questions, but no answers.'

He shook his head.

'Only one question that's important.'

Sarah sighed and closed her eyes.

'Am I going to like the question?'

'Irrelevant whether you like it or not. The only thing that's relevant is this: you're in a bad situation and it's probably going to get worse.'

'Great. You're making me feel better already.'

'You can't go backwards, Sarah. You can't go back to a time before this happened, before you made a deal with the Russian. That door is closed now – you have to go forwards, deal with the world as it is. And so here's the one question: what are you going to do about it?'

Sarah knew he was right. She had known for days, weeks. Since the phone call that had sent her through the looking glass into another life.

'Do?' she repeated. 'What *can* I do about it?'

'Well, you have a choice to make. Just like when you were sixteen and you had to decide what path to take. You're at another crossroads now and it seems to me you have three choices.'

Sarah took a sip of her tea, feeling the burn as it went down. Her calm, methodical dad had always been the same. The man who'd spent his career analysing risks, always good at breaking a situation down and looking at it from every angle. Always good at stripping away everything that was irrelevant and pinpointing the facts.

'Life's not as simple as that,' she said.

'Life can be complicated if we choose. But it doesn't have to be.'

'So what are they, these three options?'

'Are you sure you want to hear them?'

'No,' she sighed. 'Yes. Go on, then.'

'Without stating the obvious, I've assumed that doing nothing is a non-starter.'

'Correct. Doesn't bear thinking about.'

'So, the first option is the obvious one: you can cut your losses and run, admit that the system sometimes fails, that bad things happen to good people, that the odds against you in your current situation are simply too great. Admit that sometimes there simply isn't an effective and fair solution – accept that's just how life is. Make a fresh start somewhere else, in a different field, a different city. I can help you to do that.'

'Everything I've worked towards here will be lost.'

'Yes. You'll have to start again.'

Sarah slumped back against her chair with a sigh.

'Believe it or not, Dad, that's not wildly attractive as an option.'

'I know.'

'There comes a point when you start feeling too old to start again. What's option two?'

'Put your faith in the powers that be. Make a full formal complaint to the university and go public if you have to. Find a good solicitor – and get ready to have Lovelock come at you with this accusation about the Russian. Deny ever meeting him, stand firm and try to hold your nerve longer than they can. Hope that there's no evidence out there of you and Volkov having a conversation.'

'Trust a broken process while I lie through my teeth? I might as well surrender right now.'

'I wouldn't put it like that.' He cocked his head to the side. 'But surrender is not always the worst option, you know. It can save a lot of pain and grief, a lot of unnecessary trauma.'

She looked up at her father through bloodshot eyes.

'But you would never surrender, would you?'

'I did when it came to Lee Goodyer. Sometimes, it's the right thing, that's all I'm saying.'

Sarah closed her eyes, relishing the momentary blackness.

'What's the third option?' she said.

'The third one is the hardest, Sarah.'

'Harder than running away or lying for the rest of my life?'

'Well,' he said. 'That rather depends on your point of view.'

66

Sarah loaded the shopping bags into the boot of her car, working quickly and keeping an eye on her surroundings. The multi-storey car park at Brent Cross shopping centre was almost full and she didn't want to bump into anyone she knew, anyone from work who might ask awkward questions, however unlikely that was at seven o'clock on a Wednesday evening. The shopping centre at Wood Green was nearer to home but she was desperate to get away from her own neighbourhood, to be anonymous, doing something that might take her mind off her problems if only for an hour. She had left the children at home with her father and gone shopping.

She didn't want to talk to anyone. What she really wanted to do was curl up in a corner and hide.

She slammed the boot and took the trolley to the collection point, walking quickly back to her car, keen to be out of this claustrophobic place. The cars were packed in so tight here that someone could creep up and you wouldn't see them until they were right on top of you. Her nerves were stretched taut as it was, and every extra second she had to stay in the multi-storey was a second too long. She had come to hate places with only one exit. Two was better, three preferable. The more the better if she had to get away from somewhere – or someone – in a hurry. But this car park only had one exit, the concrete ramp down to the ground floor. The sooner she was out of here, the better.

She saw him everywhere. Lovelock. Glimpsed him moving in crowds, at the end of a supermarket aisle, on her street, watching her from behind windows. The back of his head, or his distinctive walk, his booming voice; and every time there was a little stab of fear twisting in her stomach. She knew it *wasn't* him, not really, just her imagination. Just her exhausted mind projecting him onto every tall man she saw.

But she also knew it *could* be him, any time, on any day. And one day it would be.

She needed to get home. Draw the curtains. Lock the door. Put her phone on silent.

She turned the ignition, put the Fiesta in gear and was reversing out of her space when out of the corner of her eye she saw a flash of grey metal, heard a squeal of brakes echoing off the car park's low concrete ceiling. Instinctively she slammed on her own brakes and her car rocked to a stop, bare inches away from a collision. A huge grey 4 x 4 had stopped behind her and now sat, unmoving, blocking her. The windows were tinted so dark that she couldn't see in. Without thinking, she hit her car's horn with the palm of her hand, the noise echoing loudly off the car park walls.

On a normal day she would have dismissed it as just another crap piece of driving in a city full of it. But this wasn't a normal day. It hadn't been a normal week, a normal month.

The 4 x 4 stayed where it was. No one got out.

A trickle of fear crept down Sarah's spine. *What the hell?*

She hit her horn again, the shrill tone sounding louder in the silence as it bounced and echoed away. The big grey 4 x 4 still didn't move.

Sarah turned left and right in her seat, desperately hoping there would be someone else there, a witness, someone who could help her.

There was no one.

The fear was flowing now, turning her stomach liquid. Bile rising in her throat.

For one mad moment she thought about flooring the accelerator and trying to ram the big car out of her way. But it was twice the size of her Fiesta, and probably twice the weight too. It wouldn't work. With shaking hands, she dug in her handbag for her phone, found it, and decided to run. She would dial 999 then get out and start running before –

A tall bearded man in sunglasses got out of the front passenger seat, wearing jeans and a dark suit jacket. He came around the Mercedes 4 x 4 and opened the rear passenger door, then walked to the driver's side door of Sarah's Fiesta and pulled it open. Up close he looked huge, the muscles of his neck and back stretching the jacket taut across his shoulders.

He reached down to the ignition of her car, turned off the engine and pocketed her keys, gesturing with his other hand towards the Mercedes' open passenger door.

Sarah stayed where she was, paralysed by fear.

The bearded man bent towards her and reached down into the Fiesta, across her body. His face was only inches from hers and the car seemed to fill suddenly with the smells of cigarettes and sweat and sickly-sweet aftershave. Sarah pushed herself back into her seat, balling her hands into fists ready to hit him, or the car horn, or both. Then she saw the gun tucked into the shoulder holster beneath his jacket, and froze.

He released her seat belt and stood up, gesturing again towards the 4 x 4.

Sarah got out of her car slowly and the man pushed her door shut. He took her mobile from her hand and gestured again towards the Mercedes idling a few feet away. Sarah could see the car's creamy white interior. It looked like one person was seated in the back.

The bearded man took her by the arm and led her to the SUV. Sarah had time for one final desperate look around the car park for someone, anyone, who might hear a cry for help, call the police or try to intervene to help her.

But there was no one.

Then the bearded man's hand was in the small of her back, pushing her towards the open door of the Mercedes.

She got in.

67

'Hello, Sarah.'

Volkov sat, relaxed in a white shirt and dark blue jeans, legs crossed, in the car's spacious leather interior.

She sat down on the far side of him, her heart juddering in her chest.

'What's going on?'

'Put your seat belt on.'

'What?'

He gestured towards her shoulder.

'Your seat belt. Nikolai likes to drive fast.'

She reached up and clicked the seat belt into place, pressing her body half against the window so she could keep her eyes on him. The bearded man got into the front passenger seat and the car moved off smoothly, leaving her Fiesta behind. The driver guided it down the ramp, through the exit and out into the evening traffic.

Volkov pressed a button in the door console and a glass partition slid into place between the driver's compartment and the rest of the car. The car was even quieter now, the noise of the engine and the outside world muffled to a distant hum. Sarah kept her eyes on the Russian the whole time, trying to read him, to work out where the car was headed.

If they were going to kidnap you they wouldn't have done it in a public place. There are CCTV cameras on that car park. And they wouldn't have left your car there.

'Are you going to tell me what's happening?'

'How are you, Sarah? You look tired.'

'I'm great. Never better. How did you know where to find me?'

He shrugged as if the answer was obvious.

'How does anyone find anything these days?'

'I thought you said we'd never see each other again?'

'I did say that. But unusual circumstances mean we have to adapt. The truth is, Sarah, I'm worried about you.'

'Me? Why?'

'Are you sleeping?'

She was momentarily disarmed by his question.

'On and off.'

'And you have spoken to the police yesterday morning, yes? Detective Inspector Kate Rayner?'

'How do you know about that?'

'I know many things. How did your conversation go?'

'She wanted to talk to me about Alan.'

'What did you tell her?'

'I told them I didn't know anything about it.'

'And what did you say about me?'

'Nothing. Nothing at all.'

'What about the mobile phone I gave you?'

'I disposed of it.'

He considered this for a moment.

'All right. But consider this a warning and a personal guarantee. If you tell the police one word about our conversation, about my offer, I will know about it. I promise you, I will know. Do you understand what this means?'

Sarah nodded, remembering the pictures he had shown her of her children's schools. Grace, oblivious, photographed in the middle of the playground.

'Yes.'

'Good. It is good to understand each other.'

'What about your man? The police have him. They found Lovelock in the boot of his car.'

'What about him?'

'What if *he* talks to the police?'

Volkov grunted as if this was funny.

'Let me tell you about Yuri – about how he got his scar. One of my rivals in Moscow sent four men to take him, some years ago. He killed one and put another in the hospital for a month. The others beat him unconscious with iron bars and took him to a basement where they beat him for another three days straight. They pulled out all his fingernails, one by one, and put out cigarettes on the wounds. Cut off three of his toes with bolt cutters. They tortured him with electricity. They sliced his scalp from his ear,' he motioned with a finger over the top of his head, 'and peeled it back over his forehead so they could put more cigarettes out on his bare skull. And all this time, *all this time*, he said not one word to them. Not one word.'

'What did they want from him?'

'Information about me and my family – so they could get to me. But even though they beat him for three days, he still gave them nothing. So in answer to your question: no. He will not be talking to your soft British police, even if they try to force him. He has already seen the worst that men can do and he still kept his silence. Hell will freeze and the Devil will beg on his knees for repentance before this happens. You would do well to follow his example.'

'I have nothing to gain by talking to the police. And everything to lose.'

'Good. Then we understand each other.'

She looked at the leather upholstery of the expensive car, the seatback screens and minibar. Listened to the soft powerful thrum of the engine as they were driven through the busy north London streets.

She spoke without looking at him.

'So what the hell happened?'

'What do you mean?'

'Your man Yuri, the scarred man. How on earth did he manage to get himself arrested with Alan tied up in the boot?'

Volkov shrugged.

'Our usual process is we wait a few days after taking the subject, wait for any initial attention to calm down a little. We wait until the subject is weakened, more docile. Only this time, when Yuri was on his way out of the city to complete the task he had a piece of simple bad luck – it happens. Sometimes fate intervenes. For this, I apologise.'

'Well, I'm glad, anyway.'

Volkov frowned.

'Glad the professor is still alive?'

'Yes. No. Not exactly. I still hate his guts but I'm glad he's not dead, I suppose. I'm glad I'm not responsible.'

'Two weeks ago you wanted him gone.'

'I know. I was angry.'

'You are a fickle woman.' He smiled slightly but there was sadness in it. 'My wife was the same.'

The car stopped, and Sarah looked out of her window. They were back in the car park, her little blue Fiesta just where she had left it. The driver got out and came around to her door, scanning their surroundings and then opening it for her.

Volkov held out his hand.

'Goodbye, Dr Haywood. I wish you luck.'

68

She stared at him.

'So that's it? That's all? You just wanted to warn me about talking to the police?'

She felt like a swimmer who had let the tide take her so far out that she couldn't touch the bottom. Just treading cold water, fighting the panic and trying to keep her head up. But how long could a person do that?

Volkov nodded, once.

'That,' he said, 'is all.'

You can't tread water forever. Sooner or later, you go under.

Unless you grab on to something, anything, to keep you afloat.

There was the tiniest glimmer of a plan in her mind, so far away it was virtually disappearing over the horizon. But desperation lent anger to her voice.

'I thought you were a man of your word.'

'I am.'

'*No.* You made me a promise, and you broke that promise.' She saw anger darken his face, but she ploughed on regardless. 'You said you were a man of honour, a man who knew what it meant to pay his debts.'

He gestured to his driver and the man closed her door again.

'Things have changed,' he said. 'Circumstances have changed.'

'*My* circumstances have not changed,' Sarah spat back. 'Actually, they have – they've got ten times worse. And your debt is still not paid.'

He frowned. The anger left his face then he nodded slowly.

'This is true. The debt is not paid.'

'When you made me this offer you said there would be no going back. That was one of your conditions.'

'True.'

'But you've gone back on your word. *You have.*'

Volkov pointed at her.

'It is good to see the tiger is back. But you just said you were glad the tall professor is still breathing.'

'Something still needs to be done. Things can't carry on the way they are.'

'The *volshebnik* cannot perform his vanishing trick for a little while.'

'I know that. But there are other ways of making someone disappear.'

'Not in my world. In my world, there is only one way. The oldest way.'

'I'm talking about *my* world.'

He studied her for a moment.

'And how does it happen in your world?'

'Let me worry about that.'

He considered this for a moment.

'Now I am intrigued. Tell me more.'

'There is more than one way to make a person vanish. I need you to do what you promised me. I need you to settle our debt – but not your way. My way.' She summoned the one Russian phrase she had learned, trying her best with the accent. '*Ugovor dorozhe deneg.*'

He laughed and clapped his hands.

'Ha! Very good, I like this. Do you know what it means?'

She shrugged.

'A bargain is a bargain.'

'Yes. And also that a man's word is his reputation. This is very important.' He smiled. 'Your accent needs some work, however.'

'So . . . will you help me?'

He looked at her, his dark eyes boring into her.

'This depends, Dr Haywood. What is it you need?'

'I need something your countrymen are famous for.'

'We are famous for many things,' he said, spreading his hands. 'You will have to be a little more specific.'

And so she told him.

He listened, keeping his eyes on her. He took no notes, but Sarah knew that he would remember every word of their conversation.

Finally, he nodded.

'I will think about it.'

'Give me the tools and I will do what's needed. I will do it myself.'

'There are many risks.'

'The biggest risk for me is doing nothing.'

He considered this for a moment.

'Perhaps. As I said, I will think about it.'

'How will you let me know when you've decided? How do I contact you again?'

'You don't. I will be in touch if we are to proceed.'

He lifted up the central compartment between them on the back seat. Inside were half a dozen identical mobile phones, vacuum-packed in clear plastic like prime cuts of steak. He selected one and handed it to her.

'Single-use phone. Charge it and keep it switched on at all times. Do not use for anything else. If you do so, we will know and that will be an end to it.' He leaned forward. 'But if I decide to help you in the way you suggest, one of my colleagues will be in touch by six tomorrow. Then remove SIM card and destroy both card and phone.'

'And if I don't hear from you?'

'Then I wish you luck, Dr Haywood.'

The meeting, it seemed, was at an end.

Sarah got out, closing the door behind her. The big 4 x 4 pulled away in a squeal of tyres and disappeared back down the exit ramp, leaving nothing behind but an echo bouncing off the low concrete walls.

69

Sarah gathered up books and papers spread across the seminar room table as the last of her final year students filed out. It was a good group, bright third-years with a genuine interest in the subject, but she couldn't concentrate at more than a superficial level. She let them do most of the talking, holding just enough of the thread to make sure she could keep the discussion going until the allotted hour was up. Picking up the last of her papers, she heard a *click* as the seminar room door shut behind her. She froze, an animal fear flooding her veins, knowing who was there even without turning around.

'Good to see you back in harness, Sarah,' Lovelock said, his deep baritone filling every corner of the room.

It was Thursday morning, her second day back at work after he had assaulted her in the lounge of her house. She had determined to avoid him as far as possible – to limit their contact to an absolute minimum – while she tried to get everything in place.

She turned to face him, holding her bag across her chest.

'I have to get to my next seminar group,' she said quietly.

He turned the door lock in its latch and leaned back against the frame, blocking her exit.

'Don't worry, this won't take long. I just want to be clear about our new arrangement, after our conversation the other day.'

'All right.'

'You see, I know women like you. I know how your minds work.'

'Really.' She did her best to keep her voice even.

'Oh yes. You're thinking you can just up sticks and run away from the little mess you've created here. Resign from your post.'

'No,' Sarah said.

'Good, because if you do decide to resign, I will suddenly remember what our Russian friend said to me, and I will have to tell Detective Inspector Rayner. Imagine how that will go down.'

Sarah felt she was falling, plummeting, and put a hand out to the desk next to her, to steady herself.

'You're saying I can't leave?'

'You can do whatever you like.' He folded his arms across his chest. 'I'm just telling you what the consequences will be.'

'Until when?'

'Until I get bored with our new weekly arrangement.'

'So basically, you won't give me a permanent role but you won't let me quit either.'

'I hate that word. *Quit.* I've never quit in my life – there's a lesson for you there, Sarah. And just think about this: if you choose that road and you end up going to jail for conspiracy to kidnap, what do you think will happen to your children?'

'What? What about them?'

He let her consider it for a moment before continuing.

'They will be taken away from you and given to your faithless, wandering husband, who will probably divorce you. The little brats will have to learn to live without mummy. And who knows? With a criminal conviction, you might never see them again.'

Somehow, among all the events of the last few weeks – all the choices she had made – it had never occurred to her that the consequences might rebound upon her children. That they might end up being the biggest losers of all, cut adrift from their mother and left with their feckless father. What hope would there be for them then? She told herself that everything she had done, *everything*, had been about safe-guarding their future, about doing what she needed to do as a mother to bring up Grace and Harry. Having the stability and security to bring up her little family single-handed, if she had to.

And now this.

She stared at him, feeling her anger building.

And at that moment, in that instant, the dam that had been holding back all of her pent-up emotions cracked wide open and they surged through her like a burning tide – despair, fear, the desperate rage of a cornered mother whose young are threat-ened. She knew with absolute certainty then that she could kill this man if she had to. It took all the control she had to stop herself throwing herself at him, climbing over the desk and stabbing him through the heart with whatever she could lay her hands on. Tearing his throat out, plunging her thumbs into his eye sockets and –

Lovelock continued with his monologue, but Sarah could barely hear him above the blood rushing in her ears, the anger pounding in her temples.

'And career-wise?' he said. 'You can forget it. You'll be damaged goods, Sarah. No one in academia will touch you with a barge-pole. You might get a job teaching spelling to spotty sixteen-year-old drop-outs at the local FE college, but you can forget any kind of university position. That will be gone forever.'

Be calm. Walk the line.

She swallowed hard.

'I realise that.'

'Good. I'm glad we understand each other. I can see you're angry with me, but it's not my fault, is it? We have to consider the consequences of what we do.' He gestured at a framed print on the wall, the cover of Christopher Marlowe's most famous work. 'Faustus knew this when he sold his soul to the Devil. You should have known it when you got involved with the Russian.'

'I know how to make it right.'

'Good! So: Saturday evening. You're coming to my house, as you suggested.'

Marie was right, she thought. *The kidnapping has pushed him over the edge.*

'As we agreed,' Sarah said quietly. 'Could you email me your address again?'

He smiled, shaking his head.

'Nice try, Sarah, but better not to have any electronic records of our new arrangement, don't you think? Let's just keep it between us: word of mouth. I'm sure you can remember my address, from the party.'

Sarah looked away from him, embarrassed to be caught out.

'I'll dig out the invitation.'

'Caroline's away Saturday night, down in Devon. So you and I will inaugurate our new weekly arrangement.' He leaned down and whispered into her ear. 'With you on your knees.'

She looked up and nodded.

'I'll be there.'

70

She carried the little flip phone with her everywhere, praying it would ring. It was another fairly unremarkable Alcatel handset, small and cheap-looking, not much bigger than a packet of para-cetamol. She flipped it open for the tenth time. Still no calls, no messages, no texts. She had left work, pleading illness again, and sat in her silent kitchen, in the semi-dark, holding the little mobile and willing it to come to life. The Russian had said he would call by six if he decided to help her, and there were only a few hours left.

Please. I can do this but I need your help.

She jumped as the landline rang on the kitchen counter. A withheld number. Possibly someone from work? Best not to answer. She waited for the caller to ring off.

It rang again. She ignored it a second time.

A minute later, there was a knocking at the front door. Four loud, confident raps on the wood, then a pause, then four more.

She waited for the visitor to get bored and go away.

The knocking came again.

She crept up the stairs, across the landing and into the front bedroom, peering out from the side of the curtain and down to her little driveway.

There was no one at the door.

Her own mobile phone buzzed where it sat charging on her bedside table. A text message.

Open the door, Sarah. Kate R.

Sarah went downstairs, feeling foolish for being caught out, and opened the front door. It was DI Rayner.

'Sorry about that,' Sarah said, reddening. 'Thought you were a Jehovah's Witness.'

'I went to your office, but they said you were off sick. Can I come in?'

'I was sort of in the middle of something.'

'It'll only be ten minutes.'

Sarah unhooked the door chain and let the police officer inside. DI Rayner waved away the offer of a cup of coffee and the two of them sat in the closed-curtain gloom of the lounge, facing each other on the two little sofas.

DI Rayner took a notebook and pen out of her bag.

'Are you all right? You look exhausted.'

'I've not really been sleeping very much. I've had pills but they seem to get less effective the longer it goes on.'

She caught herself, realising she'd already said too much.

'The longer *what* goes on, Sarah?'

'Everything. Life.' She reached for a convincing lie. 'My husband and I, we've been having some . . . problems. He's not here at the moment.'

'Yes, I remember you saying. And your boss?'

Sarah looked up.

'What about him?'

DI Rayner laced her fingers together and regarded Sarah with a look of professional sympathy.

'I know about it, Sarah. I know about it all.'

Sarah felt her stomach drop.

'About what?'

'What he's like. What he's *really* like. Not the TV persona. Not the brilliant academic. Not the tireless charity fundraiser. The real man behind all that, the one that most people have never seen. We've seen it with Jimmy Savile and all those others.' She leaned forward. 'You've seen the real Alan Lovelock, haven't you?'

Sarah nodded, but said nothing.

'I know it's not been easy for you,' Rayner continued. 'There are plenty of arseholes like him in the police force, believe me. Men who talk down to you, belittle you, just because you're a woman. Men who make assumptions about you they'd never make with a male colleague.' She paused, holding Sarah's gaze. 'Men you want to make sure you're never alone with.'

Sarah looked away.

'I know what it's like to have to deal with men like that, day in, day out. So why don't you tell me what happened between you and him?'

'Nothing happened,' she said in a monotone.

'It's time for you to come clean, Sarah.'

'Come clean?'

A phone began to ring. A mobile. The muffled ringtone sounded like a cheap, tinny imitation of the standard iPhone Marimba tune, but it was not one that Sarah had ever used. She assumed it was Rayner's phone, but the detective made no move to answer it. With a jolt, Sarah realised where the sound was coming from: the little flip phone Volkov had given her the day before. It was just a few feet from where they sat, on a side table next to the sofa.

She felt the blood drain from her face, willing the caller to hang up and leave a message instead.

The two women looked at each other, the conversation paused while the ringtone cycled round and around.

'Do you want to get that?' DI Rayner said.

'No, it's fine.'

'You sure?'

'They'll leave a message if it's important.'

Finally, the phone stopped ringing.

'Do you want to check it?'

'I'll do it later. You were saying?'

'I was saying that it's time to get things off your chest.'

Sarah's heart was still fluttering from the missed call. She waited a moment to get her breathing back under control.

'You make it sound easy.'

'It *can* be easy: tell me what's really been going on between you and Alan Lovelock. Get it out in the open.' She put a hand on Sarah's arm. 'I promise you, I absolutely guarantee you, that it will feel better once you've done it. *You* will feel better.'

'What did my husband tell you, when you talked to him on the phone?'

'Why?'

'I'd just like to know.'

'He said Lovelock made your life very difficult at work. Did you ever ask Nick to confront him about it?'

'No.'

'Why not?'

'My husband's not that sort of man.'

'So you found someone else to do it?'

'No.'

'Someone who would teach Lovelock a lesson?'

'No!'

The detective took Sarah's hand. She had large, kind eyes, her brow furrowed with concern. And suddenly the urge to tell her was overwhelming. The problem was, she was right – and Sarah knew it. She knew she would feel better if she set down this secret, this heavy load that she had been carrying, and let someone else pick it up.

'I'm on your side, Sarah. I want to help you.'

The urge to confess was almost a physical force pushing against her chest.

Forget what you were going to do. Just tell her. Tell her.

Sarah dropped her eyes to the floor so she wouldn't have to meet the detective's gaze any longer. The room suddenly seemed oppressive, too small for the two of them. There was an honourable way out of this: confess everything, get it all out there in the open. Rayner clearly understood what it was like, she knew what men like Lovelock were like – and she wasn't going to get a fairer hearing from anyone else. Sarah felt like a tightrope walker heading into the void. Suddenly she felt like telling it all. Spilling everything. Every last detail.

Then she looked up and saw the detective's look of compassion replaced by the focused intensity of a hunter waiting for her quarry to move into the crosshairs. The anticipation of a lion about to make its kill. Just a tiny flicker, but it was enough. The mask had slipped, if only for a moment.

By the time it was back in place, Sarah had seen what she needed to see. She shrank back into the chair, arms crossed tightly across her chest.

Don't trust her. Don't trust any of them. She is not your friend.

'There's nothing to say. Nothing between me and Alan. He had a certain reputation but I didn't suffer worse than anyone else.'

'I know there's more to it than that. I think I have a pretty good idea of what he's like.'

Sarah shook her head.

'Trust me, you have no idea.'

71

Sarah showed the detective out, locked the door behind her, and watched out of the window as she got in her car and drove away. Only then did she fetch the phone Volkov had given her and flip it open. One missed call showed on the display. The caller had not left a voicemail and his or her number was withheld – but there was a text message. No words, just a mobile phone number. Sarah dialled the number and put the phone to her ear.

'Speak.' A male voice at the other end of the line.

'You called me, just now.'

'What is your daughter's date and time of birth?' Accented Russian, a voice she had heard before. A young man.

'Pardon?'

'Date and time. Your daughter. No hesitation please.'

Sarah pulled the memory into focus.

'She was born on 17th of December, 2009 at 11.35 a.m.'

'Weight?'

Her confusion cleared. *He's testing me. Checking my identity.*

'Uh, six pounds ten ounces.'

A pause, then: 'Good.'

'How do you know that's right?'

'Hospital database,' he said, a shrug in his voice. 'Now listen: same car park as before. Same floor, same place. One hour.'

'Does this mean –'

But it was already too late. He had hung up.

*   *   *

She entered the Brent Cross multi-storey fifty-five minutes later, found a spot near to where she had been penned in by the big 4 x 4 the day before, and parked. She got out of her car and walked up and down the row of parked vehicles, looking to see if any of them were occupied.

An unremarkable white van pulled up next to her Fiesta. The driver was the man with the sunglasses she had seen here before. Sarah leaned forward to peer past him but he seemed to be alone in the front cab. The van's sliding side door opened next to her, revealing a small table in the back. Sitting at the table was the young man with the ponytail, a laptop and an array of other items in front of him. He beckoned to her. *Come on. Get in.*

Sarah got out of her car and climbed into the van, sitting opposite the young Russian.

He slammed the sliding door behind her.

72

As soon as she was back at the house, Sarah got to work. She still had a couple of hours before the kids would need to be picked up from after-school club.

First, she made four phone calls, noting down times, places and various other details. She arranged two meetings for the following day, and an appointment. Booted up her laptop, logged onto her online banking and made a transfer to another account, typing in the numbers carefully from a piece of paper she had jotted them on. Then she went into her wardrobe and selected three outfits, laying them out side by side on the bed. One for a smart evening out – a black jacket and skirt long enough that her mother would have approved – and a work-casual outfit that she might wear to the office. Alongside the latter, she picked out sunglasses and a knitted hat with a brim that she had started to wear again now winter had arrived. The third outfit was Nick's old boiler suit, which he used to wear for occasional DIY around the house and jobs in the garden.

Next, she dug in her bedside drawer for her old mobile phone, a Sony Xperia. She found the charging cable and plugged it in, then sat on her bed with sheets of A4 paper, writing lists and planning what she still needed to do. Timelines for what she had in mind.

She slept intermittently.

The next day – Friday – she had a lecture and two seminars in the morning, but as soon as the last of them was done she sneaked out of the department and drove to the train station at Enfield Chase. She bought a one-day travelcard with cash and got the next train to Finsbury Park, where she switched to the Tube and took the Piccadilly line to Holborn. She had a number of items on her shopping list. There were shops nearer to the campus, and nearer to her house too, but the risk of bumping into someone she knew would be higher, and she didn't want to be seen anywhere close to where she lived or worked. It was better to be somewhere where there were lots of people, where she could get lost in the crowd.

She found a small independent phone shop and – copying what she had learned from Volkov – paid cash for the three cheapest pay-as-you-go phones she could find, and a new pay-as-you-go SIM card to go into her old handset.

She was fifteen minutes early for her first meeting, so she made her way to the back of the little café just off Russell Square. It was tucked away down a side street, off the main tourist track, and fairly quiet with the mid-afternoon lull in between lunch and knocking-off time.

She used to meet Nick here, in their first year after university. When he was taking his first steps into professional acting and she was embarking on her doctorate at UCL. It was a friendly little Italian place with low beams, cosy booths and the best coffee

Sarah had ever tasted. She ordered a cappuccino and settled down in a back booth to wait.

While she waited, she got the new SIM card and the old Sony Xperia out of her bag, took the back off the phone, slotted the card into place and reassembled the handset. The screen came to life and the phone started its setup with a new – and more importantly, anonymous – electronic identity.

The fragments of her plan were starting to come together. A plan that – even when her conscious mind had not been aware of it – had been quietly coalescing in the back of her mind from the very moment she realised Lovelock was still alive. A plan that she knew would be her last roll of the dice.

Her first visitor arrived right on time. Sarah smiled and gestured at the empty seat across the booth.

'Hello again. Thanks so much for meeting me at short notice. Let me get you a drink.'

Exactly an hour and a half later, her second visitor arrived. A different conversation, same goal.

She had called in a debt. She had asked for help. All that remained now was to offer the chance of redemption – or maybe revenge.

73

'Well?' Laura said, uncorking a chilled bottle of Pinot later that day.

'I've had enough.'

'Finally!'

'And I've got a plan. But I'm going to need your help. And Dad's.'

'Count me in,' Laura said. She pulled the cork out with a pop and filled Sarah's glass.

'Don't you want to hear what the plan is, before you decide?'

'Whatever it is, I'm up for it.' She filled her own glass. 'So, what *is* the plan?'

'I'm going to do what you've been saying all along, what you've been telling me to do for a year. It's all about evidence, isn't it? I'm going to give the university something they can't ignore.'

'How?'

'I'm going to get Lovelock on audio, telling me that I have to sleep with him to keep my job.'

'Okaaay,' Laura said. 'And if the uni tries to sweep it under the carpet, like they have before?'

'Then I'll go to the media. The *Guardian* will have a field day with something like that.'

Laura put her glass down.

'Are you serious?'

'Dead serious.'

'Fuck. You are, aren't you? What's made you change your mind?'

'Things have just got worse,' Sarah said, picking up her glass. 'A lot worse. He's gone off the deep end, big time.'

'Since the kidnapping thing?'

Sarah nodded.

'Yeah. That.'

'So have you got a mate at MI5 who can bug his office?'

'Not quite. I'm going to record him.'

'At your next meeting?'

Sarah shook her head.

'He won't talk about it at work, not now – but he might if he's at home and he lets his guard down. If he's pissed. If it's just the two of us and he thinks I'm going to play ball.'

'Woah!' Laura said, holding a hand up. 'Back up a minute. What did you just say?'

'At his house.'

'You've got to be fucking kidding me! That means deliberately breaking every single one of the Rules.'

'Yes.'

Her dad walked in, putting a finger to his lips.

'The children are asleep.'

'Thanks, Dad.'

Laura gave him a thumbs up and turned back to her friend, her voice quieter.

'And how exactly are you going to make him think you'll play ball?'

Sarah shrugged.

'Act the right way. Say the right things. Pick the right dress.'

'Holy Christ!' Laura said, loudly again. She threw her hands up. 'Sorry. But have you been smoking crack?'

'I know it sounds mad, but bear with me – it makes sense. Let's break it down for a minute: first of all what do we know about him? What is the fundamental essence of Professor Alan Lovelock?'

'He's a massive twat?' Laura said.

'Yes, but that wasn't quite what I was driving at.'

There was silence for a moment while they pondered Sarah's question.

'Ego,' Roger said. 'He has an ego the size of Big Ben.'

Sarah pointed at her father, smiling.

'Absolutely. And that means what?'

He shrugged.

'Colossal, unshakeable self-belief.'

'Right. Keep going.'

'So even despite all your knock-backs, he still believes that deep down you're attracted to him. Because, of course, you are, right? You're a woman, what woman wouldn't be?'

'Bingo,' Sarah said. 'He thinks he's irresistible. That's his weakness.'

'*And* he's a massive twat,' Laura added.

'It gives me a way in, a way to exploit his weakness. But I'll have to go about it in a convincing way.'

Laura crossed her arms tightly over her chest.

'And how are you going to do that?'

'I'm going to play a role. Just like Nick played a role with me the last few years.'

'Acting?'

'Yes. I'm going to give the performance of a lifetime.'

'You're talking about entrapment.'

'I'm talking about proof. Saving my job – and my sanity.'

Laura spoke more calmly now, her voice softened with concern.

'You know, at work we have to categorise potential reputation issues for the company in terms of them being low, medium, high or critical risk. From what you've told me so far, this plan of yours would be ranked somewhere north of critical, probably in the category of "totally shitting bonkers". Do you follow me?'

'I know it's high risk, Loz, but I've run out of options. Anyway, I thought you said you were up for it?'

Laura frowned.

'I am, of course I am. He's spent his whole life fighting dirty – why shouldn't we fight dirty, too? But how are you going to record him?'

'He's invited me to his house on Saturday evening. Well, I actually sort of invited myself.'

'What about his wife?'

'She's away in the West Country, seeing her mother. And he's been busy telling people at work that he's locking himself away at home for the weekend to finish writing his book – no visitors, no calls, no distractions. Says he's going to spend two days in splendid isolation to finish his magnum opus.'

'Hang on a minute, you're going *this* Saturday? You mean tomorrow?'

'Yes.' She picked up the box that Mikhail had given her in the Brent Cross multi-storey, lifting it up onto the kitchen side and slicing it open with the boning knife. 'So we've not got long to prepare.'

74

'This is a really bad idea,' Roger said. 'It's far too dangerous.'

'I agree,' Laura said.

Sarah looked from one of them to the other, across the table.

'I know there's risk,' she said calmly, 'but it's my best shot as well. And it's the best I could come up with. I might only get inside his house once – I *have* to take this chance, it could be the only one I get. It's now or never.'

Her dad leaned forward, his face grim.

'Why does it have to be at his house?'

'Because that's his domain, his kingdom; it's where he's most likely to let his guard down.'

'It just feels like you're playing right into his hands.'

'Look, I've got a better idea,' Laura said. 'We do this in a public place, in a park maybe, or a café, or even at your office, and the two of us can be waiting around the corner ready to step in if things go wrong. We could be twenty yards away the whole time, rather than bloody miles away.'

'Agreed,' Roger said, nodding.

'Won't work,' Sarah countered. 'He's too smart for that. He'll smell it a mile off. It needs to be on his own turf, with plenty of alcohol to loosen his tongue.'

'But that's *exactly* what makes it more dangerous for you, love,' Roger said, his voice rising. 'The risk is too great.'

'The risk is necessary,' Sarah replied, her own voice flat. 'Dad, you're the one who told me what my options were. This is the option I choose.'

'I'm with your dad on this,' Laura said.

Sarah crossed her arms on the table in front of her.

'Look, I'm going to do this whether you help me or not. I think I'll have a better chance of making it work if I have backup, but I'm going to do it anyway. I've got the kit to do the job, and I'm going to use it. Solo, if I have to.'

'You can't pull this off on your own.'

'Watch me.'

Her father and her best friend stared at her across the table, then looked at each other.

Finally, her father nodded.

'OK then. You better show us the equipment.'

* * *

'The quick brown fox jumped over the lazy dog,' Sarah's dad said to her.

'The rain in Spain falls mainly on the plain,' she replied.

More quietly, he said: 'All work and no play makes Jack a dull boy.'

Sarah paused for a moment.

'Lean back a bit and say that again.'

He did as he was told and they looked at each other as he repeated the same sentence. Sarah picked up her phone, lying on the coffee table between them, and moved it onto the arm of the sofa next to her.

'Try it again,' Laura called from the next room. 'I can hear you OK, Sarah, but your dad is getting really muffled.'

They went through their lines again and a minute later Laura came into the room, sitting down with the laptop.

'You're going to need to get the phone as close to him as you can, especially if there's background noise.'

'That's why I have the other kit.'

'Yeah. About that . . .'

Laura called up another tab on the screen of the laptop the young Russian had provided, showing an image from the room they were in. She selected the rewind option and the picture skipped backwards, jerking up and down. She paused it and the only things visible were Roger's knees, the coffee table and a section of carpet.

'There's a lot of movement on this little camera. That's not so good.' She studied the new brooch pinned to Sarah's blouse. 'We're going to need to secure it, somehow, so it's more stable. Also, you'll need to stay as still as possible, slow and steady, otherwise the image quality is going to be shite.'

'I'm going to have to move, Loz. I can't just sit there like a statue.'

'The less you move, the better the video is going to be. That's all I'm saying.'

'Easier said than done.'

'Ideally, we want to take the image from the brooch camera and the audio from the phone, and sync them together to give the full picture of what's going on. You've got the bag as well, but I don't think we should rely on that.'

'But they're all recording OK?'

'Yup. Audio and video wirelessly transmitted and captured right here.'

Laura patted the laptop.

Roger stood up and headed for the kitchen.

'I'll put the kettle on.'

When he'd left the room, Laura said more quietly: 'We should have an alert word, too.'

'A what?'

'A word you can use to raise the alarm, to drop into conversation without him realising. Something innocuous that won't raise his suspicions.'

'If it gets to that stage, it'll probably be too late anyway.'

'But we need a way for you to tell us if you're in trouble – if you need help. And when we hear the word, or if you text it to your dad, all bets are off and we come to get you out.'

'What are you going to do, kick the door down?'

'Maybe,' Laura said. 'Or call the police.'

Sarah shook her head.

'No. Not the police.'

'You can't just rule it out. What if things go wrong, or he gets violent, or something?'

'Let me worry about that.'

'Bollocks!' Laura said, throwing her hands in the air. 'That's just bollocks, and you know it.'

'No police,' Sarah said again.

'Why?'

'You know why.'

Laura couldn't hide her exasperation.

'This thing of yours, this plan, it could easily get to the point of no return. As in, it could go seriously wrong if he figures out what's going on.'

'I think we all know that already,' Sarah said quietly.

'I mean it could go *catastrophically* fucking wrong. You realise that, don't you?'

Sarah looked down at the floor.

'Yes. I know.'

Laura lowered her voice.

'He might try to rape you. He might do anything.'

'He has to be confronted.'

'And if the really bad stuff happens, if things go wrong, it's going to be very hard to explain why you went to his house willingly, on a Saturday evening, when his wife wasn't there. You know what I'm talking about, don't you?'

'Yes.'

'You know how risky this is?'

Sarah nodded again but couldn't speak. She had thought of little else since coming up with the plan.

'Christ,' Laura said. 'Come here.'

She went to her friend and put her arms around her. The two of them stood like that, in the middle of Sarah's lounge, no words between them. Each trying to comfort the other, and themselves.

'I'm sorry,' Laura said finally. 'But I don't like the idea of you going to that bastard's house, alone with no one to back you up. For the third time of asking, I'm now going to try and talk you out of this mad plan. Because it *is* totally mad.'

Sarah hugged her back.

'I know, but that's what I'm relying on. If it wasn't a bit crazy, he'd see it coming from a mile away.'

'Sometimes I think you're even more pig-headed than me.'

'No chance.'

'We should think of an alert phrase, though. It needs to be something unusual enough that you won't use it in normal conversation. So we'll know what it means when we hear it.'

'Such as?'

Laura's eyes lit on the cheap new throwaway phones that Sarah had bought for Laura and her dad to use. Both charging on a side table.

'How about something to do with your phone? Then I'll know you want to make a call, but can't. You could use the words "brand new phone" in that order.'

Roger came back into the lounge, holding three steaming mugs of tea.

'I suppose that's as good a phrase as any,' she said. 'What happens if I say it?'

Roger frowned. 'If we hear you're in trouble, I drive straight to the house and hammer on the door until he lets me in. I'll be waiting down the road in the pub car park – I can be at his house in two minutes from there.'

Laura put her hand up.

'Hang on a minute, if she gives the alert phrase our rescue plan is that you're going to *knock on the door*? What if he just ignores you?'

'Have you got a better idea?' Roger said.

'Take a sledgehammer to it. Kick it in.'

Sarah shook her head.

'It's solid oak, two inches thick. No one's smashing the front door down.'

'OK,' Laura said, 'but then what's the point of having an alert phrase if we can't come in and get you?'

'Let's just hope it doesn't come to that. Stick to the plan: you call me on the mobile at exactly 8.10, you tell me Harry has fallen down the stairs and you're in an ambulance on the way to hospital. You tell me that Dad's on his way to pick me up.'

'Why 8.10 again?'

'The timing is important: I'll arrive at 7.30 so it will give me forty minutes to get what I need.'

'A lot of shit could go wrong in forty minutes.'

'I know that. So if you hear me say the words "brand new phone" at any point, you just call my mobile straight away, give me the spiel about Harry and the ambulance, and we stop it right there.'

'What if you can't answer?'

'Don't worry. I'll keep it within arm's reach the whole time.'

75

They sat at the kitchen table, the three of them. With an hour until the allotted meeting time, everything was in place. Laura had the laptop in front of her, showing the live video and audio feeds on its screen, a phone connected via USB and ready to record everything. Her dad had his coat and shoes on, car keys in hand, looking exactly like what he was: a harmless retiree in his mid-sixties. Sarah was in a smart jacket, blouse and long skirt that she had not taken out of the cupboard for months. Where before the jacket had fitted just about right, now there seemed to be room to spare. The consequence of barely eating for weeks on end, she supposed. A new crystal brooch decorated one side of the jacket, over her heart.

'You look fab, honey,' Laura said, taking her friend's hands in hers.

'Thanks,' Sarah said.

'I wish I could come with you. But since you won't let me, I've got something else for your handbag. A bit of insurance.'

'I'll be fine.'

'Bollocks to being fine,' Laura said. She reached into her pocket and pulled out a slim rectangle of black plastic, pressing a button at one end. A wicked four-inch blade sprang out of the handle, snapping into place.

'Bloody hell,' Sarah breathed. 'A flick knife?'

'It used to be my brother's. I nicked it off him one day when we were kids, and I've kept it ever since.'

'Aren't they illegal?'

Laura raised an eyebrow.

'I think we're a bit beyond that, aren't we?'

She retracted the blade back into the handle and dropped it into the handbag.

'Thanks,' Sarah said. 'Have you both got your throwaway phones switched on and ready?'

They held up the cheap pay-as-you go handsets.

'Why do we need these again?' Laura said.

'Because if it all goes wrong, I'll be able to say you weren't involved and had nothing to do with any of it – and there will be no mobile phone data to contradict me. I've got those numbers if I need them, but whatever happens, tomorrow both these phones are going into the Thames, never to be seen again.'

'I don't like the idea of it going wrong.'

'It's not going to go wrong, Loz.'

Laura nodded and gave her a tight smile.

'Good,' Sarah said. 'So are we all ready? Everyone know what they have to do?'

'Are *you* ready?' her dad said.

'Not really, but if we waited until we were ready we'd never get anywhere, would we?'

'And you're sure, you're absolutely sure, that you want to go through with this?'

She stood up.

'Yes, I'm sure.' She picked up her handbag. 'Let's go.'

76

Sarah walked carefully up the drive of Lovelock's six-bedroom detached house, her heels crunching on the gravel. She was grateful for the way her jacket now hung off her thinner frame. It left more space for the items concealed beneath her blouse. Her hair was pinned up and she carried the brand new handbag in her left hand. It was slightly bigger than she would have chosen for herself and didn't quite go with the rest of the outfit, but she didn't think a man like Alan Lovelock would notice.

A security light clicked on as she approached, bathing the top of the drive in a bright halogen light. The house behind was a huge shadowy mass, looming up out of the cold November night. The only other light she could see was glowing faintly in one of the long bay windows – the rest of the house was in darkness.

It was the second time she had been here in a matter of weeks. That first time, at Lovelock's annual charity fundraising party, the place had been loud with chatter and music and Sarah had been hopeful that her invitation was a prelude to good news for her job and her career prospects. *How we delude ourselves*, she thought as she approached the front door. She was grateful for one thing at least: the party was where she had met Gillian Arnold. A woman with whom she had a great deal in common.

Tonight would be different. This time, the house would not be full of guests. No safety in numbers. No witnesses to keep his behaviour in check. She wouldn't have a colleague by her side, riding shotgun. In fact, she was breaking the Rules so completely that she thought she'd probably broken new ones that they hadn't even thought up yet. She would be alone with Love-lock behind a closed door, he would likely be drunk, and on his home turf. If Marie had known what she was about to do she would have begged her, pleaded with her, to walk away. Though of course they were no longer on speaking terms.

Marie didn't know, anyway. And that was the way it had to be.

She looked up and saw the little CCTV camera in its discreet housing above the front door, nestled among the ivy. Its tiny red light, unblinking in the shadows, indicating the camera was live and filming everyone who came up the drive. *This will have to be the performance of a lifetime*, she reminded herself.

Her heels clicked on polished flagstones as she walked up the broad steps that rose to the door, which was flanked on either side by large Roman-style pillars. She raised a hand to the brass button of the doorbell –

And stopped. Stood on the broad welcome mat, her finger inches from the bell. Two seconds, five seconds. Ten.

Last chance to turn back. You don't have to go into the lion's den. You could just walk away now. What's the worst he could do?

Last chance.

She said a silent prayer and pressed the doorbell.

77

Lovelock greeted her with a slow smile, showing her through to the lounge and gesturing to the sofa. He wore brown corduroy trousers and a cravat tucked into an open-necked white shirt, belly straining over his belt buckle. It was only 7.30 but his cheeks already had the red-vein flush of alcohol. Logs blazed and crackled in the huge fireplace, and a low burble of discordant jazz played out of speakers in the oak-beamed ceiling, the music so low it was almost inaudible. Thick fabric curtains, closed against the dark November night, made the room feel as if it was hermetically sealed off from the outside world.

Sarah had never felt so alone in her life. She told herself to be calm, took slow breaths in and out to calm her racing heart.

Lovelock looked her up and down with approval.

'Gin and tonic, isn't it?'

'Please.'

He busied himself at a large drinks cabinet before handing her a large cut-glass tumbler filled almost to the brim.

'Thanks.'

Sarah sat down on the deep leather sofa, shoes sinking into the thick cream carpet, placing her mobile phone carefully on the coffee table in between herself and Lovelock's large glass of whisky. She put her handbag next to it. The bag's flat base meant it stood upright on the table, and she lined it up so one end was positioned directly facing the leather armchair opposite her. She was gambling on the assumption that he would sit there first, then move across to sit next to her on the sofa before too long. *Of course he would.*

'So,' she said. 'Here we are.'

Bringing over his own drink, Lovelock sank down in the leather armchair, as predicted, and crossed his legs.

'Indeed.'

'Is it just the two of us?'

'Caroline's away visiting her mother as I told you and I've sent the cook away.' He stretched an arm across the back of the chair. 'So it's just us.'

Sarah fought the urge to adjust the position of the bag on the table. *What was the camera's field of view? Sixty degrees?* She couldn't remember what Mikhail had said, but she didn't dare touch it in case it was too obvious.

'The house is certainly quieter than the last time I was here.'

'The party? Yes. A shame that it was rather tainted at the end by an unexpected guest.'

He paused, placing his palms together as if in prayer. 'First of all, Sarah, please let me say something.'

She shifted in her seat.

'OK.'

'I want to apologise for my behaviour.'

It was the last thing she expected. She had never heard him apologise to anyone before, for anything.

'Apologise?'

'The other day I let myself get a little . . . carried away.'

That's one way of spinning it, Sarah thought.

'It doesn't matter,' she said.

'Oh, but it does. I wanted to be sure that you didn't take things the wrong way.'

'It's fine, Alan.'

'Are you sure?'

'Yes.'

'Wonderful.' He smiled and leaned back in the big armchair. 'So, my girl. What shall we talk about?'

She took a sip of her drink. There was so much gin in it that she could barely taste the tonic or lemon. *Was there another taste in there as well? Something in the background, masked by the gin?*

'Whatever you want, Alan.'

'How about the Boston trip – have you decided whether you can make it?'

'Actually, I've been thinking about it and I've decided –'

The doorbell rang, a two-tone clang of bells echoing through the large entrance hall.

Sarah froze, panic etched on her face.

'Who's that?' she said in a low whisper. 'I thought you'd arranged to be left totally alone to write, this weekend?'

Lovelock held up a calming hand.

'Don't worry, I'll get rid of whoever it is.'

Sarah covered her mouth.

'Oh God, what if it's Nick?'

'Does he know you're here?'

'No. At least . . . I don't think so.'

Lovelock gave her a slow smile.

'Glad to hear it.' He put his drink down on the low, glass-topped table and got to his feet. 'Stay there. Whoever it is, I'll get rid of them.'

He went out into the hall. Sarah heard the front door open for a few heartbeats, a brief exchange of words and then the door slammed shut again. The metallic *click* of a lock slotting into place then a door chain being replaced. A moment later Lovelock reappeared holding a shoebox-sized parcel. He tossed it onto a side table and – ignoring the armchair he had previously occupied – sat down on the sofa next to Sarah.

'Don't worry – not your hubby checking up on you. A courier.'

Sarah sat back, crossing her legs and smoothing her long skirt out over her knees. One shoe tapping nervously.

'Anything important?'

'Just Caroline's daily delivery. Honestly, I've no idea how she filled her days before Internet shopping was invented.' He picked up his whisky again. 'Where does hubby think you are, anyway?'

'He's not ... we're having a little bit of time apart at the moment.'

Lovelock smiled, showing small, yellowing teeth.

'Really? Taking a break, are you?'

'Something like that.'

'Probably wise.'

She stared into her drink, steeling herself against the intense discomfort of revealing such personal details to this man. But she had to speak openly, let her guard down – so that when the time came, he would do the same.

'He took himself off again,' she said. 'Went to stay with some-one. He said he was trying to find himself, whatever that means.'

'A woman?'

'Sorry?'

'He went to stay with a woman?'

'Yes. He met her at an audition last year.'

'A shame,' he said, without conviction. 'You must be lonely, on your own.'

'It's tough, with the kids and everything else going on. But it's thinking time for us both, so we can get a few things sorted out. Work out what happens next.'

'And what do you want to happen next?'

Sarah took another sip of her drink, the gin sharp on her tongue. She glanced at the clock over the aquarium: 7.42. Twenty-eight minutes left.

Bait the trap. Do it now.

'I've decided that I'm prepared to do what I have to do,' she said, her tone heavy with resignation. 'And I want to go to Boston with you. The two of us.'

78

'Ah!' He clapped his hands together. 'You've decided to join me after all. Marvellous.'

'I want to meet the Atholl Sanders people, I want to help you win this grant and work with you on the project.'

'So you've finally come around to my point of view. I knew you would, in the end! It really is most gratifying, Sarah.'

'I understand the situation. Like I said: I'm prepared to do what I have to do.'

'Go with the flow?'

'Yes.'

His grin was as wide as she'd ever seen it, a gaping rictus of victory. Sarah suppressed a shudder.

'That's my girl,' he said.

She swallowed hard, searching for the right words.

'You said it would be good for my career, to meet the funders and develop some contacts at the foundation.'

He edged closer to her, draping one long arm along the back of the sofa.

'Undoubtedly. And besides all that, we're going to have *such* fun, you and me. I'll tell Jocelyn first thing Monday morning to get you a flight booked and have the hotel booking amended. We'll get adjoining rooms, shall we?'

She felt herself nodding, as if on autopilot.

'I don't know Boston at all.'

'Oh, it's an absolutely terrific city.' He leaned forward. 'It will be my pleasure to give you an intimate guided tour.'

'Great.'

He studied her, a look of immense satisfaction on his face, and clapped his hands again.

'I'm *so* pleased that you've come around to the idea, Sarah. It'll be a wonderful trip.' He picked up his glass and clinked it against hers. 'Cheers.'

'Cheers,' Sarah said in return.

Now close the deal. Get what you came here for.

'I'm looking forward to seeing Boston,' she said, taking another small sip of her drink. It was strong enough to make her wince.

'Oh, you'll love it. There's a conference in Chicago in February that you should come to, as well. I'll be able to introduce you to some really rather fascinating members of the American academy. Have you been to Chicago?'

'I've not been to America at all, Alan. Just never had the chance.'

'Well,' he said, toasting her again with his raised glass, 'now you shall, my dear.'

Keep him talking.

'What are the dates?'

'Four weeks from now. BA business class – naturally – I'll have Jocelyn send you all the details. Boston in January is something special, I can tell you.'

'I'll have to read up on the city.'

'Oh don't you worry about that,' he said, giving a mock bow. 'I will be your guide. I'll show you *everything* worth seeing.'

Sarah raised the glass to her lips again and took a small sip.

'So I just wanted to ask you about the – the terms of the arrangement.'

His smile faded.

'Terms? How do you mean?'

You know exactly what I mean, she thought, remembering his words from just a few days ago.

Once a week, every week, you'll come to my office. We'll lock the door, I'll sit back and you'll get down on your knees and go to work. Or on your back. Perhaps on your front. Perhaps all three.

'I mean what happens after tonight?' she said, choosing her words carefully. 'You spoke about us having a weekly arrangement? With the changes in the department, I mean.'

'Slow down, Sarah. You've lost me.'

She leaned a little closer to him, shifting her body so that she was facing him.

Go on. Say it.

'The restructure in the department. You said some people were going to lose their jobs, and my name was near the top of the hit list.'

Lovelock was close enough for her to smell the stale tang of whisky on his breath.

'There are some tough decisions coming, that's a fact.'

'You said my job was at risk.'

'That's true. As are others.'

'But there was one thing I could do to avoid the chop.' Their conversation about the scarred man was burned into her brain. 'And for you to – to keep certain things to yourself, rather than telling the police.'

He tossed the rest of his whisky back in one gulp and went over to the drinks cabinet for a refill. Sarah watched him: an inch of whisky and an inch of water, each from identical crystal decanters. He returned to the sofa, unfastening the second button of his white linen shirt.

'We don't need to talk about these things now, do we? How about we discuss it . . . later. Afterwards?'

'If it's all the same to you, I'd like to talk about it now.'

A flash of anger crossed his face and she thought he was about to refuse again. But then his frown lifted.

'Of course, why not.' He crossed his legs towards her, leaning into the sofa so their legs were almost touching. 'What is it that you'd like to know?'

79

'I want to know if my job will be safe,' Sarah said.

'Are any of our jobs truly safe?'

'You know what I mean, Alan. You told me in your office, you made it very clear.'

'It is good to be clear, is it not? *A matter that becomes clear ceases to concern us.*'

'What?'

'Friedrich Nietzsche.'

'Remember you told me that once we start this new arrangement, you'll make sure I'm not made redundant in the restructure. That the threat disappears if we have sex.'

'Are you hungry?' he said abruptly.

'I'm sorry?'

'I've got a couple of juicy rib-eye steaks and a stunning bottle of '91 Mouton Rothschild open and breathing. Just let me know when you're getting hungry.'

Get him back on track.

She willed him to say it, to repeat the words he'd spoken to her just a few days ago. The clock on the wall said 7.51. Nineteen minutes before Laura called her mobile with the prearranged message that would be her signal to escape.

'I'd rather get things straight between us, first. If we start the new arrangement tonight, just like you told me, then what?'

She pictured herself sitting in a meeting room with Peter Moran, the school manager, the dean and the head of HR, as she played them the recording of this conversation. The looks on their faces as they understood what it meant: first disbelief, then denial. Followed swiftly by panic. That look, that moment, might go some way to balancing out the nightmare she'd had to live with for the last two years.

Lovelock leaned back, running a hand over his balding pate.

'Want my signature in blood, do you?'

'I just want to make sure we're on the same page. I want to hear you say it.'

'Say what, exactly?'

'That I can keep hold of my job if I agree to the arrangement. If I agree to sleep with you.'

Say it, just once. That's all I need.

He smiled. A long, lazy smile that didn't reach his eyes.

'I love your outfit, by the way.'

Sarah was momentarily thrown by the change of direction.

'Thanks.'

'And I love what you've done with your hair and make-up. Can't recall ever seeing you look so good.'

She made herself smile back.

'Just trying to make the effort. Show willing.'

'There's only one problem, Sarah.'

She shifted uncomfortably in her seat.

'Problem?'

'I'm afraid so, yes.'

She felt a tingle of fear in her stomach.

Abruptly, Lovelock stood up and walked out of the room into the hallway. A moment of silence, then she heard the heavy metallic *thunk* of a deadbolt being shot home. Then another.

The front door. He's bolting the front door.

He came back into the lounge, pocketing a set of keys. Closing the door behind him, he sat down again on the sofa beside her.

'There. That's better.'

Sarah could feel her heart thudding against her ribcage.

You're trapped now.

'What's the matter, Alan?'

His greedy eyes ran over her.

'Here's the thing, Sarah. You've done a wonderful job with your make-up, your hair, your outfit, your shoes, your perfume. It's all absolutely lovely.' He stared at her a moment longer. 'The only problem is, I don't believe you.'

80

Sarah stared back at him.

'I don't understand.'

'It's simple, really.' He gestured at her blouse with a wave of his hand. 'I don't believe you'd come here all dolled up with your nice outfit and your best shoes and your most expensive perfume. I was fully expecting you to cancel at the last minute, make some excuse that one of your little brats had a sniffle, something along those lines. I didn't believe you'd come – and I certainly didn't think you'd come looking like this.'

'It's what we agreed.'

He shook his head.

'You gave in too easily. *Far* too easily. I think, deep down, in your heart of hearts, you think you're above it all. You think you're too good, too virtuous, to have to do something like this.'

Sarah felt the flutters of panic taking flight in her chest, Laura's words of warning echoing inside her mind: *This plan could go seriously wrong if he figures out what's going on. As in, catastrophically fucking wrong.*

The clock on the wall said 7.53. Twenty-three minutes since she had arrived, and still seventeen to go before Laura's rescuing call.

Seventeen minutes is going to be too long. Far too long.

'Too good for what, Alan? I don't understand what you're talking about.'

'The truth is that we all have to make sacrifices. All of us are sinners, Sarah. All of us. Marlowe said it himself: *'If we say that we have no sin, we deceive ourselves.'*

'You've got it wrong, you're –'

He put a finger to his lips. His eyes gleamed with a strange intensity, his pupils reduced to tiny black pinpricks.

'Shush now.'

Get out. Use the alert word now. Just get out.

As she opened her mouth to speak, he snatched up a black remote control from the table and hit a button. The jazz music coming from the ceiling speakers rose and swelled until it was almost deafening, an onslaught of trumpets and saxophones.

'What are you doing?' She could barely hear her own voice against the noise.

He grabbed her mobile from the coffee table, made the screen come to life and shifted over to sit down heavily on the sofa next to her. He took hold of her right hand, gripping the thumb, and pressed it against the Sony Xperia's home button. Registering her thumbprint, the phone unlocked. She tried to grab it from him but he pushed her hand away, studying the screen. He found what he was looking for and showed it to her.

The recording app was live, the digital counter showing twenty-five minutes elapsed. He hit the *end* button and the counter stopped. He moved right up close and shouted into her ear.

'What were you planning to do with this recording?'

Sarah's heart was slamming so hard against her ribcage she could barely speak.

'Nothing.'

'Nothing useful, anyway,' he shouted over the music.

She shook her head.

He went into the app's file manager and erased the recording of their conversation.

'No matter. Gone now.'

He switched the phone off and walked to the tropical fish tank, holding it over the water.

'Alan, don't!' Remembering the alert phrase again, she shouted: 'It's my brand new phone!'

He shrugged and dropped the phone into the fish tank.

'Oops,' he said, as it sank rapidly to the bottom.

Had Laura even been able to make out her words, against this noise? It didn't seem likely.

Lovelock came back to the table and picked up her handbag, going through its contents and feeling the lining. He studied the flick knife before putting it into his trouser pocket, then returned his attention to the bag, looking closely at what appeared to be a decorative stud at one end, studying it from different angles. Finally he raised an eyebrow and nodded slowly to himself.

He dropped the bag and its contents into the fish tank before sitting down next to her again.

'Those little spy cameras are amazing, aren't they? Virtually invisible if you don't know what you're looking for. Can't hear me or see me now, can they? Your friends? Can't hear you either.'

One camera left. One last chance to make this work.

'Alan, please,' she shouted over the swooping, lurching cacophony of jazz music. 'Let's just talk.'

'Stand up.'

'Why?'

'Just do as you're told, my dear.'

She stood up, taking a step away from him as she did so.

He studied her, his head on one side. Beads of sweat had appeared on his forehead.

'Turn around. Slowly.'

She did as she was told, eyes searching the room for something she could use as a weapon. A poker by the fire. A vase on the mantelpiece. She finished her circle and faced him again.

There was a look of triumph on his face.

'I knew it,' he said slowly. 'It's the brooch, isn't it? It doesn't quite work with the rest of your outfit. Almost, but not quite.'

'It was my mother's,' Sarah said. The lie didn't sound convincing, even to her own ears.

'Why would you ruin a lovely smart jacket with a fussy little thing like that?' He gestured with his hand. 'Take it off.'

'I don't want to dam—'

'Take it off!' he shouted.

She began fumbling with the brooch, trying to unclasp it with shaking fingers, knowing that she couldn't, that it would be the final confirmation of her motive in coming here tonight.

'It's stuck, I can't get it off.' Her voice was cracking. 'I'll damage the jacket. Please, Alan.'

He stepped up to her and grabbed the little silver brooch, ripping it from her lapel, tearing a hole in the fabric. Held it in his hand for a moment, studying it close up. A tiny black wire trailed from the brooch, back into her jacket. He tugged on it, pulling her towards him.

'Just as I thought: another bloody camera.' He produced the flick knife from his pocket, snapping out the blade. Four inches of wickedly sharp steel tapered to a needle point. 'Enough of this nonsense.'

Sarah's mind scrambled for options, all the while trying to fight the ball of fear at the base of her throat. She shot a glance at the clock on the wall: 7.56.

But that's no help: you can't receive Laura's call anymore.

'Alan, please.'

He ignored her, using the flick knife to cut through the wire attached to the brooch. He tossed the hidden camera into the fire, where it was instantly lost among the flames.

He pointed the knife at her, firelight glinting off the polished steel blade.

'Now then. What other concealed devices am I going to find, you devious little bitch?'

'Nothing, Alan. I swear!'

'Hmm. Unfortunately, there has been rather a breakdown of trust, hasn't there? So you leave me no choice.' He took a step towards her, towering over her as he hooked a finger into the new hole in her jacket. 'You're going to have to take it all off. Everything.'

81

She put her arms across her chest and took a step back.

'What do you mean?'

'You know very well what I mean. Strip, right now.'

'No,' Sarah said.

'I beg your pardon?'

'I said no. I won't do it.'

'You've misunderstood, my dear. It wasn't a request: it was an instruction.' He took his mobile out of his pocket. 'If you're unable to comply I will simply have to call my friend Detective Inspector Rayner and tell her what I just remembered about our Russian friend. I've got all her numbers stored.'

Sarah felt a wave of cold panic washing through her.

Lovelock gestured towards her with the knife.

'I won't ask you again.'

She stared at him a moment longer, letting the anger build, then kicked off her shoes. Eased her jacket off her shoulders. Pulled her blouse over her head and then reached down and unzipped the back of her skirt, letting it fall to the floor. She stood in front of him, cheeks burning, in nothing but her bra, pants and tights.

She felt more vulnerable and alone than she had ever done in her life.

Lovelock regarded her with hungry eyes, a flush of blood reddening the skin of his neck and face.

'Turn around again.'

A slim wireless transmitter and power pack was clipped to the back of her bra, secured in place with a length of thin black duct tape wound around her abdomen. He unclipped the tiny electronic devices and threw them, too, into the fire. Finally satisfied that he was no longer being recorded, he picked up the black remote control and killed the jazz music.

The silence was suddenly all around them.

She backed away from him, around the side of the sofa. He followed her. She took another step back, moving so that he was no longer between her and the door out into the hall.

'And the rest,' he said, his voice thick now. 'The rest of your clothes.'

'No. That's all there was. There's nothing else to find.'

'DO AS YOU'RE DAMN WELL TOLD!' he roared.

She flinched backwards and took off her tights, moving another half-step away from him as she rolled them down to her ankles and stepped out of them.

He rubbed a hand over the stubble on his jaw.

'And the rest,' he said again. His voice was breathy and hoarse now, a bead of sweat running down his cheek.

She unclipped her bra and let it fall to the floor, then her pants, using her arms to cover her nakedness.

This is it. This is what Laura warned you about.

Blushing so deep she could feel her face burning, there was one overriding thought pushing all the shame and fury and hatred aside – one animal instinct ringing in her head. *Get out of this room and find a door you can lock behind you. Put a barrier between him and you. Then you can worry about the next thing, and the one after that.*

Because this is how it ends.

He took a slow step towards her, his right hand reaching for her breasts.

She dodged away from his grasp, and ran.

82

The air of the hallway was cold against her naked skin. She instinctively turned to the right, running for the stairs and hitting a set of light switches on the way, bathing the wide staircase in light.

Find a door you can lock.

She took the stairs two at a time, fear forcing her on as she heard his heavy tread behind her. At the top was a large landing with five doors and corridors left and right. Directly across the landing was an open door, a tiled floor and the side of a bath just visible. She bolted for it, praying that there would be a lock.

She threw herself into the bathroom and slammed the door behind her. To her huge relief she saw a silver lock beneath the handle, and turned it to slot the lock home. Standing, panting, with both palms against the door as if she could hold it there through her strength alone.

Safe. For now.

The only thing she was still wearing was her watch. It was 7.59. She did a quick calculation in her head, wondering whether this door and its lock would be able to withstand him.

Heavy footsteps reached the door and the handle turned as Lovelock tried it from the other side. The door stayed shut. Sarah held her breath, expecting him to start hammering on it, but instead his footsteps retreated away across the landing. Her eyes scanned the bathroom wildly, looking for something with which she could cover up. There was a pile of large white bath towels on a wooden chest in the corner, and she grabbed one, wrapping it around herself.

What else? Escape route? The row of small windows were locked shut, the key nowhere in sight. Too small to fit through, anyway.

Weapon? She pulled open the bathroom cabinet, praying that there might be razor blades inside, or scissors, or *something*. No such luck. Instead she snatched up one of the electric toothbrushes and pulled off the brush head, leaving only an inch-long spine of steel. It would penetrate flesh if wielded with enough force.

The heavy footsteps returned, stopping on the other side of the bathroom door. She turned to face it, quickly checking her watch again. One minute past eight o'clock, just over thirty minutes since she had sat down in his lounge. She felt as if she had aged ten years.

There was nothing but silence from the other side of the door. Silence throughout the house.

She backed into the corner of the bathroom, holding her makeshift weapon down by her side. Fighting back the undercurrent of panic that was creeping back in to replace the little beat of reassurance when she had turned the door lock. Only a small spine of metal, but it was all that stood between her and him.

As she stared at it, the door lock began to turn.

Before she could react, before she could even move, the lock clicked and the door swung open.

Lovelock filled the doorway, a long screwdriver in one hand, whisky glass in the other. He leaned against the frame and gestured at her with the screwdriver. It was almost a foot long and tapered to a shiny blade.

'Easy enough to open up what is locked,' he said, 'if you have the right tools.'

'Don't come any closer,' she said, trying to keep her voice level.

'So, you came to my house, tried to trick me, tried to entrap me with a recording. It was an interesting idea, a valiant effort. Clearly, I underestimated you, my dear.'

'I think you've been underestimating women all your life.'

His face turned hard.

'But you failed. And now it's time for you to start making amends. What's it going to be? Are you going to play the game like a big girl?'

She clutched the towel more tightly around her.

'Just let me leave. I promise I won't tell anyone what's happened tonight.'

He tutted and shook his head.

'No. I don't think so. I think we're a bit past shaking hands and calling it quits, my dear. A *long* way past. Time to prove whether you're more than just the little housewife playing at academia.'

'Please, Alan.' She hated hearing the pleading tone in her voice. 'Don't do this.'

'I like to hear you beg,' he said, his eyes running up and down her. 'Now take the towel off.'

'No.'

'I'll tell you what,' he said, fumbling for his belt. 'If you're really, *really* good in bed tonight, I might decide not flush your career down the lavatory.'

'You can't do to me what you did to Gillian Arnold.'

'On the contrary, my dear: I can. I win, you lose. That is how tonight's game ends.'

She stared at him for a long moment, her father's words echoing through her mind.

The third option is the toughest, Sarah.

'So, I'm going to ask you one more time, for the last time.' He blinked once, twice and took another deep slug of his whisky, emptying the glass. His face was shiny with sweat. 'What's it going to be?'

She stood, drawing herself up to her full height, gripping her makeshift weapon in a white-knuckled hand. Feeling all of the surrender drain out of her, all the reason, and logic and common sense, all the worry and concern. Drawing on all of the frustration and anger of the last year, drinking deep of all the fears that had kept her awake for months on end, letting the emotion rage through her body and focusing it all on this man, this man who had kept his true self hidden from so many people, until he had climbed to the top of his profession.

It had to stop, one way or the other.

She felt the rage boiling in her veins, the blood pounding in her neck. Marie's words coming back to her. *If you go to war with him, only one of you will be left standing at the end of it.*

'This is where it ends, Alan. You want my answer? Here it is.' She brandished the steel point in her right hand, pointing it towards him. 'You can go to hell.'

83

Sarah finished marking the paper and moved on to the next one. She had left the lights off and the door closed, so the office was gloomy and only half-lit from the window's weak winter light. But this was how she liked it now. Quiet. Alone. Almost invisible. *Keep your head down, don't cause any ructions, just get on with the job for as long as possible.*

She had come to terms with what she had done and she was ready to face the consequences when the time came. She had done her best, and that was all anyone could do, wasn't it? She had made a choice, and she would have to live with it.

It was as simple – and as complicated – as that.

There was a small sense of relief that a decision had been made, a path chosen, that she had shaken off the paralysis of doubt and made a choice. Perhaps the only choice.

She stood up and went to the window. It was one of those overcast December days when it never seemed to get light properly, heavy grey clouds low in the sky. She'd grown to love this view over the two years she'd occupied the little room, a second-floor office at the end of the building, looking across the parkland campus towards the lake and the clock tower. There were students wandering to lectures, perhaps heading towards the union building for an early lunch, some looking as if they had just crawled out of bed.

It would be so nice to be there again, she thought. Eighteen years old, no responsibilities, no expectations on you to do anything apart from what you felt like from one day to the next. In charge of your own destiny, free from all the things that gradually encumbered adults as they grew older. She wondered if she would make the same choices, if she had her time again. If she knew those choices would bring her to this room, this place, this situation. This turning point in her life.

It was an easy question to answer now.

At the turning circle in front of the building, someone – most likely a member of the rugby club, she thought – had climbed up the statue again and placed a bright yellow Afro wig on Neptune's head and a wastepaper bin over his trident. Another job for Mr Jennings, the porter.

She wasn't sure how long she stood there. She was about to go back to her marking when a car appeared from behind the row of trees and turned into the arts faculty car park. An unremarkable saloon car, with a man and a woman in the front. It was followed by a police van with the words 'Scientific Support Unit' on its side. They pulled to a stop in front of the statue, directly in front of the faculty building's main entrance. Two uniformed officers got out of the van and the two detectives Sarah recognised as DI Rayner and DS Neal emerged from the unmarked saloon.

The figures all gathered around DI Rayner for a brief conversation, heads leaning towards her as she spoke to them.

Sarah studied them. She tried to summon up some feeling but there was nothing – not fear or despair, not anger, not sadness. It was as if all the emotions had been scoured out of her, leaving her blank and empty and exhausted.

What would be, would be.

After a minute or so, the four police officers turned and headed into the main building, with DI Rayner in the lead. They disappeared from Sarah's sight.

She went back to her desk.

Quickly, she stacked the essay she had been marking in the pile with the others, placing all the papers together in a desk drawer before locking it and putting the key in her pocket. She capped her pen and turned off her PC, went to the hook by the door and put her jacket on, then sat back down at her desk, and waited.

The police were here again. They were here in numbers.

And this time, she thought, they would be making an arrest.

FOUR WEEKS LATER

84

Sarah sat back in her seat, trying to get comfortable. They were packed in tight, her and the others, these strangers who surrounded her.

Grace and Harry were far away now. She couldn't remember the last time she had spent more than a few nights away from them. The thought of her children made her feel weak and strong at the same time, a dizzying mix of emotions that left her terrified and exhilarated, now more than ever. She would tear down mountains for them, she would stand up against any danger and shield them with her own body, until she had nothing left to give. She was more proud of them than she was of anything in the world.

She hoped that one day they would know that.

It had been a crazy day, waking early in an unfamiliar bed, without her children, away from home. Waiting in endless queues, and then more queues, and security everywhere. Uniforms and radios, metal detectors and pat-downs and weapon searches. Then more waiting and walking and standing in line.

She would need to get used to it. This was the path she had chosen, the choice she had made with one phone call, and she would have to cope with the consequences. That was just how life was.

She thought back to how she'd been as a teenager. What would that seventeen-year-old think, if she could see her older self now? She would be shaking her head in disbelief – never in a million years would she have thought her path would lead her here, to this.

The nerves were there again, just below the surface. That was only natural, she supposed: she was going to a strange place and didn't really know what would be waiting for her at the end of the journey, more importantly, *who* would be waiting for her.

What would they be like? Would she cope? Could she do this? Was she tough enough to see it through?

There were so many unanswered questions.

But she knew she would do it. For the simple reason that she had to. Because what other choice was there?

Should probably try to get some sleep, she thought. *This is going to be a long day.*

She closed her eyes for a moment, trying to shut out the strangers packed in around her. Life had become complicated in the last couple of weeks – there was a lot to think about, a lot to stay on top of. But deep down in her heart, in her gut, she felt like she was going to be all right. She could make it. She could do this.

As long as she remembered the Rules.

The *new* Rules.

85

And just like before, the new Rules were simple enough.

Never talk about the night at Lovelock's house. Because according to everyone apart from him, it had never happened.

Never mention the custom-mixed cocktail of drugs that Sarah had slipped into his whisky when he went to answer the door a few minutes after she arrived.

Never refer to the 'courier' who had distracted him for those vital seconds – a young Russian named Mikhail with a particular talent for computer hacking.

Never talk about what Mikhail had added to the hard drive of Lovelock's computer that night.

The grey-haired lady across the aisle from Sarah was engrossed in a copy of the *Daily Mail*. The front-page picture was a familiar face, snapped as he was led out of the arts faculty building in handcuffs. He looked like he'd been caught off-guard, his mouth half-open, his face a mixture of fury and alarm as he saw the long-lens photographer a second too late.

Alongside the picture there was a headline in heavy black capitals, 'BBC SACKS STAR PROF IN PAEDO PROBE'.

Sarah tilted her head to read the first paragraphs of the story.

TV academic Alan Lovelock has been dropped by the BBC after detectives launched a wide-ranging child porn investigation.

Professor Lovelock, 56, was the star of BBC1 show Undiscovered History *and patron of a number of children's charities. The BBC has confirmed that the rest of the current series will be pulled from schedules and filming of the new series has been halted indefinitely.*

A university spokesman confirmed Lovelock had been suspended from his position with immediate effect pending the outcome of criminal proceedings.

The story was everywhere, and the tabloid attack dogs were baying for blood. Lovelock was a combination of all the things they hated the most: an ivory tower academic, a BBC luvvie, and a millionaire socialist. They scented blood and wouldn't be satisfied until his reputation was smashed beyond repair. With a twinge of irony, Sarah noticed that the byline on the front-page story was Ollie Bailey – the journalist who had first given her the idea. A random question tossed into a car park conversation: *'Is it true that he's been picked up as part of Operation Yewtree?'* The police operation that had uncovered a string of high-profile paedophiles and sexual predators from Jimmy Savile onwards.

The grey-haired lady caught Sarah's eye as they both read. She tutted and shook her head.

'Disgusting, isn't it? Mind you, I always thought there was something not quite right about that fellow. Didn't you?'

Sarah shrugged.

'I never really watched his show.'

'No smoke without fire, trust me.' She turned to a double-page spread inside the paper, pictures of police officers carrying box after box of personal belongings out of Lovelock's house, and the same at the faculty office at work. The woman tapped the page with a delicate index finger. 'Look – they're bound to find something in all that lot, aren't they?'

They've already found plenty, Sarah thought.

She had spiked Lovelock's drink with a particularly potent cocktail of the drugs GHB and Rohypnol – provided by Volkov along with the surveillance equipment – that rendered him unconscious within thirty minutes and shredded his short-term memory. Combined with alcohol, the combination of drugs was known to erase memories several hours *before* it was even taken. And within twelve hours of ingestion, all traces disappeared from the victim's system. The dosage had to be exactly right, using precise details of size and weight – calculations made possible using the dimensions of Lovelock's tailor-made ceremonial academic regalia.

A regalia kept in immaculate order by his PA, Jocelyn Steer.

With her target unconscious, Sarah had opened the package from the 'courier', removed a throwaway phone to summon Mikhail back to the house, and then let him in. Also inside the package was Nick's old boiler suit and two pairs of rubber gloves. While Sarah got changed and began to erase all physical traces of her presence in the house, the young hacker had gone to work. And while Laura and her dad believed the plan was all about catching Lovelock on tape – hence the covert recording equipment – the real reason for Sarah's visit went deeper. Much deeper. They had to be shielded from this real reason. And her efforts to record Lovelock had to be convincing enough so that he wouldn't realise it was all a decoy.

Because when he turned on his PC the next day, a self-replicating virus corrupted every single file – including his new book – and crashed the machine. On Monday, the technicians at PC World trying to fix it made a grim discovery: more than 9,000 child pornography images in the computer's hard drive. A call to the police had brought simultaneous Tuesday morning raids to his house and office, where they had discovered thousands more images on his work computer and still more on an external hard drive concealed in his study at home, with date stamps going back fifteen years. A second external hard drive, concealed beneath his desk at work by Jocelyn, contained thousands more. Associated email traffic linked the professor with a notorious paedophile ring – and suggested that a recent falling-out over payment had led to his kidnapping two weeks previously.

Sarah knew there was a risk Lovelock might remember some of what had happened between them, and that he would have his suspicions. But there was no physical evidence of her ever being at his house – and she had a rock-solid alibi. She had been caught on CCTV going into work, and her mobile phone had connected to the university Wi-Fi. She had sent a text from work to her dad. Logged into her work computer at 7.34 that evening and stayed there for the best part of an hour. She had been caught on CCTV again on the way home – when she stopped to use the cashpoint.

Sarah had done all these things on Saturday evening – her electronic footprint proved it.

Or at least, someone who *looked like* her had done so: another slim brunette in her early thirties. Same height and hair colour, with Sarah's clothes, bag, hat and sunglasses. Driving her car. Someone else who fitted Lovelock's very particular type to a T.

Someone like Gillian Arnold.

Mikhail had even dealt with the recording from the CCTV camera over Lovelock's front door. He had deleted the sequence showing Sarah's arrival – and his own dressed as a courier ten minutes later – and replaced it with an unremarkable hour from the previous evening. Leaving nothing to suggest anyone had visited on Saturday evening.

Sarah settled back into her business class seat, giving her lap belt a little tug to make sure it was tight enough. It was a seven-hour flight to Boston and it was going to be a full-on four days in the city, to make sure she landed the Atholl Sanders funding. It would be a huge coup for the university, for the department, for *her*, if she could pull it off. All the signs were good so far. The dean of the faculty had been very quick to clarify with the Atholl Foundation that all of the work, and research, would be led by Dr Sarah Haywood – who, after all, had made the initial contact. That Alan Lovelock had only been brought in to oversee the early part of the process and would not be involved with the work in any capacity whatsoever from now on. The department was bigger than one person, they insisted. It was bigger than one individual. Much bigger.

With a rising whine the jet engines spooled up to full power and Sarah sat back in her seat, ready for the rush of acceleration that would start them on their way. She thought about her dad, about a conversation in a moment of crisis. A conversation that led to a decision. A decision that led to a plan – and a carefully orchestrated sting.

There are only ever really three options in life, Sarah.

You can cut and run, make a fresh start somewhere else.

You can trust the process, the powers that be.

Or you can stand and fight.

She had chosen to stand and fight. Even though it meant getting right down in the gutter with her opponent, and fighting dirty. Because it was no more than he deserved. And sometimes – just sometimes – maybe it was true that an impossible situation required an unthinkable solution.

The plane started rolling down the runway, slowly at first, then picking up speed, dashed lines on the tarmac blurring into a continuous white stripe. The Boeing's nose lifted, then the rear wheels, and finally they were airborne, climbing out of Heathrow en route to Boston.

Sarah watched the roads and houses diminish beneath her, the big jet turning towards the setting sun as it headed for the Atlantic.

She closed her eyes, and smiled.

THE END

Acknowledgements

That thing they say about the difficult second album? It's true. Luckily, I had a lot of people to help me bring 29 SECONDS into the world.

First and foremost, thanks to you for picking up this book. I appreciate it. And thanks to everyone who has taken the time to leave a review, tell a friend or share with their reading group.

Thanks to my agent, Camilla Wray, at Darley Anderson, who always manages to offer the right mix of encouragement, guidance and insight. Thanks also to the brilliant rights team at DA for bringing my stories to new readers in countries around the world. Mary, Sheila, Emma and Kristina – you're all fab.

A huge thank-you to Sophie Orme, my editor at Bonnier Zaffre, and the wonderful team there, including Bec Farrell, Katherine Armstrong, Kate Parkin, Emily Burns and Felice Howden. Also, thanks to Joel Richardson, for opening the door in the first place.

I am grateful once again for the help of Chief Superintendent Rob Griffin of Nottinghamshire Police, for his guidance on evidence and procedure; and to Dr Gill Sare, for her help on medical matters. Thanks also to Charlotte, who suggested Christopher Marlowe as the ideal subject specialism.

I'm indebted to the investigative reporting of the *Guardian*, which has worked hard to expose some of the issues that feature in 29 SECONDS. Also to Laura Bates and her powerful book *Everyday Sexism*, which makes for grim, but eye-opening, reading.

A shout out to my wonderful former colleagues, who have been very kind with their comments and encouragement. In alphabetical order: Anne (those badges!), Charlotte, Debs, Emma H-B, Emma L, Emma R and Emma T, Esther, Katy, Leigh, Lindsay, Lisa, Liz C, Liz G, Paul, Paula, Rob, Ryan, Tara, Tom. I miss you all. Particularly the tea.

To Team Twenty7 (you know who you are), it has been great to get to know you all – an unexpected delight since first getting published. Thanks for all the support, solidarity and sensible advice. And to the Doomsday Writers, for all the same reasons.

Thanks to John, Sue, Jenny and Bernard, whose help and encouragement is invaluable. Also to my big brothers, Ralph and Ollie, who have been enthusiastic supporters of my writing.

A massive thank-you to my wonderful wife, Sally, for steering me in the right direction at an early stage of this story, for being one of my diligent first readers and for always telling me which parts she'd skip. To my amazing kids, who make me proud every day and keep me grounded in a way that only teenagers can: Sophie, who succinctly (and very accurately) described what I do as 'sitting in the spare room making stuff up'. And Tom, who still asks me when I'm going to get a proper job again.

Lastly, thanks to my Mum and Dad for their love and support over many years. I don't think it's a coincidence that the heroes of my first two books are a teacher and an academic. Thank you, both – for everything.

A message from TM Logan . . .

If you enjoyed 29 SECONDS, why not join TM LOGAN'S READERS' CLUB by visiting **www.bit.ly/TMLogan**?

First of all, I want to thank you for picking up 29 SECONDS. Even though this is my second book, it's still slightly surreal to be writing full-time and to have had so much positive feedback about my debut thriller, LIES. I feel incredibly lucky to be creating stories that people have embraced, and I'm very grateful that you've given your time to reading my latest.

I've always been fascinated by the boundary between right and wrong – the shades of grey in between the two; the tension between what is *just* and what is *right*. How might that boundary become blurred if you were to find yourself in a situation where your options are being taken away, where the laws and rules intended to protect us *fail* us? How much pressure would it take for you to make a decision you never would have considered under normal circumstances? And what happens when you do?

These questions were the inspiration for 29 SECONDS, a 'what if' story that pivots on a single question and a single decision.

I started writing this novel in the autumn of 2016, a year before the *New York Times* broke its story about sexual harassment in Hollywood. The ripples from that brilliant piece of journalism have underlined the damage that can be caused by a powerful individual, operating with impunity, who has total control over the careers of those around him: a man like Professor Alan Lovelock. The *New York Times* story reminds us of the potential for situations like this to develop, not just in the film industry, but anywhere – wherever there is a major imbalance of power and a vested interest in maintaining the status quo.

My next psychological thriller has the working title SEVEN DAYS. It's set in the south of France where three families are holidaying together, the women having been best friends for as long as they can remember. But one of them – Katy – has a secret: her husband is having an affair. And this trip is the perfect opportunity for Katy to catch him in the act, because all of her instincts point to *the other woman* being one of her two best friends. But Katy realises too late that the stakes are far higher than she ever could have imagined – and someone in the villa is prepared to kill to keep their secret hidden . . .

If you would like to hear more from me about my future books, you can visit **www.bit.ly/TMLogan** and join the TM Logan Readers' Club. It only takes a few moments to sign up, there are no catches or costs, and new members will automatically receive exclusive content from me that features a scene cut from the original draft of my debut novel, LIES – think of it as a novel version of a DVD extra, with a bit of author's commentary! Your data will be kept totally private and confidential, and it will never be passed on to a third party. I won't spam you with lots of emails, but will get in touch now and again with book news, and you can unsubscribe any time you want.

And if you would like to get involved in a wider conversation about my books, please do review 29 SECONDS on Amazon, on GoodReads, on any other e-store, on your own blog and social media accounts, or talk about it with friends, family or reading groups! Sharing your thoughts helps other readers, and I always enjoy hearing what people think about my stories.

Thanks again for your interest in 29 SECONDS, and I hope you'll return for SEVEN DAYS and what comes after . . .

Best wishes,

Tim